Crashing
into Her

Crashing into Her

LOVE ON CUE

MIA SOSA

AVONIMPULSE
An Imprint of HarperCollinsPublishers

CRASHING INTO HER. Copyright © 2019 by Mia Sosa. All rights reserved. Printed in the United States of America. No part of this book may be used or reproduced in any manner whatsoever without written permission except in the case of brief quotations embodied in critical articles and reviews. For information, address HarperCollins Publishers, 195 Broadway, New York, NY 10007.

Digital Edition FEBRUARY 2019 ISBN: 978-0-06-287874-8
Print Edition ISBN: 978-0-06-287876-2

Cover design by Nadine Badalaty
Cover photographs © PeopleImages/iStock/Getty Images (couple);
© ASDF_MEDIA/Champiofoto/Shutterstock (2 Images)

Avon Impulse and the Avon Impulse logo are registered trademarks of HarperCollins Publishers in the United States of America.

Avon and HarperCollins are registered trademarks of HarperCollins Publishers in the United States of America and other countries.

FIRST EDITION

19 20 21 22 23   HDC   10 9 8 7 6 5 4 3 2 1

This book is dedicated to my readers.
Thank you for embracing my stories.

Crashing into Her

Chapter One

(sings to the tune of *West Side Story*'s "I Feel Pretty")
*I feel grumpy • Oh so grumpy • I feel grumpy and grimy
and gray • And I pity anyone who fucks with me today
Lalalalalalala la-la la-la*

Eva

*Bradley International Airport
Windsor Locks, Connecticut*

"MY APOLOGIES, MS. MONTGOMERY. This flight is over capacity, and you were the last person to check in. Unfortunately, there are no other flights to your destination this evening, so we won't be able to get you home tonight."

I'm gasping for air as I try to process the agent's words, my chest on fire because I just sprinted the length of a football field to get to the gate. The strap of my weekender has burrowed itself so deeply into my skin it's going to leave a permanent dent in my shoulder. And my hair is making an admirable effort to take all the humidity in Connecticut back to Philly as a souvenir. Fuck me sideways.

Delivering a tirade would be immensely satisfying right now, but this weary-eyed airline employee isn't responsible for my predicament—or my jacked-up hair day. I let the bag fall to the floor and kick it between my legs before I collapse against the counter. "This is . . . what . . . I get for . . . buying the cheapest ticket, right?"

Oh, lovely. I'm wheezing. I don't care how well conditioned I am, running 120 yards with a big-ass bag isn't easy.

The man—Steven, according to his perfectly positioned nameplate—tries to hide a grin. "Not so, Ms. Montgomery. If a flight is full—"

"*Oversold.*"

"*Over capacity* is how we describe it," he says, tugging on the hem of his sweater vest.

"I'm sure you do."

"In any case," he says, stepping back as though new battle lines have been drawn, "we make every effort to get passengers to voluntarily give up their seats. A few did, but we simply do not have space to accommodate you, and I'm *very* sorry for that."

His emphasis on the word *very* sounds earnest even to my jaded ears, so I save what little energy I have left and accept my fate. "Okay."

He cocks his head, eyeing me with suspicion. "Really?"

"Yes, really. What else do you expect me to say? You've advised me of the problem, and I'm waiting to hear the solution." My phone buzzes in the back pocket of my jeans. "Excuse me, I need to take this."

After nudging my bag across the floor with my foot, I move to the side of the counter and check the number. My stomach drops when I see that the caller's my best friend, Tori, who married her famous actor boyfriend, Carter Stone, this morning and should be on a plane headed to Aruba *this minute*. In fact, their surprise wedding, which they hid from the paparazzi and most of their guests by disguising it as a weekend-long family reunion in his hometown, is the reason I'm trapped in New England.

"What's wrong?" I ask without preamble.

"Everything's fine. Well, our flight's delayed, but only by an hour. I just have a quick question."

Now that I know her vacation isn't ruined, I relax my shoulders. "Shoot."

"The . . . uh . . . items you encouraged me to take on our honeymoon. Will I have any trouble getting them through security?"

I mentally tick through the gifts I gave her, genuinely not understanding her concern. "The crotchless panties shouldn't be an issue. The oral sex light looks like a regular telephone headset, so that should be fine, too. Maybe you should toss the warming massage oil. It's probably more than three ounces. Wait. Are you worried about the butt plugs?"

Steven snickers as he clicks away at his computer.

"Yes," Tori whispers into the phone. "That's exactly what I'm worried about. I didn't think it through. What if the TSA screeners mistake them for bullets?"

"Don't worry. The rainbow tails will throw them off. And if they ask, just say the plugs are part of a *My Little Pony* stationery set."

"Oh, good cover. I'll go with that." She blows out a relieved breath. "So what about you? Heading out soon?"

"No, they bumped me."

"What? Those *pendejos*."

"Yeah, I've been grumbling about it, too, but I'll survive."

In the background, Carter hustles her off the phone.

"Look, I've got to go," she says. "But text Ashley, okay? She's a flight attendant. Maybe she can help."

"I will. Now go get your swerve on."

"On it. Love you, *chica*."

"Love you, too."

My bestie's happy, and I'm overjoyed for her, so every time I think about the inconvenience of not getting home tonight as planned, I'll focus on those facts instead. As promised, I type a quick text to Ashley, Carter's younger sister, praying that she'll bless me with her insider knowledge.

Me: Hi, Ash. Eva here. Airline bumped me and

it's the last flight to Philly out of Bradford. Any advice?

Not long after, the three dots appear like a lifeline.

Ash: Do you need to get home today?

Me: Not necessary, but it would be nice.

The three continuously moving dots indicate she's typing a lengthy response. The woman's chatty, so I'm not surprised. If people were sentences, she'd be a run-on with an exclamation mark at the end.

Ash: Ok. They're required to compensate you. Can't recall the specifics, but it's at least double your one-way fare if you're delayed more than a couple hours, might even be triple. Ask for cash, not a voucher. They need to put you up in a hotel. The airlines have arrangements with area hotels for this very reason. You're welcome to come back to the house, though!

More dots.

Ash: And food! For that, a voucher's good.

Me: This is great. Thank you.

Ash: Good luck! And let me know how you make out.

Me: Will do.

Minutes later, having secured an early morning flight, a free hotel stay, food vouchers, and the promise of a check for 300 percent more than the price I paid for my original ticket, I drag myself back through the main terminal and follow the signs to ground transportation. I'd still prefer to sleep in my own bed tonight, but getting bumped off a flight apparently has many perks if you ask for them; amusing the gate agent responsible for doling out those perks probably helps, too.

I send a quick update to Tori and Ashley. The latter responds with a combo of thumbs-up and heart-eyes emojis. The former sends a two-word reply: Hang on. In the meantime, I hustle behind a dozen or so people waiting for cabs.

Tori sends a longer text a minute later:

Anthony's at the airport. He just dropped off my parents and Bianca. They're heading to NYC for sightseeing. He can pick you up outside the terminal and take you to the hotel. Says he's coming around again and will look for you. Ok, Carter's giving me some serious side-eye. Going on airplane mode. Love you.

A heavy weight settles in my belly when I finish reading her message. Shit. Tori's cousin—I've secretly dubbed him the square root of Thor—is the *last* person I want to see. My hand flies to the unruly strands on my head. Argh. This hair travesty alone is spiking my blood pressure, which doesn't bode well for him. When I'm not at my personal best, I'm more irritable than usual, and judging by our interaction this weekend, Anthony's very presence makes me cranky. This should be fun for everyone involved.

It isn't long before he finds me. In truth, I spot him first and duck my head, giving me a minute to watch him as he rounds his rental car and surveys the line, his eyes hidden behind silver lens aviators that are pure overkill given that sunset is fast approaching. To me, a white T-shirt and jeans typically read basic; on him, they add dimension to his appearance, emphasizing the assured, relaxed way he carries himself. And although I'm aware there's no correlation between the size of a man's hands and the girth of his penis, I still glance at his long fingers—for pseudoscience. The man's an eggplant emoji, for sure.

He shouts to get my attention, his smoky voice pulling my mind out of its permanent residence in the trash bin. "Eva! Over here!"

The woman in front of me twists her upper body around and meets my gaze. "Dayum. Are you Eva?"

Stifling the urge to laugh, I nod.

"No offense, but I'm considering stealing your identity," she says.

Ha. Imagine how she'd react if I told her he's a Hollywood stunt professional. She'd probably shank me. "No offense taken, and yeah, I know what you mean."

Because yes, there's no denying the man's physical gifts: broad shoulders, dark brown wavy hair that's a smidge too long for my liking, and full lips that probably predispose him to better-than-competent-kisser status. He's a mishmash of muscles and scruff, but in a refined package, like the construction worker in a music video who struts around with manicured hands, spotless jeans, and a single, perfect streak of dirt across his cheek. All of this means Anthony takes up more than his fair share of physical space in my mind's eye, not because he's huge—although he *is* big considering my five-foot-two frame—but because there's so much to absorb when I look at him that I trick myself into giving him a larger blueprint. Oddly, no single trait stands out from the rest; rather, it's the *totality* of the man that holds my attention hostage. *Free me, damn you.*

It's been this way since I met him a few days ago. In that moment, the idea of a hookup planted itself in my brain, an unfortunate and all too common occurrence when a sexually frustrated woman gives up on pricks but still wants dick. But then Tori warned me against pursuing him, explaining that he's "emotionally unavailable," whatever that means, and I grudgingly backed away. In short, *bitches before itches*. Still, the thirst is strong with this one. Until he opens his mouth, that is.

Since I can't ogle him forever, I step out of line and give him a weak wave, readjusting the strap of my bag across my body.

He saunters over to meet me, a lopsided grin broadcasting that he's poised to say something annoying. "Philadelphia decided it couldn't handle you either, huh?"

And this is the crux of the problem: He speaks. What I wouldn't give for a roll of duct tape. I'd use it on his mouth and anywhere with a surplus of hair. His crotch, probably. "Ahhh, so *that's* what happened. You decided you couldn't handle me." I scan him from his head to the tops of his derby shoes. "Makes sense. I spy a lightweight."

Folding his thick arms over his impressive chest, he takes a step back and tilts his head. "Whoa, whoa, whoa. Why the hostility, Eva? I thought we were friends."

"We're acquaintances, not friends, and I'm good with that."

He pouts at me and runs his index finger from his lower eyelid down to the hollow of his cheek. Sad face. I press my lips together, refusing to laugh at his antics even though that's exactly what I'd do if our roles were reversed. When he gets no reaction from me, he lowers his arm and sighs. "Not interested in being my friend because . . . ?"

I give him a halfhearted shrug. "Not sure, exactly. You just rub me the wrong way."

He leans in and waggles his eyebrows. "Teach me how to rub you the right way, then."

The epiphany smacks me upside my head: Anthony's my male counterpart. As evidenced by the swagger, the self-confidence—in his case, it's *overconfidence*—and the mouth that must have the last word, no matter how inappropriate it may be. There's only room for one of me in my life, however, and if I were looking for someone to balance out my ridiculousness, this man would fail miserably. On one end of the spectrum is a shy, quiet type who'll cower in the center of my tornado; on the other end of the spectrum is someone like Anthony, who'll grab the funnel with his bare hands and swing it around in the hopes of wreaking even more havoc. Neither one will do. Well, given my abysmal track record when it comes to men, *no one* will do.

But that doesn't mean I can't extract a little fun from the situation. So I drop my bag, round the front of his rental car, and hop onto the hood, resting my feet on the bumper and spreading my legs wide. Waving him over, I say, "You want to learn how to rub me the right way? Go ahead. Break me off a little something right here and show me what we're working with."

I raise my face toward the sky and close my eyes. A woman somewhere in the vicinity cackles. Car horns blare with impatience as drivers try to navigate the airport traffic. Anthony, however, doesn't say a word. I drop my head and open one eye to sneak a peek at his reaction. But he's not in my line of sight. Someone else is, though—and the scowl on his face suggests he isn't friendly at all.

Fuck me sideways twice.

Chapter Two

Anthony

THIS WOMAN NEEDS her own reality TV show. And this could be the first episode. I'd call it, "That's What You Get, Eva."

The airport security officer standing in front of her raps his knuckles on the hood. "All right, folks, no idling vehicles in the passenger pickup lane. Take your selfies somewhere else."

Wearing a sheepish expression, she slides off the car and brushes dirt off her butt. Thanks to me, the rental's spotless, though, so I know it's a nervous gesture. But her voice is calm when she says, "Sorry about that, sir. My boyfriend and I got a little carried away."

The little devil on my shoulder—I think of him as my inner *maldito*—bangs his pitchfork on my shoulder and makes a brilliant suggestion. Unable to resist messing with her, I sidle up to Eva and shake my phone in the air. "Hey, man. This reunion's been a long time coming. Any chance you'd take a picture of us together? It would mean a lot to us."

Eva clears her throat and shoves me away. "Don't be silly, sweetheart. He doesn't have time to do that."

Unsure I'll be able to do it justice, I try my best impression of a man in love: looking at her with longing in my eyes and blowing a kiss. "It's just . . . this is such a special day, *honey*." Given the way Eva crinkles her nose, I'm assuming I wasn't as convincing as I had hoped to be. Not a shock since I'd need to swat away the cobwebs in my brain to recall my memories of being in that state.

The officer, meanwhile, scans the immediate area, shakes his head in resignation, and puts out his hand. "One picture and then you're out of here."

Grinning way more than this small triumph warrants, I give him the phone and steer Eva back onto the hood. It's underhanded of me to do this, of course, but she went down this path and I'm following it to its logical—and entertaining as fuck—conclusion.

She loops arms with me and lifts her face toward mine, her mouth grazing my ear as she whispers, "You are so dead when this is over."

The touch of her lips is fleeting, a minor brush of contact that shouldn't register at all, but my inner *maldito*'s working overtime, and now I'm picturing a different ending to this scenario, one that involves a bed and multiple orgasms for us both. Messing around with my cousin's best friend would be a supremely stupid thing to do, though. Casual sex is a dish best served anonymously, an arm's length encounter that leaves no room for seconds. Knowing this should be enough to reprogram my brain, but the wiring's all screwed up in there today.

"I can't wait to see how you'll make me pay," I tell her under my breath, wanting to keep this encounter as light as I know it should be and reminding myself that this is nothing more than a game. To our amateur photographer, I say, "All you need to do is tap the circle when you're ready."

He gives me a blank stare, probably regretting that he didn't make us vacate the premises immediately. "Yes, I know how to use an iPhone. Let's do this on three. One, two, three."

When we're done, Eva scrambles off the car and busies herself with riffling through her humongous bag while I thank the officer and confirm that he took a decent pic. It's better than I could have hoped for. Not surprisingly, Eva's bright eyes dominate the photo, the mass of copper ringlets that surround her face like party streamers coming in a close second. But it's the gritted teeth masquerading as a smile, along with the barest hint of a flared nostril, that I enjoy the most about the shot, because it's photographic evidence that, contrary to what she said earlier, I can keep up with her just fine.

I slip the phone back into my pocket, pop the trunk open, and reach for her bag, wearing a conspiratorial grin that I hope will distract her from exacting any mean-spirited retribution. "You must be dog-tired. Let's get you to your hotel. Which one is it?" For a minute, I prepare myself for a bit of resistance or a curt response warning me of my impending doom. Instead, she rams the bag into my stomach; says, "It's the Marriott in Windsor;" and slides into the front passenger seat, leaving me with the impression that nothing about the past ten minutes was funny to her. Maybe I've gone too far, and if that's the case, I'll apologize.

The first thing I notice when I climb into the car is Eva's hair, which is piled on top of her head through some force of magic; from here, it looks like a thick band of it is holding everything else in place. The second thing I notice is that she's resting with her eyes closed, the smooth brown skin on her neck and shoulders that was previously hidden by her curls now on full display. Technically, that's more than one thing. Which is why the final thing I notice is that I shouldn't be noticing anything about Eva. *Move on, maldito.*

I strap myself in and use a phone app to map out the hotel route. It's only five miles away. She's buckled in, too, so I start the engine and ease into traffic, and still, she doesn't budge. It's no hassle to drive her the short distance, not when it means I get to spend a few minutes with a woman who makes me smile as much as she does. And that reminds me . . . "Listen, I'm sorry about that stunt. I didn't mean to piss you off, but I obviously did."

Her eyes flutter open, and she turns her head in my direction. "I'm not mad at you." She opens her mouth, hesitates, and then says, "If I'm being honest, I was just irritated that you one-upped me."

The pleasure I feel in hearing this admission is way out of proportion with what's at stake, which is to say, not a goddamn thing. Still, it feels like an accomplishment for some reason. "Oh, I see. You're having a hard time accepting that you've finally met your match."

"Settle down, big boy," she says in an amused tone. "I wouldn't go that far. Let's just say that you've dampened my urge to snarl at you. Anyone who can catch me off guard like you did back there can't be all bad. Truce?"

She caps the offering with a wink. It's all . . . too easy. And nothing about this woman strikes me as easy. My prank antenna goes up, but I'll play along, because whatever she's planning will be good for a few laughs. "Didn't know we needed one, but yeah, truce."

We arrive at the hotel within ten minutes of leaving the airport. Her mouth drops when I pull into the circular driveway. "We're already here? God, what a waste of your time."

I wave her off. "It's no big deal. I was at the airport. Plus, my flight doesn't leave until morning and all my family's gone, so it's not like I have tons to do."

Eva lays her fingers on the door handle, her brows pulled in as though she's carefully weighing what she's about to say, and then she blows out a long breath. "So, would you be interested in joining me for a drink at the bar?" She peers out the passenger window. "Assuming they have one."

My brain knows this routine by rote. A drink at the bar leads to a hookup somewhere else, after a frank two-way discussion about what precisely this is and isn't. I stop myself from running through the usual preliminaries, because that won't be happening here. Not with Eva. Besides, chances are high this is the first step in an elaborate revenge scheme. I don't care, though, because Eva's fun to hang with. If I remain alert around her, I should be okay. "Sure. Since you need to check in, let's meet there in ten minutes? Cool?"

"Cool."

Again, too easy, but I'm interested to see how this'll turn out. I give her my cell phone number in case she's delayed in her room.

"I can get a tab started," I tell her. "What'll you have?"

She shrugs as she opens the door. "I'm partial to drinks with cranberry juice. Surprise me."

Her grin grows in stages, starting small and secretive and ending wide and welcoming. Maybe this is just my overactive imagination, but a split second along the way it appears devious, too, and now I have a hunch that if anyone's doing the surprising tonight, it'll be her.

"So, how'd you meet Tori?"

Eva waits for our second round of drinks to be placed in front of us—a rum punch for her and a Corona for me—before telling me how she met my favorite cousin. We're facing each other in a sparsely populated bar, her feet resting on the bottom rung of my wood stool. After thanking the bartender, Eva places an elbow on the counter and leans in. The top of her sweater falls from her shoulder, and I catch a glimpse of the yellow tank top underneath. As much as I'd like to enjoy the view, I force my gaze to hover around her face. It's a safe zone, both for her comfort and mine.

"We were in the same physiology class our sophomore year," she says. "After midterms, the professor assigned a class project and posted the group assignments outside the lecture hall. I was standing behind her trying to locate my name, but her cloud of hair was in the way and I told her so."

I cover my mouth, shaking my head and easily picturing their first meeting as a battle of wills. Eva takes a long sip of her cocktail and flicks her tongue out to lick away a drop of moisture at the corner of her mouth. Unfortunately, I stare too long and she catches me. If she calls me on it, I'll fess up, but as she assesses me, I silently pray she'll ignore my lapse in good judgment and finish the story.

"So Tori's standing there, her back to me," she continues with a smile, "and for a few seconds I'm thinking she didn't hear my comment. But then she turns around slowly, shields her eyes like she's peering out over the horizon, and says, 'Is someone out there? I could have sworn I heard yapping.' And I said something like, 'Bitch, you know you see me down here,' but I couldn't keep the laughter out of my voice. We've been best friends ever since."

I throw my head back and slow clap my approval. This is the perfect beginning for them. Explains why they've been inseparable for so long: instant chemistry. "Yeah, Tori caught a lot of grief about her hair growing up. One Thanksgiving, my parents and I were visiting Tori's family in Philadelphia and she came home crying about the kids in the neighborhood calling her Chia Pet. My father wiped her tears and told her, '*Tu cabello es tu corona.*'"

"Which means what?"

"It means, 'Your hair is your crown,' and ever since then I've called her *princessa.*"

Eva smiles as she swirls the straw through her drink. "That's sweet." She opens her mouth—to pose a question, I think—but then she takes another sip of her rum punch instead. Until now, the conversation's been flowing, so I'm not sure what I could have said to make her hesitant to ask me something. I rewind the last minute and snag on the obvious. My mother and father. "They're both alive, if that's what you were afraid to ask. My parents, I mean."

She drops her shoulders and gives me a shy smile. "Sorry. I know your father's alive. Tori's mentioned him a few times. But I don't think I've ever heard her talk about your mother. And, well, since neither of them was at the wedding, I wasn't sure what to think."

Honestly, I wish we could move on to another topic. Not that my father's an issue. My mother, though, is a different story—a long, drawn-out one—and I'd rather not talk about it. "I can see now why you'd wonder about that. They're not together anymore, and she lives in Puerto Rico."

She nods in understanding. "So where's your father? I expected him to be here."

Now there's a man who has no chill. He's pining for a woman who's been out of his life for more than a decade, trying to convince her they still belong together even though she finally asked him for a divorce three weeks ago and wants him to foot the bill. The more he begs, the more my mother pulls away. "He's on the island helping her with the house. Hurricane Maria ripped through her steel roof. The government's given her a blue tarp to cover the gaping hole, but hurricane season is about to roll around again and that's not enough."

She grimaces. "What's happening there is criminal, and the way some people here are acting—like our government doesn't have a duty to help—is ridiculous."

And watching the destruction on TV, knowing there wasn't much we could do until the storm passed, was a nightmare. My mother managed to let us know she was okay through a Facebook message, but only after charging her phone with what little gas she had in her car because the power had been out for days. She and I may no longer be close, but I want her to be safe, and the people who call the island their home deserve better. It's a relief to know Eva's on the same page. "Half of the people here don't even realize Puerto Ricans are US citizens, so most discussions about giving aid start in a bad place from the get-go. It's frustrating, to say the least."

Why the fuck are we talking about this? Bar chatter isn't supposed to be this deep. "Anyway, I was the person designated to represent our side of the family this weekend. Good thing, too, because I wouldn't have wanted to miss Tori's wedding for the world."

"She adores you."

"And I adore her."

Eva shifts on the stool, leaning in another fraction. "You know, Tori's suffering from a bit of hero-worship when it comes to you. She described you as this larger-than-life guy in LA doing stunt work for TV and film. Honestly, I pictured you as someone who'd always have a person hanging on their arm, so I was surprised you came alone. Couldn't find a date in time?"

My eyes snap to hers. Oh, we're going down this road, are we? "Fishing for information about my relationship status?"

She pulls back and huffs at me, swinging her legs back under her own stool. "Excuse you, it was a simple question. You don't have to answer, makes no difference to me."

I steal a glance at her profile, amused by the stubborn tilt of her chin. If someone asked me to describe her on paper, I'd probably answer like I was filling out a government form: "Let's see, she's African American, twenty-five to twenty-nine, brown hair, brown skin, brown eyes, less than average height." Eva in 3-D is more than those basic traits, though. Her brown skin glows with vitality, and the apples of her cheeks always look like she's just tweaked them. Until I met Eva, I would have laughed in someone's face if they told me a person's eyes twinkle. But I swear, hers do. And that hair—it frames her face like a heart. She'd probably clock me if I told her how adorable that feature is to me.

I straighten once I notice that she's giving me a narrow-eyed stare. "Okay, okay, I'm not seeing anyone, if that's what you wanted to know."

Her chin cranks up one more level. "It wasn't."

"Fine. But let's say, hypothetically speaking, we were exchanging that kind of information for no reason at all, and I was interested in finding out who keeps Eva warm at night. You'd say . . . ?"

She turns toward me again and leans in close, her eyelids falling to half-mast. "My down comforter does an excellent job. It's plush. And soft. And decadent. I highly recommend the brand. Let me know if you want info on where to buy it."

I don't think I've ever envied an inanimate object, but suddenly I want to *be* the comforter that keeps her warm. Wrapping myself around those curves would be a spectacular experience. For tonight only, though. And . . . that's my cue to break the fuck out of here before I make an ass of myself and ask her to take me upstairs. "Excuse me a minute. I need to use the restroom."

She smirks at me. "Sure."

I don't sprint out of the bar, but I come damn near close to a jog. And when I return a few minutes later, my face freshly splashed with water, she's gone.

The bartender lightly bangs her fist on the counter to get my attention. "Your friend wasn't feeling well. Said she was heading up to her room."

I stand there like an idiot, massaging the back of my neck. Right. That's so Eva. She must have been humoring me the whole time.

"Said to give you this," the bartender adds, handing me what looks like a hotel room key card.

I drop back onto the stool, clutching the card like it holds talismanic power over me. What am I supposed to do with this now? I have no idea what room she's in. Suddenly I hear everything. The laughter on the other side of the bar. The clank of the dishes being bussed in the adjoining restaurant. The pounding in my chest as I consider my next move. I will apply myself to the task of finding Eva in the same way I committed to solving the Rubik's Cube last year. Then my phone dings.

Eva: I miss my down comforter. Care to replace it? For one night. JUST one night.

It's the text message to end all text messages. I'm framing this beauty when I get back to LA. And yes, I should probably pause and think this through, but I don't want to. Simple as that. Instead, I text her back.

Me: I can be the best fucking comforter you've ever had.

Eva: Literally?

Me: I'll make it my life's mission.

Eva: Cum to room 308 then.

Eva: Oops, typo. ☺

I love the way this woman thinks. And I can't wait to get upstairs.

Me: Coming soon . . . but not TOO soon.

A one-night stand with a funny, sexy woman who has no interest in ever seeing me again? There's no way I'm passing up that opportunity . . .

Chapter Three

There's a reason the word manipulative begins
with the letters M-A-N: namely, it's always a
man doing the manipulating.

Eva

Los Angeles, California
Three months later

"EVA, HONEY, I'VE decided not to give you any money
for this move to California."

My father's ill-timed announcement makes the vein
at my right temple throb like a drumbeat. He's telling
me this *after* I left my job in Philadelphia and relocated
to LA, a decision I considered less daunting because he'd
promised to help pay some of my first-year expenses.

Okay, Satan. Today it is.

Blowing out a long, slow breath, I tighten my grip
on the phone and stifle the urge to let out a string of
cuss words that would make a navy SEAL blush and

clutch his Glock. Instead, I speak calmly, mimicking my mother's patented you-are-getting-on-my-last-nerve tone. "You agreed to help me get settled. For a year at least. What's changed?"

On the other end of the line, my father sighs as though he's put out by the question. I know from experience I'll be put out by his answer.

A calculated few seconds pass before he says, "Well, the more I think about it, the more I think this whole venture is a bad idea. If you were in your twenties, I'd say go find yourself. But you're going to be thirty soon. It's well past the time for you to focus on a solid career."

Right. I see. Manipulation 101 is in session, and he's mastered the material so well he could write scholarly tomes about it. "Dad, it doesn't bother you at all that you're reneging on a commitment?"

He talks in a soothing voice, the one he adopts when he's speaking with my mother and realizes he's gone too far. "Sweetie, don't be mad at me. The money will be here when you return."

His words fall on my head like acid rain: innocuous on the surface but toxic once you understand their long-term implications.

When you return.

In other words, my father's rooting for me to fail. Makes me wants to scream mindlessly into the void. If I killed him within the next twenty-four hours, would I still fall safely within crime-of-passion territory? I make a mental note to research that handy factoid.

"What happens when you get hurt?" he asks in an exasperated tone. "Or sick? Or you can no longer move the way you once did? You need a backup plan. I can't imagine what I would have done without one."

My father, now a tenured history professor, never fails to remind me that his own dreams of playing professional football were dashed when he broke his leg during a game in his third year of college. His plan B saved him. In his view, a fitness career isn't a plan A at all, let alone a stable one.

"As soon as you're ready to take those accounting courses," he continues, "I'll gladly pay for them. But if you're satisfied being an exercise instructor, it should be on you to make this gig work."

"Yeah, I get it." My tone is clipped and emotionless, but my stomach is churning like an overstuffed washing machine during the spin cycle. I hate that my mother correctly predicted an outcome along these lines weeks ago: "If you want to make it on your own in LA, then do exactly that," she'd said. "Because if you rely on your father, his help will come with strings attached." I hate even more that I anticipated a power move of this kind, never including my father's pledge in my budget calculations. It isn't even the loss of income that bothers me; it's what that money represented: support, encouragement, a sign that he wanted me to succeed.

Sure, I *know* he loves me. He's proven it time and again. When my parents split in my first year of middle school, he became my primary caregiver while my mother pursued her goal of starting a second career as an emergency room nurse. Long hours and night shifts meant she missed lots of moments, big and small: my first school dance, the day my braces came off, the afternoon I left school early because my menstrual cramps made me nauseous. He was there through it all, guiding me, wiping my tears, *being* a father. But he doesn't trust me to figure out life on my own, even if it means I'll make a few well-intentioned mistakes along the way.

"All right, I need to get to work," I say, unable to keep the emotional fatigue out of my voice. "My first class starts at five."

"Give me a call when you're not busy, okay? And be careful out there, sweetheart."

He says this as though he's done nothing upsetting, the past few minutes set aside and forgotten. It's like I'm dealing with two different men. One of them yanks the rug out from under me; the other one drapes a soft blanket over my body and tells me to get some rest.

"Of course. Talk to you soon."

I end the call and shove my phone into my fire-engine-red gym bag, a welcome gift from Tori. Rolling my shoulders to ease the tension in them, I scan the living area of my freshly painted one-bedroom apartment and try to recapture the excitement I felt about the its features: a cozy window seat straight out of a Hallmark movie; the tiny wrought-iron terrace overlooking the quaint courtyard; my very first granite countertops. But now I'm questioning if any of it matters, if I've moved across the country only to remain in the same place.

No, I'm not going to let my father steal my joy, and more important than that, I'll prove him wrong. I refuse to return to Philly with my tail between my legs, no matter how much my father wants me to.

Inspecting my reflection in the mirror, I set aside my parental woes and focus on the positives: I'm an unattached, employed woman with a nice apartment who's embarking on an adventure in a new city. Also, my ass looks *amazing* in these yoga pants.

Satan can shove it.

WHEN I ARRIVE at Every Body in West Hollywood, Tori waves at me from behind the reception desk. The studio's general manager, Valeria, stands at her side, a bright smile revealing the sexy gap between her two front teeth.

Tori drums on her chest as I approach. "You can't begin to understand how happy I am to see you walk through that door. My heart can't take it."

I'm just as thrilled as she is, honestly. After Tori moved to California last year, Philly wasn't the same without her. When she brought me in to tour the space a few months ago, I could easily picture myself working here. "We're stuck with each other, *chica*—for better or better."

She rounds the desk, hands me a manila envelope, and tackle-hugs me. "This is going to be great."

My arms hang loosely at my sides, and my cheek is smashed against her chest. "Tori, honey, I need air."

"Oh, sorry about that." She draws back, scans me from head to toe, and points at the envelope. "Your ID, access card, locker combo, and staff room codes are all in there. Valeria will give you the necessary employment forms. You know your way around, right? Because my class starts in a few minutes."

I roll my eyes at her. "You have four exercise studios in a seventy-five-hundred-square-foot space, woman. I think I can figure this place out on my own."

She bumps my hip with hers, a familiar move that brings a smile to my face. "Fine, my lovely crab apple. I'll introduce you in Advanced Zumba at five. The people who signed up for that class can't wait to get started. I've been talking you up for weeks."

A wave of jitters hits me. Advanced Zumba has always been one of my most popular classes, but what if the regulars here don't like it? What if the music doesn't suit their tastes? We did a few trial runs while I was considering Tori's job offer, but maybe the students were just being polite when they said they enjoyed themselves. More than anything, I don't want Tori to regret her decision to bring me on staff. This gym is her new venture, too, and I'd hate to hold her back in any way.

Goodness, Satan's working overtime today. I rub my temples, inwardly chastising myself for overthinking the class and undervaluing my skills. This isn't me. This is my father throwing me off balance—and it's up to me to regain my equilibrium.

After placing my belongings in a locker in the staff room, I stroll through the fitness center, familiarizing myself with the layout. Water fountain. Got it. Emergency exits. Check, check. Gender-neutral, accessible restrooms with signs that say, "Everyone. If you can't deal, hold it." Yes, Tori, yes. My BFF never fails to make me proud.

Because it's midafternoon, the place isn't packed yet, so I duck into the empty studio where I'll be teaching and walk along the perimeter. Twice the size of my exercise room in Philly, it's bright and airy, with floor-to-ceiling mirrors along the front and back, a light blue wall to the right of the stage, and a clear glass wall and door to the left. It's perfect, and according to Tori, mostly mine once I complete my six-month probation.

I step onto the platform, its suspended wood floor easy on my joints, and bend at the waist to stretch my lower back. Not long after, a whoosh of cool air brushes over my shoulders, so I straighten and turn to the door, my mouth falling open when I see Anthony—the man formerly known as my one-night stand—watching me, a black canvas gym bag in his hand and a dazed expression on his face.

Images of our night together flash in my head, each one brighter and more blinding than the one before it. Tangled limbs, his ridiculously soft lips trailing a path from my belly button to my breasts, the uninhibited way I shouted his name, his large hands kneading my ass like he was trying to make the finest pizza crust in all the land. I don't know much about this man, but I know that when we were together that evening, he wanted nothing more than to give and receive as much pleasure as our bodies could handle. And I was right: The eggplant emoji is accurate as hell.

For a moment, it's a stand-off, both of us eyeing each other warily, gauging our respective reactions to this unplanned reunion. But then he shakes life into his limbs and strides into the room like he owns it, the outline of his thick thighs visible through his navy-blue dress slacks. If he were wearing black-rimmed glasses and cleaned up that five o'clock shadow, I'd wonder if he were cosplaying as Clark Kent.

"If you wanted to get my attention, all you had to do was say hello," he says, dropping his bag on a chair near the stage.

Okay, so we're pretending we didn't spend several hours in each other's arms a few months ago. Understood. And now that I think about it, a mutually agreed-upon memory loss is the perfect approach, allowing us both the freedom to do what we do best: needle each other. I cross my arms over my chest and smirk at him. "This might be hard for you to grasp, but not every person lives and breathes for your attention."

He grins at me as he removes his jacket. "But is anyone really living without my attention?"

Oh, gross. He's messing up the fantasy, making my decision to sleep with him back then more ill-advised with each passing moment. "Do you ever think about what you're saying? Like, try it out in your head first and revise when it's clear that what you're about to say makes you sound like an asshat?"

His eyes crinkle at the corners as he widens his smile, but a flush stains his cheeks, and I hope with all my heart it's a sign of his embarrassment, because if it isn't, he's hopeless.

"It's a skill I'm working on, I promise," he says. "But yeah, sometimes the edit feature in my head malfunctions."

I'll grant him some latitude, because Lord knows I've said some jaw-dropping nonsense in my lifetime, but I need him gone so I can regroup. It's then that I first notice the stark differences in our attire. I'm dressed to get my heart pumping; he's dressed to get my clit thumping. Argh. Why is he even here? Today of all days? "So, are you planning to take Advanced Zumba at five?"

He snorts. "Never in a million years." When he spots the eye daggers flying his way, he realizes his edit button's jammed again. "I mean, I'm sure it's a great class, but I'm not down with embarrassing myself in public spaces."

"Your loss," I say, shrugging. "Well, if you're looking for Tori, she's in Studio A."

"I'm not looking for Tori," he says. "I'm teaching a free self-defense class for women at four. As part of

Tori's goal to incorporate community service into her business plan."

"Here?"

"Here."

"In this room?"

He nods, a mischievous grin dancing across his rugged face. "Yes, in this studio. Been doing it once a week for about a month."

Right. How convenient that the class is geared to women. Very Anthony, indeed. "And sharing your many gifts with the ladies, I assume."

He doesn't bother to deny it. Instead, he gives me a blank stare, as though my dig wasn't surprising at all. "That, too, of course." For a few seconds, he appears thoughtful, biting into his bottom lip as he considers me. "So, how long will you be visiting? I'd offer to show you around during your stay, but I'm guessing you wouldn't be interested. *Que pena*."

I know what that means, and it's not a pity at all. "Tori didn't tell you? I moved to LA this week, and I'm working as an instructor here. But yes, you're right, I'll pass on the guided tour."

Brows knitted in confusion—a state I'm thrilled to have caused—he stares at me and says nothing. I don't think I spoke those words in another language, but he sure is looking at me as though I did.

"I'm sorry?" he asks with a jerk of his head. "What did you say?"

"I said I'm here to stay. Well, if LA is nice to me, that is."

"You're moving here?"

"I've already moved, Anthony."

The brightness in his brown eyes dims, and his maddeningly broad shoulders tense. The change in his demeanor reminds me of a rose dying in a time-lapse video. Despite this, he says, "Well, good for you. Welcome." Then he tugs on his tie as he clears his throat. "So uh . . . listen . . . about that night. It was great, and I hope you enjoyed it as much as I did, but we're on the same page about this, right? That was a one-off."

Oh. My. God. I want him to stop talking. He's going off script, and I'm terrible at improvising when a conversation enters the awkward zone. In times like these, my bravado fails me. I wish I were wearing wood-paneling camouflage pants so I could drop to the floor and make myself invisible. "A one-off?"

I inwardly cringe at the strangled tinge to my voice.

He blows out a breath. "Yeah, you know. A one-time thing. Like you didn't move to LA expecting that we'd pick up where we left off."

Oh, wait a minute now. He's suggesting that I packed up all my belongings and uprooted my life to chase after a guy I hooked up with once? That punts me out of the awkward zone and drops me squarely— and comfortably—within pissed-off territory. Heat suffuses my face and the pounding at my temples resumes as I line up for the tackle. There's so much I could say, but I go with an essential truth, a maxim every self-respecting person knows. "Anthony, sweetie, no dick's that special."

I gather from his silence and the gray tint to his skin that my answer's a direct hit. Hopefully that'll teach him to use his edit function more often. And I still can't get over his presumptuous question. I'm moved to scream mindlessly into the void for the second time today.

Well played, Satan. Well played.

Chapter Four

Anthony

¡Coño! I'm FUCKING up big time.

I want to apologize to Eva, but I don't know where to begin or how to explain myself without sounding like an asshole.

Sorry, although it was cool to hook up with you in another state, now that we're living in the same city, I don't want you to get the misimpression that I'm interested in you.

Shit. Maybe I *am* an asshole. No, that can't be right. Papi would disown me if that were the case. Let me try this again.

Sorry, although it was cool to hook up with you in another state, now that we're living in the same city, I don't want to send you mixed signals. You see, my policy is simple: No repeats. Ever. No matter how much I want to. Side note: I want to. Badly. Which is reason alone to stick to the policy.

That's a little better, I guess. Shows it's not about her specifically. I still sound like an asshole, but if it ensures neither one of us gets hurt by a rash decision we made months ago, I'll live with it. I raise a fist to my mouth and blow out a forceful breath, prepping myself to clarify what I meant, and then I make the mistake of looking at her, and this tumbles out instead: "I was just kidding, Eva. Foot-in-mouth disease is running rampant in LA. Let's just forget I said anything."

She regards me with a tilt of her head and a squiggly line between her brows, as though I'm a painting that just sold at auction for millions of dollars and she isn't sure why. "Fine."

I need to fix this somehow, but I can't focus on that problem now, not when twenty-five women are waiting for me to teach them how to split a man's balls in half. So I grab my bag and take several backward steps until my butt hits the door. "Class is going to start soon, and I need to get ready. Maybe we can catch up some other time." I slip through the door, unable to tear my eyes from the pretty picture she makes standing there, a hand on her hip and her curls piled on top of her head in that knot thingy she does with it.

After changing into athletic shorts and a T-shirt, I leave the restroom and peek inside the studio. Eva's gone, but the memory of how poorly I handled seeing her again remains. I don't have the luxury of wallowing in a puddle of shame, though, so I pace the length of the hall and try to get into the right mindset to teach the class.

A few of the students arrive and wave at me, reminding me that Kurt should be here, too. I glance at my sports watch and confirm he's late. How am I supposed to demonstrate today's self-defense moves without an experienced opponent? Grumbling, I whip out my phone and bang out a quick text.

Me: Class starts at 4. Where r you?

He responds within seconds.

Kurt: Traffic. Be there in 20.

Which really means he'll be here in 30. Damn. I shove the phone in my pocket and growl at no one in particular. This is LA. What the fuck is new about traffic? At this point, it's like saying your dog ate your homework. Lightly pounding my fists together as I continue to pace, I try to come up with a solution while cursing Kurt's notoriously late ass. *Think, Anthony. Think.* Asking for a volunteer isn't out of the question, but it's risky. The person might be cool with it at first but feel awkward when they're asked to execute a move. And part of my technique is to demonstrate the sense of power you gain when doing it correctly. I won't feel comfortable unleashing my full strength on a student.

"Hello? Everything okay?"

I halt midstride and find Eva waving a hand in front of my face.

She takes a small step back now that she has my attention. "You look out of sorts. Just being a good *neighbor* and checking in."

I don't miss the way she emphasizes *neighbor* as though it's a filthy word. Letting out a quick breath, I grab the back of my neck and try something groundbreaking, like having a normal conversation with her. "We're about to start," I say, pointing my chin at the women in the class who are mingling and chatting in the corridor. "My boss promised to show up for the first half of the class—to help me demo a few defensive moves—but he's running late." Another glance at my watch still puts Kurt twenty-five minutes away.

"Maybe I could help?" she asks.

My head snaps up, and her big brown-eyed gaze meets mine. For a second, I'm taken aback by how pretty she is—her skin is glowing and she's wearing this deep burgundy lipstick that highlights her sensual mouth—but I force myself to concentrate, for everyone's sake. It's not a bad idea. I'll never forget when she schooled me about her tae kwon do experience when we first met. "Seriously? You'd do that for me?"

"Sure, you're in a jam, and it wouldn't be *neighborly* to leave you hanging. What's today's lesson?"

"We've been working on defense moves from a distance, and next up is the groin strike."

Her face screws up in a way I'm 99 percent positive means she's trying to hold in a grin. She manages to suppress it, though, and I'm glad to see my earlier comments didn't alter her sense of humor around me.

"I think I can handle that," she says, rubbing her hands as though she's excited about the prospect of jumping into the demo. "Let's do it."

She trails behind me as I jog to the door. Seconds later, I cringe at the ear-splitting squeak of sneakers coming from a small stampede of women to our right. Eva gets to the door before them. Over her shoulder, she says, "I see you have an avid following."

I lean close to her ear, a misstep that forces me to breathe in her sweet, vanilla scent. Christ, she smells good. "I'm an excellent teacher," I manage to say. "Are you suggesting there's some other reason for my popularity?"

She shrugs, her eyes twinkling again. "It's a mystery, I'm sure."

I'd like to press the issue further, but we have an audience. Holding the door open as everyone else rushes in, I tell them, "Please choose a partner and for each pairing decide who's on offense and defense."

Once we're all inside, Eva asks, "Where do you want me?"

She's messing with me, I guarantee it. There's no way Eva doesn't understand the implications of an open-ended question like that. Besides, the answers are obvious. In my bed. On the floor. Against a wall. Draped over the couch. In a closet if it has room enough for two people—and maybe even if it doesn't.

"I mean, where do you want me to stand?" she clarifies, a lopsided grin revealing what's going on in that head of hers.

This is a good development. She's being open and friendly, no evidence of a grudge in sight. Makes me hopeful that we can still be friends. "Let's do the demo at the front of the room," I say with a grin. "I'll introduce you and say a few words. Last name's Montgomery, right?"

She lifts her eyebrows in surprise. "You remember."

I could never forget it, but I'm not confessing to that. "It stuck with me. I think Tori mentioned it recently." All true.

"Huh," she says, her lips pursed as though she's deep in thought. "I don't think I ever caught yours."

"It's Castillo."

"Anthony Castillo. I like it. Rolls off the tongue quite nicely."

Yeah, not touching that one, either. I *know* I don't have the stamina to discuss tongues with Eva. "Okay, everyone, listen up. This is Eva Montgomery. Some of you may know her as one of the new instructors here, but what you probably don't know is that she's a black belt in tae kwon do."

"I see some of you are confused," she chimes in. "All that really means is that I can kick Anthony's ass."

Most of the women laugh; a few of them egg her on by shouting, "Yes, girl."

I put up a hand to quiet them down. "Okay, let's get to work." Then I place both hands behind my back and walk across the room as I address them, their eager faces a reminder that what I'm trying to convey in this course is important to them and to me. The idea that any person could be overpowered and sexually assaulted fills me with rage, and if I can pass on my own expertise to help even one person avoid that fate or instill in them enough confidence that they can fight off an attacker, I'll consider this class an overwhelming success. "In today's session, I want to give you strategies for dealing with an assailant who's not in your personal space. At least not yet. And one of the most effective ways to deal with someone who's within your zone of contact but doesn't have their hands on you is a groin strike."

"Kick 'em in the balls," someone in the back shouts.

"Well, maybe, depending on who you're dealing with," I say. "But bear in mind a groin kick is gender neutral. That area is vulnerable for everyone."

Beside me, Eva shifts, her arms going behind her back to mimic my stance. "Well, everyone's vulnerable, yes. But testicles don't have any structural protection, and men don't tolerate pain as well as women do."

"Debatable," I say, flashing her a look of warning.

"Not at all shocked you'd say that."

Stopping in front of her, I lean over, whispering for her ears only. "Hey, I didn't ask you to be my verbal sparring partner, too."

She maintains a straight face while she rubs her lips together and listens intently. Then she says, "No need to thank me. I'm a giver like that."

She amuses me. Distracts me with her wit. Just two of her many talents. Still, it's time to get this class on track. I pick up the strike pad and turn to face Eva. She bends her knees and raises her fists to protect her face. "We're going to show you what you're aiming for," I tell them. "Before you think about kicking, a couple of things to keep in mind. First, your feet should be planted firmly on the ground with your hips leaning forward. That will help you kick with power. Second, most of the impact should be on the top of your foot, not your toes. Kicking with your toes could land you in a cast. Third, don't kick straight on. Kick at a thirty-degree angle at least. That'll ensure your attacker doesn't clock you with his head. Anything to add, Eva?"

She straightens to address the class. "The key is not to think of it as a strike to the groin. Really what you're trying to do is split this person's groin in half and rip them apart from the balls up. So your task is to crack this person's head open, but you've got to go through the groin first."

The more she speaks, the more my balls shrink away in protest. Out of the corner of my eye, I see Kurt slip into the studio. He's here sooner than I expected, but there's no point in making a switch now. It would be too disruptive. "All right, all right. Let's talk about engaging with your attacker. In short, you want to make eye contact, because if you don't, you're likely looking at their crotch, which is telegraphing that you intend to kick them there. Let's show them how that can go wrong, Eva."

Without missing a beat, she stares at my crotch before she strikes the pad. I evade the kick easily and scramble behind her, applying a light choke hold. "So you see—"

It happens fast. So fucking fast. Before I can fully process it, Eva presses a thumb against my hold, side-steps it, and then pivots to elbow me in the center of my chest. Really hard.

The swift blow knocks the wind out of me and I double over, partly to catch my breath and partly to recover from the pain. Fuck, this woman's dangerous. And somewhere in my adrenaline-spiked brain, an unwelcome thought comes to me: *In more ways than one, Anthony. In more ways than one.*

Eva

OOPS. I DIDN'T mean to do that—instinct is a curious thing—but I'd be lying if I claimed I didn't enjoy that just a bit.

Before I can check on Anthony, a stocky middle-aged white man with bulging biceps for days lumbers forward and places a beefy hand on my victim's back. "You okay there, A?"

Anthony breathes heavily through his nose as he responds. "Yeah. I'm all right. She just caught me off guard."

The beefy man, who I assume is his tardy boss, chuckles. "Kind of the point, isn't it?"

Anthony narrows his eyes into slits and shakes off the man's assistance. He presses his lips together, his face contorted into an incredulous expression. "You're late, which left me at Eva's mercy. I'll find a way to make you pay for this." He points at his boss, a stern look in his eyes, but with a smile to signal he's not serious. "You. Stand in the corner for now."

Anthony recovers from my unintentional pummeling with remarkable ease, straightening to his full height and stretching his chest wide. Turning to the class, he says, "All right, here's what this is supposed to look like."

Silently, Anthony and I move into our respective positions; he holds the strike pad in front of his groin, and I bend my knees with my hips leaning forward as he instructed.

My leg flies up to his crotch with as much force as I can put behind it, landing with a loud *thwap* that echoes in the room. He absorbs the kick easily, his arms locked in front of him. "Excellent, Eva. Again." Bending at the knees, he repositions himself and waits for another kick. This time I strike harder, swinging my arms up and then behind me to add more power to the move.

Anthony shouts his encouragement. "*Yes, Eva, yes. That's it.*"

We straighten immediately, exchanging guilty glances. I know what I'm thinking. Is he thinking the same thing? Because that sure sounds like what he said to me in Room 308 of the Marriott in Windsor.

Anthony swipes his free hand down his face—as though he's putting on a mask—and turns to the class. "Okay, everyone. Now you try it. Targets, make sure you protect the groin area. Strikers, settle into your stances without giving your target a warning as to when the strikes will occur."

As everyone shuffles into position and practices, I slink over to Anthony with the intention of apologizing for what he probably thought was a cheap shot earlier. But our latecomer thrusts his hand in my direction before I can say anything, and Anthony goes off to watch the students—actually, fleeing might be a better description of what he's doing.

"That was a fantastic move, my dear. Where'd you learn it?" He reaches out for a handshake. "I'm Kurt, by the way."

I take his hand and pump it with confidence, just the way my father taught me to. "Eva, good to meet you. Took a self-defense class a few years back and got certified after that."

"She's being too modest," Anthony says over his shoulder. "Eva's a black belt in tae kwon do."

Kurt's eyebrows rise like a Phoenix. "Really? What degree?"

"Made it to third."

"Hot damn," he says, slapping his thigh for emphasis. "You'd be a perfect fit for my training class. Ever thought about getting into the biz?"

I suppose *the biz* is shorthand for the entertainment business, and the answer is definitely not. "Acting, you mean?"

"Well, some acting, yeah," Kurt says. "But mostly we're talking really physical stuff. Stunt work. Standing in for the actors who are too chickenshit to do the dangerous stuff themselves. We're always looking to grow our list of stunt people on standby. Especially women. I'm sure you'd get a few gigs in no time at all."

LA's a trip. I've been here less than a week and someone's already proposing that I make a living crashing into stuff. "Um, sounds interesting, but I'm good."

"Well, if you ever change your mind, ask Anthony about it. You never know when you might need a few extra thousand dollars in your pocket. Not bad for a few days' work."

He ambles off to join Anthony, and I stare after him. Back the hell up. Did he just say a few extra thousand dollars? For a few days' work? Does anyone ever *not* need a few extra thousand dollars? Do *I* not need a few extra thousand dollars?

Anthony makes a couple remarks and calls a five-minute break while I process the possibilities. I have so many questions, which I'm eager to ask once I can speak to him alone. After the last student sails through the door with a jaunty wave in our direction, Kurt following a respectable distance behind her, I pounce on Anthony. "This training Kurt mentioned, how long is it? And how much does it cost? How big's the class? And when and where is it held? Do you help with job placement? Would I need to join a union? How does that work?"

He stares down at me, his brows knitted in confusion. "What are you talking about?"

Obviously, he's never heard of context clues. Or he's being purposefully obtuse about this. "I'm talking about stunt training, of course. Kurt thinks I might be a natural, and he mentioned you have some kind of program in place."

He crosses the room and tosses a towel onto his duffel bag, and then he scrolls through his phone as though my questions aren't worthy of serious consideration. "Stunt work isn't a hobby, it's a career. It's not something to do on a whim. And it's dangerous. And there are no guarantees you'll even get work. That's Kurt's thing. Shooting off at the mouth. Don't take him too seriously."

Well, damn. Someone's a Davey Downer. I'm still curious, though, so I refuse to let up. "But what if someone wasn't doing it on a whim, and they'd thought long and hard about it. How much would it cost for such a person to take your course?"

"Wouldn't matter," he says as he strides to the door. "It's sold out, and we have a waiting list a mile long." He spins around to face me and uses his back to push the door open. "Thanks for your help today. You saved my ass. Since Kurt's here now, I'll finish up the demo with him. Hope your first class goes well."

And then he's gone, not having answered a single question I posed. What the hell? What is this man's problem? Now that I think about it, I should have kicked him in the balls for real when I had the chance.

Chapter Five

When life hands you lemons, squeeze the juice
of those lemons right into life's eyes. That'll
teach it not to mess with you.

Eva

THE THREE DUDES in the back of the studio help me get
over my new class jitters—and distract me from overthinking Anthony's puzzling behavior. They'll rue the
day they decided to take Advanced Zumba for the sole
purpose of staring at women's asses. I'll make sure of it.

With a friendly wave and a welcoming smile, I
beckon them to the front. "Hey, guys. Would you mind
coming up here? Most of the moves for the second half
of the class will be facing the back wall, so I want to be
sure everyone can see. You're all so tall."

Their heads swivel back and forth between them,
and then the lankiest of the three, a white guy with a
man bun, steps forward and motions his friends to do
the same.

As I see it, my job has three main parts: illustrate the dance steps in an easy-to-follow way; regulate the class environment to ensure a positive and safe experience for everyone; and motivate each student to do their best and have fun. I'm in regulation mode, and given my day so far, I'm going to relish the task ahead of me.

I had them pegged before the end of the first song. They walked in here dressed to play pickup basketball on the court across the street. Two in the trio didn't even bother to tie their shoelaces, so one of them lost a sneaker after the first sequence with a skip-and-a-hop combo. Plus, they don't know any of the basic steps. And the biggest clue: They're literally staring at women's butts while pretending to dance. The result is that most of the class, including a few men with excellent coordination, are doing a kick-ass job of following my lead, but these three look like they're making their own dance video for "Rhythmless Nation."

I need to establish from the outset that I'm not to be trifled with, and although I can't kick them out, I *can* use them to demonstrate the complexity of the moves our students will be learning over time—and make them suffer while doing so. But I'll give them one more shot to save themselves. "Before we begin again, I just want to make clear that there's no shame in deciding these moves are too advanced for your skill set, and I won't be offended if the choreography or music isn't to your liking. I want everyone to enjoy themselves, but if this class isn't a good fit for you for whatever reason, feel free to step out now."

It's a risky statement to make, but it serves two purposes. One, it helps to ensure the students are enthusiastic. Group fitness feeds off the collective energy of its participants, and if that's low, your class will be a dud. Two, it gives my three stooges a chance to leave without embarrassing themselves any further.

No one's leaving, though. In fact, people are shaking out their limbs and stretching in anticipation of the next dance. Okay, then, embarrassment it is.

My heavy-handed claps get everyone's attention, and I'm gratified to see several students looking at me expectantly, their bodies and faces vibrating with positive energy. "Okay, everyone, I've been playing around with a few new routines of my own that add strength training to the mix, and I'd love to try them out with you. Sound good?"

Most of the students cheer me on, but my three Zumba drop-ins aren't taking part in the celebration. Instead, they're exchanging furtive glances, probably because we're still facing the front of the room, and that's where they're positioned.

"Now, I recognize some of you may not be familiar with these moves, so I'm going to break them down for you. And to do that, I'll need a few volunteers." I spin around and ignore the enthusiastic hands in the air. "How about you guys? You're strapping young men, right? This should be a piece of cake for you."

There's a moment's hesitation as they consider my request, but then the ringleader pivots to face the class and hams it up, alternating between poorly performed salsa moves and bicep curls.

I can't help picturing Lin-Manuel Miranda performing *Hamilton*'s title song, and in my head, I'm singing along with him, my voice sure and strong: *"Just you wait. Just you wait."*

"First, we're going to begin with twelve burpees, each one in four counts." I get in position to demonstrate the sequence, walking everyone through each part of the exercise. "Down. Back legs out. Back legs return. And stand up." I turn to my unwitting assistants. "Okay, show them twelve burpees and finish with a salsa travel in two counts."

There's a lot of eyebrow scrunching and frowning going on, but I pretend not to see it. Eventually, they get in position and perform twelve burpees. When they're done, they shake their hips in a sad approximation of a salsa travel.

Each is huffing from the exertion. Splendid.

Next, I demonstrate a plank followed by a salsa side step in plank position. It's a dance and exercise combo that was very popular in my Philly classes; it's not as popular with these three, though. And I am here for it.

"Okay, now we're going to add a few basic moves and see how it all looks together." I click the remote and shuffle to "Macarena."

I'm so petty, and given the way some of the students

are trying to hide their laughter, they are, too. This is going to work out just fine.

AT THE END of the class, Tori meets me at the door. "So, how was it?"

She's biting her lip, her nose scrunched as if she hopes it's not bad news. I'm certain she's nervous because she wants me to be happy, and if this job doesn't work out for me, she'll feel partially responsible for selling me so hard on the idea. But I'd never blame her. I'm determined to succeed despite any obstacles that dare to block my way.

"It was great," I say. "The people were enthusiastic, and I was feeding off their good vibes. I had a few guys who treated the class like a check-in meeting at Ass Watchers, but I set them straight."

Tori places a hand on my wrist, a sneaky grin on her face. "What'd you do?"

"Broke out the good ol' 'Macarena.'"

She throws her head back and cackles. "Love it."

I slip my arm through hers as we walk toward the staff room. "I do have something I want to talk to you about, though."

She looks down at me, a grave expression on her face, and motions me inside when we get to the threshold. "What's going on?"

The staff room contains several steel round tables, each with seating for six. We drop into the seats at the table closest to the door. I hate that I'm bringing this up on my first day, but if I can't talk to Tori about this, I'll explode. And every woman needs that one friend who'll let her vent and then squeeze her arm when she's done. "Turns out my father isn't going to help me with the move. Says he thinks it's a mistake and he doesn't want to enable me." I wipe at the tears welling up in my eyes. "I don't know why I'm being so emotional about this. So I won't buy a used car like I planned. I'll survive. It's just—"

She nods, throwing on her puppy dog eyes. "You feel betrayed."

"Not exactly. Betrayal would mean I didn't see it coming, but I wasn't surprised. Above all, I was disappointed."

Right on time, Tori leans over, takes my hand, and squeezes it. "You're allowed to feel that way."

"A part of me knows that to be the case. Another part of me—a teeny, tiny part of me—thinks maybe he's right. Maybe I will fail, and he's just trying to save me a ton of grief."

She pins me with a *now you listen to me* stare, her gaze fierce and commanding. "That teeny, tiny part of you needs to shut the fuck up."

I burst out laughing, just as she intended.

"You are a badass," she continues, "and we're not going to let your father's games throw you off track, okay?"

She's right. I *know* this. My father wants to force me

to make different choices, and he's doing what he can to facilitate his objective. Now that I think about it, I wouldn't be at all shocked if he offered to help me, fully intending to back out once I got here. He would call it tough love, but love isn't manipulation, and this latest stunt is exactly that. I slump down into the chair and rest the back of my head against the top rail. "No, you're right. It's just been a long day, and my badass mojo is spent."

"Well, let me give you some of mine, then." Lips flattened into a threatening grimace, she rises and strides with typical purpose to a black credenza, where she throws open a cabinet and riffles through it. I don't have enough energy to be angry, but she's happy to be my surrogate, and I love her for it.

"Okay, let's figure this out," she says, finally producing a fresh notepad and a ballpoint pen.

When she sits again, I notice the pen features the studio's logo. Fancy.

"What did your father promise to pay?" she asks, pulling me out of my random thoughts.

"He said he'd help with rent for the first year or so. I can cover that with savings, but that'll mean I'll need to table my plans to buy a used car."

With a wave of her pen, she dismisses that concern as though it's no big deal. "Plenty of people don't drive in LA."

"Oh yeah? Do you know any of these"—I make air quotes—"plenty of people?"

She shrugs unapologetically. "Nope."

"Figured you'd say that. But a car *would* make a big difference to a transplant like me. I'm still furnishing my apartment, and I'd like to explore everything this town has to offer. A car would make all that easier. Anyway, if I can find some way to supplement my income from time to time, I'd be in good shape to rebuild my car fund. Problem is, my schedule here is all over the place. If I try to get another job, what will I tell them? I teach class at 10:00 a.m., 11:00 a.m., then again at 3:00 p.m. some days, and at 5:00 and 7:00 p.m. every other day?"

She writes "irregular schedule" on the pad. "And technically, you're on probation here, so I can't give you extra hours. Not yet. Because if I did, I'd have a mutiny on my hands. Dammit." After writing "no additional hours for now," she drops her forehead onto the table, her mass of curls obscuring her face from view. "This sucks."

"Tori, *this* isn't your fault, so please don't go there. I came into this knowing I'd have to prove myself before you'd give me a full schedule. And it's not like I'm worried about paying rent or anything like that. As much as I'd like one, a car is a luxury for me."

She lifts her head and regards me with sad eyes. "Your father's a butthead."

I can't help laughing at the juvenile description, partly because it's true and partly because I know she wants me to.

"I hesitate to ask this, but . . ."

"Ask," I tell her.

"What about your mom?"

"That's a no."

"May I ask why not?"

"Well, the easiest answer is that my mother's not swimming around in extra cash. But the more complicated one is that I don't want to summon a shitstorm. I already mentioned to her that he'd agreed to help me. If I told her he reneged on that commitment, she'd go nuclear."

Besides, I'm not in the mood for I-told-you-so's. And if she knew he'd acted exactly as she'd predicted, she would remind me that in the hands of the wrong man, love is a weapon he'll use to control you. My problem is, they're *always* the wrong men. "This is a lot to take in, especially after the shit Nate pulled. I just want to figure this out without a man's tentacles trying to orchestrate my choices."

Nate, my ex-boss in Philly and occasional lover, who wouldn't release me from my obligation to give thirty days' notice because he thought he could change my mind about leaving in the interim. Before that, it was Jason, my first serious boyfriend after college. I thought we'd get married someday. He did, too, but he wanted it to happen sooner than I did, and his brilliant idea to accomplish his goal was to steal my birth control pills and try to convince me to have sex without a condom. I found *my* pills in *his* jacket when I was searching for the apartment keys he'd borrowed. Needless to say, Jason and I never married.

"Okay, your mother's not an option. Let's dispense with the simple stuff, then. If things get tight, you know I've got you."

"I appreciate that, but my whole point in moving here was to establish myself in a new city, so I need to come up with a long-range plan. My father's she-nanigans made me realize something I hadn't really focused on."

"What's that?" Tori asks.

"I moved across the country to do exactly what I'd been doing in Philly. I'm just doing it in a place with a higher cost of living."

Tori's face falls. "You're selling this move short, you know. This is *LA*, dammit. I'm here. Your father's *not* here. You won't have to deal with Nate anymore, either. There's a lot about this move to be excited about."

She's not wrong, but I can't ignore that niggling feeling inside me that I should be doing *more*. Proving once and for all to my father that I know what I'm doing.

Tori writes "production stuff" on the pad. "I could ask Carter about any leads in the movie industry. Maybe he'll know of some temp work that could give you a quick influx of cash."

My mind flashes to my interaction with Anthony this afternoon. "Actually, there's something you might be able to help with. Your cousin? Anthony?"

"Yes, I know who he is," she says with a smile.

"He owns a stunt training company, right? Or co-owns it?"

Tori writes "Anthony" with a question mark after his name. "He's an instructor, but he doesn't own any part of the business."

Interesting. Anthony's reaction to my inquiries suggested he was the person with the power to decide whether I could attend the boot camp, but that's not the case at all. "Then Kurt's the one I need to convince."

"Well, no. Kurt doesn't make a move without consulting Anthony first. That's just how they operate." She furrows her brows. "But what would you need to . . . oh. Really, Eva? Stunt training?"

"I know. Wacky idea, right? But you can't deny I'm a decent candidate."

"I can."

"Haters gonna hate."

She scrunches her eyebrows. For an instant, I consider telling her they'll stay that way permanently if she isn't too careful, but she'll know I'm trying to distract her.

"Eva, that's a completely different career," she says. "And I'm sure it's dangerous. And there's so much involved in pursuing it, how would you even know where to begin?"

I swipe the pen out of her hand, slide the notepad in front of me, and write, "Research stunt training."

"You're serious about this?"

I shrug. "I'm not sure, but I could be. If it's something I want to pursue, would you put in a good word with your cousin?" Referring to him by his relation to her is a good way of recalibrating my brain: He's *not* sexy. He's *not* ridiculously generous in bed. He's *not* as outrageous as I am. Nuh-uh. He's just Anthony.

She waves my question away. "You don't have to ask. Of course I will. But I wouldn't be your best friend if I didn't point out that there are like a thousand other things you could do besides stunt training to supplement your income."

"Sure, I know that, too. This just feels more meaningful. I'd be able to grow that car fund and show my father that my physical training isn't a negative thing, that it can open doors for me. And if I'm being honest, I kind of want to prove him wrong in a spectacular way." I crouch down in my seat and wince. "Is that petty of me?"

Tori purses her lips and nods. "Frankly, it's petty as fuck. Which worries me."

"I understand. You're skeptical. I'd be skeptical too if you came to me with an idea like this. Besides, I'm just thinking about it."

"While you're thinking about it, consider this." She snatches the pen back and reaches over to write "Anthony," underlining his name three times.

"What does that mean?"

"You'd have to work with him."

Oh. That. Well, that shouldn't be a problem. I'm as uninterested in picking up where we left off as Anthony says he is. And we're adults. That should be enough. "And that means . . . ?"

"I have it on good authority that he's a different person on the job. A real hard-ass. That has a lot to do with the bozos who show up and think they can become stunt performers just because they used to backflip off their roof onto the trampoline in their backyard. He says he gets a lot of those, and it's a waste of his time. You'd be putting yourself at his mercy, and that's apparently not somewhere you want to be."

The unintended innuendo in her words isn't lost on me. Honestly, being at Anthony's mercy doesn't sound all that bad. No, no, no. I can't go there. One-and-done is my new motto. I need to approach any future dealings with Anthony in a detached manner, push any memories of the masterful way he swivels his hips when he's on top way back to the dustiest recesses of my mind. "Oh, come on. How bad can he be? He's such a chill guy." And based on what I've seen, that's certainly true. Still, a frisson of unease runs through me as I remember the way he rejected my attempts to get more information about the school.

"Not about his work, though."

"That may be, but all I'm asking is that you soften him up a bit for me."

"Done."

"And as for Anthony's attitude, I'll deal with it."

"Famous last words," Tori says under her breath.

"Whatever, bitch. Mark my words, then. Anthony will be handled."

"Okay, we'll see about that. In the meantime, we

can't have your father's news souring your first week in LA. How about you come over for dinner Friday? Decompress a bit. Carter would love to see you."

I'm not in the mood to be social—in fact, this might be the first time in history that I'm experiencing sensory overload because . . . LA—but a quiet evening with Carter and Tori promises the kind of low-stress environment I need. Anything more than that could be dangerous—for the people around me.

Chapter Six

Anthony

THE SAVORY SCENT of my father's *picadillo* hits me the moment I open the front door. That must mean he's making *empanadas*. Hells yeah. I take the stack of mail with me down the front hall to the kitchen, where I find him rolling out dough, a pair of black-rimmed glasses like the ones I sometimes use for driving resting on the tip of his nose as he studies a recipe. That's unheard of in this house.

"Hey, everything okay in here?" I ask.

He doesn't look up when he answers. "Not sure. I'm making one of the recipes in *that book*. Trying to support my sister and nieces." Sighing, he shakes his head and shrugs. "Baked empanadas. Who ever heard of such a thing? *Bueno, vamos a ver.*"

That book refers to the collection of recipes my Tía Lourdes and her two daughters—Tori and Bianca—published recently. It takes the traditional dishes my aunt serves in her Philadelphia restaurant and updates them for people wanting to incorporate Puerto Rican food into their healthy lifestyles. My father's proud of them but skeptical.

He tsks as he sprinkles salt on the mountain of dough he's made. "I don't know, *mijo*. It's called *Puerto Rico Over Easy*, but maybe they should have called it *Puerto Rico Under Salted*. Who in their right mind puts just a teaspoon of salt in their dough? I think I'd rather use *Goya discos* than stuff my precious *carne* in this."

He's contemplating using store-bought empanada dough? Shit, that's saying something. "Give it a chance, Pop. Tía Lourdes knows what she's doing. And maybe you have to taste it all together before it's the real deal."

He mutters under his breath, indignation apparent in the set of his shoulders and the wrinkles in his forehead. Still, he presses a large cookie cutter into the dough. *Chacho*, even convincing him to use that technique was a feat. Before I introduced him to modern kitchen tools, he used a small plate to form the discs. "This size is perfect. No fancy tool's going to do better," he'd say. I love the man, but he's stubborn as hell.

"How was your day?" he asks, finally looking up.

"It was fine," is all I can manage. Truth is, I don't know what to make of my day. Eva's unexpected arrival threw me off center. It's as if my brain can only perceive her in one context—my cousin's sexy, outspoken friend who I thought I'd only see occasionally at a family gathering years after I'd put our amazing night together behind me—and it's refusing to adjust to the new reality: That sexy, outspoken friend isn't going anywhere, that night is still fresh in my mind, and now I need to navigate my interaction with her so I don't come off like a dick. I'm doing a poor job so far.

"Must have been exciting," he says, watching me curiously. "Any of that mail for me?"

The question reminds me that I haven't looked through the stack yet. "Not sure." I round the kitchen counter and pull the garbage cabinet open, sifting through the envelopes and glossy coupon books and tossing the junk mail in the recycling bin. Something pings in my chest when I see the letter from the bank. What's inside isn't a mystery, but seeing tangible proof that my mortgage application was declined dredges up a memory I'd rather not revisit: the day my mother told me she was leaving Papi for good and asked me to take care of him.

I can't suppress it, no matter how hard I try. "You're a man now," she'd said, taking my hand and leading me to sit on our couch. My father was in the kitchen, whistling while he stuck candles in a cake so my parents could celebrate my eighteenth birthday with me. It wasn't my actual birthday—that would have been too cruel. No, she'd waited until the next day, after I'd partied all night with my friends.

I'd puffed out my chest a bit, figuring she was going to share some motherly wisdom; instead, she told me she'd held on as long as she could, but it was time for her to go, and moving back to San Juan was the easiest way to make a clean break. She loved him, she'd explained.

Neither one had cheated on the other. They hadn't bickered or disrespected each other. She just didn't love him as much as he loved her, and she'd always felt smothered. "He's going to need you. So be there for your father like he's been there for you. You two, together, will be fine." And just like that, she mentally checked out, throwing away twenty years of marriage before I could even make a wish.

I understand her a little better now. Experience does that to you. Now I know a simple truth: In every relationship, you run the risk of either being hurt or doing the hurting. No relationship can achieve that perfect balance, that point when two halves love each other equally. In my parents' case, my father loved my mother more, and he's still paying the price.

Still, I've never viewed caring for Papi as an obligation simply because my mother placed that burden on my young shoulders. It's what I would have done even if my mother had never sat me down for that talk. But the letter in my hands reminds me that there's more to be done so my father and I can be "fine."

"Dear Mr. Castillo," it reads. "Thank you for applying for a home loan with Ridley Financial Services Group. Unfortunately, we regret to inform you that your application has been declined for the following reason(s) . . ."

I might as well emblazon the reason on my chest like a modern-day scarlet letter: "Insufficient stability of income."

Fuck.

I'm thirty years old, and the bank has deemed my

income insufficiently stable. Never mind that in some years, I can easily clear six figures. It's the other years that matter. The years when steady stunt work isn't available. Or the ones when a production budget can't absorb the cost of having both Kurt and me on set. If I can't convince him to make me a partner in the business, I'll be stuck in this adulthood limbo forever. And I need to raise this issue with him soon. For now, though, I rip up the letter and shove it under the junk mail in the bin. "Nothing for you, Pop."

Unfortunately, bending down sends a wave of pain from my sternum to my shoulder. I rub my chest in a circular motion and wince, the sound catching my father's attention.

"What's wrong?" he asks. "Get hurt on the job?"

Hardly. "No, a woman elbowed me in the chest in that self-defense class I teach."

"You taught her well, then."

"Nope, she already knew what to do."

He tilts his head and puckers his lips. "So why's she taking the class?"

"She's not in the class. I just . . ." I'm not up for explaining this tonight. "Never mind. It's not important." Knowing I'll distract him if I sample his *picadillo* before the flavor's developed to his exact specifications, I scoop some onto the wooden spoon on the stove and blow on the meat.

"*¡Para! No está listo,*" he says, trying to bat my hand away.

"That's okay. I just want a little taste." Damn, that's good. As usual, the chunky ground beef is seasoned to perfection. When I chew, a burst of onion, tomato, and garlic flavors hits my tongue like Pop Rocks. That doesn't mean I won't mess with him. "Did you put cilantro in the *sofrito*?"

"Of course."

"Might want to add some more."

He frowns at me. "Is that so?"

I take a few steps before I mention the other missing ingredient. "Oh, and you might want to add a little more salt. Seems Tía Lourdes isn't the only who undersalts her food."

The dishrag hits me in the back as I run out of the kitchen.

"These empanadas need to *bake* for thirty minutes," he calls after me. The sneer in his voice is plain when he says the word *bake*. In this house, baking an empanada is a high crime punishable by ten years in food prison.

"I'm sure it'll be great," I yell back.

"If it isn't, I made my regular dough, too."

"That's called not giving the recipe a fair shot."

"That's called being smart," he fires back.

"I'm going to take a shower before dinner."

"You do that. I didn't want to say anything before, but you stink."

As I walk to the bedroom, I laugh to myself, knowing I inherited my smart-ass mouth from him. It's true our lives may not be perfect, but we'll always have each other. And yeah, it sucks that we're still renting this house, but I'll figure out a way to buy a place outright and give him the permanent home he deserves.

It's the least I can do given the shit he's been through.

TURNS OUT, BAKED empanadas are not my thing. The best part of an empanada, the crispy, salty edges of scored dough, were nowhere to be found. In silent protest, I'm eating *fried* Puerto Rican food for lunch today. And these *chicharrones de pollo* taste so fucking good I might cry.

"What the hell are you eating over there? Stir-fried orgasm? You look like your eyes are going to fall out of your head."

Kurt's sitting across from me, our desks facing each other in the training center's sole office. He's just jealous; I would be too if my partner guilt-tripped me into eating brussels sprouts for lunch.

"It's fried chicken, man," I say between hearty chews. "From Mofongos."

He squeezes his eyes shut. "Fuck. Joel won't let me eat there anymore. Says my cholesterol's too high."

"Nothing stopping you from getting their salads, so I'm not buying it."

"When I could be eating those juicy, salty pieces of fried chicken?" he says, pouting like a small child. "That's like asking me to buy a fruit cup when there's a perfectly frosted chocolate cake for the same price. I won't tempt myself like that, kid."

I wave a piece in the air, taunting him with it. "What harm will one piece do? Moderation is my mantra."

He lifts his chin. "Fine. Toss it to me. If it lands in my mouth, then it was meant to be."

I lob the *chicharron* across the room. To no one's surprise, Kurt lurches forward to catch it, succeeds, and shudders as he chews. "Goddamn, that's good. Did you grow up on that?"

"Yup. My mom made it all the time. With rice and beans and some shredded lettuce and thinly sliced tomatoes that I never ate."

"Sounds like a dream childhood."

Most of it, yeah. But it's hard to remember the good when I know the bad that followed.

Kurt notices my hard expression. "Sorry, man. Didn't mean to touch a nerve."

I wave away his apology. "Don't worry about it."

Kurt swivels in his chair to face his computer, undoubtedly to begin his midafternoon ritual of scouring *The Hollywood Reporter* for breaking news about development deals and casting calls. His strategy is simple: If we're able to line up work for our stunt people, we can use those acting credits in our promotional materials and attract more customers to the training program. And so far, I can't argue with the results. That, along with our excellent reputation in the industry, makes us *the* training firm to beat.

For six years, I've been riding the highs and lows with him, serving as his sounding board on virtually every aspect of the business. But now it's time to take my place beside him. If he'll let me. I set aside my food and lean forward, my hands folded on the desk. "Hey, Kurt?"

"Yeah?" he asks, his eyes still focused on the computer screen.

My chest tightens in the seconds before I ask my question, because a negative answer would be just as life-challenging as a positive one. If Kurt would prefer to run the business "as is," I'll need to give some serious thought to moving on and chasing that elusive financial stability banks are so concerned about. "Have you ever thought about taking on a partner?"

He shifts away from the screen and faces me, dropping back into his chair as though I've surprised him, his eyebrows squeezed together. "Are we talking specifically about you?"

I figure being direct is the best course here. "Yes."

"Honestly? I've been so comfortable with the way we've worked together, it never occurred to me. But I can see why that would be a problem. Now that you've raised the issue, though, I can give it some thought. Fair enough?"

I nod, relieved that he didn't answer in a way that would have forced me to rethink my role in the company. "That's fair. We can—"

Outside, the side door squeaks open, and we both sit up. Training doesn't begin for another couple of hours, and we rarely get unannounced visitors here at the facility.

"Anthony," a woman yells.

We both relax again. The sound of Tori's voice is always welcome, even if it means Kurt and I will need to resume our discussion later.

"We're back here, *princessa*."

She barrels through the door, filling the room with her king-size presence. Her eyes sweep across the space and zero in on me. "I need to speak with you."

"I never would have guessed that."

"Hey, watch it. Any more sarcasm and you'll lose your favorite-cousin status."

As usual, I get nothing from her but affection—and a shitload of sass.

Kurt stands and heads for the door. "I'll give you two a minute alone."

She whips around and puts up a hand. "Please stay, Kurt. This concerns you, too."

That discreet glance between Kurt and me? It's our equivalent of *oh shit* in physical form. What topic could Tori possibly need to talk to us both about? Kurt resettles into his chair while I tilt my chair back and throw my booted feet on the desktop, trying to make clear I'm unfazed by whatever she's about to tell me even though I can feel the pulse in my neck quicken as I wait. "So what's up?"

"I want to talk to you about Eva and your training camp."

I scrub a hand down my face and place my feet back on the floor. "No."

"Anthony, why are you being so stubborn about this? Eva would be perfect for your program. It says so on the website." She pulls out her phone, and after a few taps, begins reading. "'Elite Stunt Training's ideal student isn't a daredevil or an adventure seeker but rather an individual with a background in areas that complement stunt skills, such as martial arts, personal training, and gymnastics.'" She raises her brows at me. "See? Eva wasn't a gymnast, I don't think, but she's a fitness instructor, *and* she has martial arts experience. This should be a no-brainer."

I'm fucking around with the papers on my desk for no purpose at all. Or maybe I'm doing it because I need to keep my hands busy. I'm not sure. What I *do* know is that having Eva in my work space isn't conducive to putting our one night together behind us. We need distance if we're going to keep our hookup firmly in the past, and training together is the opposite of that. But more importantly, why the hell is Eva even considering stunt work? Sounds to me like she's going off half-cocked. "Listen, I get that she looks like a great candidate on paper, but it's not as simple as you're making it out to be. We don't take everyone interested in our class, not with the doors that can open after someone takes it. We personally vouch for our graduates, so we need to be selective, and we can't take people who are dabbling in this kind of work. It's a profession, not a hobby."

She pops a hand on her hip and gives me a narrow-eyed pouty face. "Goodness, it's not like I'm asking you to take on someone unqualified. I'm asking you to make room in your class for an excellent candidate, one who needs this opportunity for . . . reasons."

Hmm, reasons? Now I'm intrigued. But not enough to distrust my gut, which is telling me working with Eva would be a bad idea. Even a minor demonstration at Tori's studio turned into a tussle that literally bruised my chest. I can't imagine weeks of dangerous training exercises would go any better, not with our shared history.

Tori takes a deep breath, and her gaze darts around the room, finally landing on the paper takeout container from Mofongos. "Are those *chicharrones*?" Before I can answer, she swipes my plastic fork off the top, flips the lid open, and spears a piece of my precious chicken.

"Yes, you can have some of my food," I tell her.

She pops the *chicharron* into her mouth. "*Sí, lo sé. That's why I didn't bother to ask." While she chomps on my food with enthusiasm, I nudge my chin at Kurt, hoping he'll chime in and support me on this. Sure, he's my boss, and maybe I shouldn't be speaking out of turn, but if I'm going to show him I'm ready for more responsibility, I need to act like a person who can handle being in charge.

Kurt's eyes widen, and then he grabs a book off his desk and thumbs through it while he figures out what to say. Good thing he mostly works behind the scenes these days because the man can't act for shit. After clearing his throat, he looks up and says, "Plus, there's the teacher-student issue."

Tori stops chewing. And I stop breathing—for a few seconds, at least.

I have no idea where he's going with this, and I don't want to know. What I'd like is for everyone to go away so I can finish my lunch.

"What teacher-student issue?" Tori asks Kurt.

"Well, Anthony and Eva are obviously interested in each other, but we have a strict prohibition on romantic connections between our instructors and students."

Tori snorts and looks around the room. "You mean all two of you?"

"We're still instructors," Kurt says with a shrug. "It's not good for our reputation, either among prospective students or in the industry. If we're going to rec someone for a job, it needs to be because we have complete confidence in their abilities and *nothing more*."

Tori reaches over the desk and pinches me like a Puerto Rican mom who's just discovered her kid was out all night—in other words, repeatedly and with annoying super strength. "Is this true? You're interested in Eva and that's the real reason you don't want her in the program? Because that would be some sexist bullshit, Anthony."

"No, no, no," I say as I dodge her torturous fingers. "Will you stop already? Kurt's off base on that one."

And I'm not aware of any official policy prohibiting me from dating someone who trains with us. The only other instructor is Kurt, and he's practically married. Still, a policy like that makes sense for all the reasons Kurt gave.

"You're not attracted to Eva, then?" Tori asks, her suspicious gaze scanning me like an X-ray machine.

Shit yeah, I'm attracted to her, but talking about relationships with me is pointless. Tori knows this. What's interesting, though, is that Eva never told Tori about our hookup. And I appreciate that—because what we did was and should remain just between us. "Look, she's an attractive woman, sure, but I don't have any plans to date her or anything. That's a given. And that's not even considering that she's probably not interested in dating me, either."

Tori nods. "Good. So I detect no problems. She's exceedingly qualified, the student-teacher policy doesn't apply, and I'm your cousin, who will harass you for the rest of my days if you don't let Eva into your program."

"She'll need to pass a physical," Kurt says. "But assuming that checks out, I think it's only right that she get a discount on the program fee since she knows you two."

Tori walks over to Kurt's desk and ruffles his hair. "You're the best, Kurt."

"Wait, wait, wait. This is getting out of hand." I point at my reckless boss. "This is *not* how we do things."

"Then how do you do them?" Tori asks.

"We have a waiting list—"

Kurt, the unhelpful motherfucker, knowing full well our waiting list is in the computer system, picks up a blank page and waves it in the air. "With zero people on it for the next session. I checked this morning."

I jump up from my chair. "There's an application process—"

"I'll tell her to apply," Tori says. "What else?"

"And an interview, either in person or on Skype."

"That shouldn't be a problem. In fact, I think the more you get to know Eva, the more you'll see she's perfect for this program."

I say nothing. What is there to say? If Tori thinks she's going to railroad us into a hasty decision, she's flat-out wrong.

Tori chews on her bottom lip, a thoughtful expression on her face. No, not thoughtful. Crafty. That little smirk raises a few hairs on my arm, but it's gone in an instant, before I can make out whether it's a sign of trouble.

"Anything else?" Tori asks.

She's obviously not going to let this go, so I'll pacify her for the time being. "We'll think about it."

Smiling brightly, she grabs the sides of my face and plants a kiss on my forehead. "*Gracias, cielito.* Bye, Kurt."

"I haven't made any promises," I say to her as she bounces out the door.

"Neither has Eva," she singsongs in return. "Just wanted to get the ball rollin'."

I can't believe this is happening. Over the years, I've been careful about my no-strings approach. I make clear that I'm not interested in a relationship, engage with like-minded women, and avoid flings with people in my social or work circles. Now I'm facing the prospect of working with a woman I've had sex with, and if that's not enough, she's my cousin's best friend. *Good job, Anthony.*

"You handled that like a pro," Kurt says after she's gone.

It's hard not to read his assessment as sarcasm given the tenor of my thoughts, but Kurt has no clue Eva and I hooked up, and I don't plan on enlightening him.

"And I'll tell you what," he continues. "I'm going to let you lead the next training program. I'll be here for some of the sessions, and I can still do the safety speeches and all that, but it's time you get some experience running things. Let's see how you do, and then we can sit down and talk numbers and specifics. See if it makes sense. Does that work for you?"

I want to pump my fist, but I play it cool and simply nod. There's no question in my mind that I bring value to his venture, so there's nothing to be grateful for. "That works."

Now I just need Eva to abandon her idea of training with us. But if she wants an interview first, she'll get one. After all, it's only fair to give her a preview of what she'd be getting herself into.

Chapter Seven

Life tip: It's never safe to go back in the water.

Eva

MY TRIP TO Tori's place Friday evening gives me a glimpse of what it'll be like to navigate LA without a car. Doable but not without its drawbacks. Exhibit A: My Lyft driver won't shut up. Ordinarily, this fact would make me giddy—I'm the person who's on a first-name basis with a driver within seconds of climbing into the car—but this guy's sharing enough information about himself that I could probably ghostwrite his memoirs.

"So yeah, I've gone out for a few parts here and there, but I'm still waiting to hit it big," he says, flashing an ultra-bright smile that sparkles in the rearview. I bet those shiny whites set him back a few thousand dollars. "My mom says it's only a matter of time."

Doesn't he know not everything our parents say to us is true? Bless his heart.

"Maybe one day you'll be telling people you met me before I became a superstar," he adds.

I grin and nod because I don't know what else to do. "Yeah, maybe."

He exhales on a heavy sigh. "It's been hard, though. Holding on to a dream when everyone makes you feel small and insignificant for pursuing it. I've been busting my ass for years. Most nights, I walk into a seedy club and take off my clothes for people who see me as nothing more than a means to their own pleasure."

Shit, this largely one-sided conversation is taking quite a turn.

He slams his hand against the steering wheel, causing me to jump in the backseat.

"And even that's not enough money to survive," he says. "So I drive people to rich neighborhoods like this one, where people are living the life I want to live. It's so fucking unfair."

A peek in the rearview confirms the emotion clogging his throat is also causing tears to pool in his eyes. I may be one of the most cynical people on the planet, but even my icy heart can't take much more of this. I open the Lyft app and increase my tip by 100 percent. "Listen . . ." I struggle to remember his name and look down at my phone. Oh, right. Dean. Because of course. "Dean, dreams aren't meant to be easy. If they were, everyone would achieve them, and we both know that will never be the case. I see your passion . . . it's inspiring, and it'll help you persevere even when—"

Dean throws his head back and laughs like a rabid hyena. Now his passion is alarming. Shit. Am I going to need to jump out of a speeding car tonight?

When he sees my wide-eyed response, he pulls himself together and settles down. "I was just testing my acting skills on you, Eva, and I can see from your reaction that I'm legit."

"So all of that about struggling and stripping was a lie?"

"Yeah, I haven't been at this very long, and I live with my parents in a very comfortable home in Los Feliz. Thing is, LA's all about making connections, and I figure there's a bunch of Hollywood-adjacent people who probably don't drive. This car will be my audition room."

That's the stupidest shit I've ever heard. I reopen the Lyft app and reduce my tip back to its original amount. Dean—if that's even his real name—can sashay his ass back to Los Feliz without the benefit of any extra help from me. "You're a genius. Truly." I can't believe I fell for that trickery. *You're slipping, Eva.*

The phone rings, saving me from my conversation with Dean.

"Hello?"

"Eva, honey. It's your mom."

I knew she'd be calling soon. My parents and I have been playing the longest-running game of telephone since I moved into my own apartment after college. He calls her, she calls me, I call him, and then we restart the cycle. And just like the game, what gets passed on in the last phone call in no way resembles what was communicated in the first.

"Hey, Mom. How are you?"

"I'm fine. Tired, but what else is new. More importantly, I'm worried about you. Your dad told me this relocation isn't going as well as you'd hoped."

I roll my eyes, imagining what loose version of the truth he shared with her.

"He says your finances aren't as solid as you thought they'd be, and you're already considering coming home."

He'd love that to be the case, I'm sure. He'd also love it if I never told my mother that he reneged on his promise to help me with the move. Luckily for him, I'm not inclined to. Pitting them against each other is never in anyone's best interest. "Mom, I haven't even been here for a week yet, so it's too early to think about coming home. My finances are fine. And you'll be happy to know I'm signing up for an amazing opportunity."

The latest of my father's machinations gives me the final push to seriously consider participating in Elite Stunt Training's boot camp. It's limited in duration, comes with the possibility of adding some serious cash in my pocket, and will finally prove to him that I can support myself without having to sit behind a desk or stand at a lectern. Yes, Anthony's part of that package, but since neither of us is interested in a repeat performance, I can't imagine that would be a problem.

"What kind of opportunity?" she asks.

"Stunt training."

"Stunt training? Oooh, can I sign up, too?"

Her reaction sums up why my parents aren't compatible. On most issues, they hold diametrically opposing views. But even knowing this, I suspect they're no longer together for a far more sinister reason: my father's cat, Simpson. A dog lover through and through, Mom never wanted a cat, but my father brought one home anyway. The year before they formally separated, "Sleep with the cat, then" was a phrase I heard often in our home. And Simpson, who's a territorial diva with no patience for visitors, is still going strong, secure in the knowledge that she's the Alpha in my father's life.

"But wait, honey," she continues. "Is it dangerous? Because it's one thing to have a little fun, and quite another to put your health and safety at risk. And please tell me you won't get on a motorcycle." She groans dramatically. "If you ever saw the injuries from that kind of spill, you'd never want to. One time, a guy came in and his limbs were so mangled that—"

I shudder, trying *not* to get a mental picture of the person. "Hello? Hello? Mom? Can you hear me?"

"Eva, can you hear me?"

I continue to pretend not to hear her, unable to bear another one of her graphic descriptions of an accident victim. "I think I've lost her," I say to myself. "Mom? Hello? If you can hear me, know that I'm okay. Everything's great. I'll check in with you soon."

When I hang up, Dean smirks at me through the rearview. "Are you sure you're not an actress yourself?"

We eye each other in the mirror, both of us smirking. "Let's just say I'm an actress in my own sitcom."

A minute later, he whistles when we arrive at Tori and Carter's place in West Hollywood. "Now I *know* someone important lives here. Producer? Director? What?"

I purse my lips in denial, a carefully cultivated picture of nonchalance complete with the requisite interest in my manicured fingernails. "Nothing like that. Just a friend."

He nods knowingly, his mouth quirked to the side like he can tell I'm bullshitting him. "Hmm, I bet. Will you need a ride at the end of the night?"

"Not sure." I wave my phone in the air. "But if I do, you're just a few taps away, right?"

"Exactly. Have a nice evening."

"You do the same."

After I climb out of the vehicle and close the door, I simply stand in awe of the structure in front of me. Carter's a bona fide star, and his home—now Tori's home, too—reflects his A-list status. Nestled in the hills, it's all white and modern, the cobblestoned walkway leading to the single front step serving as a slight nod to Old World charm. Wow, it's massive. I could live in their garage and be happy.

Before I can ring the doorbell, the door opens a crack and Tori slips outside. "Hey, you."

"Um, hey. Everything okay?"

She blinks at me, her dark eyes wide and unfocused. "Oh, yeah. Everything's fine. Why do you ask?"

This woman. "Because you invited me to your house and we're standing outside. Silly me, I thought you'd want me to come in."

"Oh, don't be absurd. Of course I want you to come in. Carter just needs a sec."

Is that a sheen of perspiration I detect on her face and neck? And what's with the dazed look in her eyes? "Tori, were you and Carter going at it before I came? Is he in there putting away the butt plugs and such?"

She snorts. "Don't knock the butt plugs until you try them."

"Who says I haven't?"

Her eyes bulge, making her naturally arched brows more prominent, and I wink at her.

She snaps her fingers. "Oh, while we wait, I should tell you that I spoke with Anthony about the course."

It's odd knowing they were somewhere discussing me. For a split second, I consider telling her that Anthony and I hooked up, but I tamp down the urge, reasoning that it wouldn't be fair to him to share his personal business. *And maybe this is the reason you shouldn't have messed around with your best friend's cousin, hmm?* "So, what did he say?"

"Well, he didn't say yes outright, but he didn't say no outright, either. Let's just say I greased the wheels for you."

"Thanks for putting in a good word, *chica*. I did

some research the past couple of days, and I'd like to go for it. I figure it's six weeks, and if I don't like it, I can withdraw. Plus, I'd always be in control of which jobs I accept. If I think a stunt's too dangerous, I just won't do it."

"Then convince him you're serious about it, and you shouldn't have a problem." She shimmies in place. "Oh, and Kurt said he'd give you a discount on the fee."

The good news keeps coming. Clearly, this was meant to be.

From inside, I hear Carter shout, "Okay, come in." And then Tori pushes the door open and pulls me into . . . a dark foyer.

"Surprise!"

A cacophony of high- and low-pitched voices assaults my ears, and I jump back, throwing my fists up to defend myself against . . . I don't know what. After my eyes adjust to the light—when Tori switched it on, I'm not sure—I see a small group of people huddled together waiting for my reaction.

I drop my arms to my sides. "Well, shit. You didn't tell me it was an orgy, Tori. Had I known, I would have scheduled a bikini wax."

They all blink at me like owls. Beside me, Tori pinches the bridge of her nose as she shakes her head and attempts to suppress a smile.

"What?" I ask her. "Is this not exactly what you expect of me?"

"Yep, it sure is." Blowing out an exasperated breath, she drags me into the living room. There, she opens her arms wide, presenting me to the guests like she's a QVC hostess. "Most of you remember, Eva, of course." She turns to me. "We just wanted to welcome you to LA and make sure you know you have friends here."

I count five sets of eyes staring back at me, one of them unfamiliar. *Well, hello there, handsome.*

Carter's sister, Ashley, with her boyfriend, Julian, in tow, rushes over and pulls me into a hug, interrupting my inspection of the new guy. "It's so good to see you, Eva. I'm still getting used to LA myself, so if you ever want to explore the city together, I'm your woman. And if you want to know the best places to buy the healthiest and most unappealing food"—she points at Julian—"he's your man."

Julian gazes at her, his expression deadpan. "I was under the impression you like *how* and *what* I eat just fine. I mean, you've always been so encouraging, but maybe you've been faking it this whole time?"

The color in Ashley's cheeks deepens. Oh my God, these two are a mess. But I like where this is headed. And Tori could be right: I may very well have found my people.

Next, Tori draws the stranger into the circle. He's a cutie all right, and he's wearing the most approachable smile I've ever seen. I'd probably destroy him in one go-round, maybe two.

"Eva, this is Gabriel Vega. He and Carter are working on a film together. Julian's his agent."

There's not much need for calculating, but I do a mental quickstep anyway. Two couples and Gabriel and me. It's a setup. Oh joy. I guess I should tell Tori that she needn't bother. The one-and-done approach will suffice for now, although at this rate I'll be applying it on a quarterly basis. Am I even doing it right? "Good to meet you, Gabriel."

He takes the hand I've offered him and covers it with his. "Same, Eva. And call me Gabe. I hope that LA treats you well and that you find happiness here."

Coming from anyone else, I'd assume that was nothing more than a well-rehearsed line, but his earnest gaze and the conviction in his voice suggest that he's sincere. I'm good at reading people—my earlier lapse in the Lyft notwithstanding—and my instincts tell me Gabe's a good guy. Plus, Julian's a well-respected businessman with no patience for bullshit. I doubt he'd agree to represent an asshole.

"Well, without revealing too much about myself, Gabe, I'll tell you that LA's the one that should be concerned here."

He gives me the tiniest of smiles, and I sigh on the inside. Gabe's sweet, sure, but he's so shy I feel excessive in comparison. He's a quiet evening at home, whereas I'm a Broadway musical complete with bright lights, jazz hands, no intermission, and multiple encores.

Carter reemerges from the kitchen with a beer in his hand and throws an arm around my shoulders. Speaking of excessive . . .

"Eva," he bellows. "I'm glad you're finally here. Tori hasn't been able to think of anything else but your move to LA."

"Knowing you, that must have been hard to handle," I tell him in jest.

He blows out a breath, feigning frustration. "The. Worst." Then he tries his hand at a Schwarzenegger impression. "This baby man needs his woman to be thinking about him all the time." Reverting to his normal voice, he says, "A few more minutes and dinner will be served, everyone."

"You cooked?" I ask, drawing back to survey him for evidence that he's been laboring in there and finding none.

He raises a single brow as though my question is absurd. "Hell no. I followed heating instructions. Our meal is compliments of Bossa Nova, a Brazilian restaurant on Sunset."

"My meat-loving body thanks you," I tell him, clasping my hands in unabashed joy.

Before he can answer, the doorbell rings, and Carter furrows his brows. "I'll get it."

Tori stops him. "No, you go ahead and get your fine ass in the kitchen where you belong. Let me answer."

A minute later, Tori returns, a sheepish look on her

face. Anthony follows her into the living area, and I do everything in my power to prevent my mouth from gaping—again—because this time I'm staring at his muscular thighs in obscenely form-fitting running shorts. Suddenly I'm craving eggplant parmigiana. *Why are you like this, Eva?*

Chapter Eight

There's no good reason a person can't hate the player *and* the game. I'm fully capable of doing both.

Eva

I HATE THAT I'm the first person Anthony makes eye contact with.

Hate it, hate it, hate it.

It's a potent reminder that we're connected in some way, even if we'd both prefer to forget it.

Tori clears her throat, giving me an excuse to focus on someone else. "Sorry for the confusion, everyone. Anthony and I have been running together in the evenings, and I forgot to tell him I'd be unavailable tonight." She turns to him and nudges his chest with her head. *"Lo siento, primo."*

"It's no biggie," Carter, the consummate host, says. "There's plenty of food, man. Join us."

Anthony's gaze bounces around the room until it

settles on Gabe. "You sure I won't be interrupting anything?"

Ah, he thinks it's a setup, too.

Tori regards him quizzically, pretending she has no idea what he's talking about. "Not at all. The more, the merrier."

He studies me for a moment, his lips curving into a secretive smile, and then he glances at his bare arms. "Could I borrow a T-shirt, maybe?"

Carter nods and jogs off down the hall. Meanwhile, Tori begins a round of introductions and reintroductions. I watch Anthony chat easily with everyone.

When he makes his way to me, we look at each other curiously and say, "We keep meeting."

I don't want to admit that I'm swooning, but my knees do dip an inch. "You're a *Hamilton* fan."

He places his hands behind his back, which has the unfortunate effect of emphasizing his pecs. "I distrust anyone who's not."

I shake my index finger at him. "No, see, this is not happening. I'm not going to like you. I wanted to kick you in the nuts the other day. A *Hamilton* reference and a smile aren't going to cut it."

"What will cut it?" he asks, his eyes gleaming with mischief.

"I'll let you know when I figure that out," I tell him.

He bows and takes a step back. "'As you wish.'"

I groan. "Dammit. *The Princess Bride*, too?"

Carter returns with a T-shirt for Anthony, and

I turn away and check my phone. No need to torture myself with a glimpse of the man's flexing muscles as he slips into a shirt. But I overhear Carter say he brought Anthony one of his longest tees, so he can "cover up," and I can't help snorting, which makes them both jerk their heads in my direction, Anthony's cheeks turning a lovely shade of pink against his tan skin.

Then Tori ushers us to the dining table, and we play an awkward game of who-sits-where that produces an Anthony-Eva-Gabe sandwich. My mind entertains the numerous positions . . . *possibilities*, I mean. As we pass around the serving dishes, I engage Gabe in conversation, suspecting that he's not as outgoing as Diet Thor over there. "So Gabe, can you tell us about this film you're working on with Carter?"

Plainly, Gabe wasn't expecting to be drawn into conversation, because he almost drops the serving bowl in his hands. He recovers quickly, though, scooping a heaping serving of black beans—*feijoada*, according to Carter—and hands the bowl to me. For a moment, I'm distracted by the onion and garlic scents wafting through the air.

"So it's a romantic comedy," Gabe says, coming to life and gesturing for emphasis. "Think *You've Got Mail* meets *How To Lose A Guy in Ten Days*. I play a reporter who clashes with his boss and gets a revenge assignment writing about my terrible dating experiences in LA. But my character doesn't have any decent material to work with, so he writes about his best friend's dating life instead. Carter's the best friend. One of the women Carter's dating reads my write-up, catches on that it's about her, and decides to make things interesting for Carter, thinking *he's* the one writing an anonymous account of his dating exploits. Things go off the rails after that."

I'm still chewing, so Ashley chimes in.

"Oooh, I already like this movie," she says. "Who does the woman end up with?"

"Carter, of course," Gabe says. "He's one of the headliners. I'm just honored he put in a good word for me with the casting director."

"And I have a great feeling about this one," Julian says. "Audiences are clamoring for rom-coms, so I'm confident we'll get a lot of excitement out the gate. And I'm really proud of the diverse cast."

"Who's your love interest?" I ask Carter.

"Tessa Thompson," he says as though he didn't just say *Tessa fucking Thompson*.

I slam my hand on the table. "Shut. Up. I. Die. I'm so obsessed with her."

Tori laughs. "Same, woman. Same."

"Sounds like a terrific premise. I can't wait to see it." I sit up straighter. "And speaking of terrible dating experiences . . . I'm a single woman in a new city. What do I need to know?"

Gabe pipes in without hesitation. "Almost every single person in this city has a roommate or two."

"Or three," Tori says.

Gabe nods. "So if you're dating someone, check out

their place early. That rooming situation could be a nightmare for your relationship."

"And remember, actors are liars by training," Ashley adds.

Understandably, both Carter and Gabe take offense, each rushing to defend his own honor.

"I'm one of the most solid men you'll ever meet," Gabe says.

Carter throws an arm around Tori. "And I'm the worst liar in the world. Just ask her."

Anthony doesn't say a word. In fact, he hasn't so much as grunted since we started talking about dating, and he's heaping food onto his plate as though he's never eaten in his life. I'm not letting him off the hook, though. "And what say you, Anthony? Any tips?"

He turns his head and looks me in the eye. "I wouldn't know. I don't date."

"At all?" I ask him.

"At all."

Message received, not that I needed it. I can do a one-night stand just as well as he can. So instead of taking offense, I slip him a curious glance. "Why not? Not that I'm knocking your stance. It's your prerogative, of course."

He pushes his plate away, all dramatic and such. "I'm what most women would consider the least eligible bachelor ever. I don't ever want to marry. I don't ever want to have kids. I don't ever want to be monogamous. *And* I live with my father. Dating's kind of pointless."

"You're up front with women about this?" Gabe asks, his voice tinged with awe.

Anthony nods. "Always. I don't gain anything by hiding it."

Wow. Tori wasn't kidding when she told me Anthony wasn't available. But this? This is next-level unavailable. He ticked off his list of no's as though they'd protect him from relationship cooties. "Wait, wait, wait. There are women who don't want kids, you know." And because I can't resist poking him, I whisper my next earth-shattering observation. "There are even women receptive to open relationships. And wonder of wonders, I've heard of women who aren't interested in marriage, too."

He curls his upper lip at me, although his eyes are flickering with amusement. "Cute."

"Admit it," I say. "I'm blowing your mind, aren't I?"

Ashley laughs, reminding me that we have an audience. *Oh, hello, everyone else.*

I turn back to him, waiting for an answer, but he doesn't give me one, and I inwardly admonish myself for expecting it. "Shoot. I'm putting you on the spot, right? Should we move on?"

He shrugs, as cool and unfazed as any person could be. "Only if you want to. As usual, I'm getting as much out of your questions as you are. This is like free Netflix."

Well, if he's cool with it—entertained by it, even—who am I to deny him? I set aside my plate and place my elbows on the table. "Okay, so let's say a woman knows your position on marriage, kids, and monogamy and still wants to date you? What then?"

"Then I'm going to assume she's lying to herself and what she really wants is to try to change my mind. If she was cool with all that, she'd just accept that I'm not dating material and move on. Either way, I'm not interested in testing my hypothesis." He grimaces. "Too messy."

"Goodness, you're full of yourself."

Tori, who's sitting across me, kicks my foot under the table and bugs her eyes out at me. "Who wants more wine?" She pours herself a second glass. "I can grab another bottle from the wine cellar."

Anthony frowns, ignoring the lifeline his cousin's thrown us. "I just said I'm the least desirable guy on the planet. How do you figure?"

"Oh, please. Guys do this so much, it's a stereotype." I raise my hands like a presenter at an awards show. "Everyone, meet 'The Commitment-Phobe.' Then I turn back to him. "Sorry to burst your bubble, but I can see right through your façade. I dated a guy like you in college. You present yourself as a challenge to be accepted. Make us think we've won a prize when you give us your time. It's one of the first tactics listed in the Commitment-Phobe Handbook, and I'm ashamed to say I fell for it, too. And *that's* why I'm on to you."

Anthony throws his hands in the air and simulates an explosion with his voice. "Wow. Just wow. Mind. Blown."

"Let me ask you this, Anthony. How do you spell manipulative?"

"Is this a trick question?"

"Just spell it."

He huffs at me. "M-A-N—"

"Stop right there. I've made my point."

"Clever," Julian says.

"Don't encourage her," Anthony tells him.

Tori clears her throat. "Could you pass the rice, please. It's *sooo* good. What kind of rice is this, Carter?"

Carter raises a brow. "Um, white rice?"

I hand Tori the bowl and wait for Anthony to say more. Based on the way he's drumming his fingers on the table, I'm assuming I've hit a nerve.

"So let me see if I've got this right. If I pretend to be something I'm not, I'm a jerk. And if I'm up front about exactly who I am, I'm a manipulator. That's harsh."

"Sucks to be you, I guess."

"It doesn't, but continue to tell yourself whatever you need to."

"So, Eva," Ashley says. "When do you start your—"

"And what's Eva's story?" Anthony asks. "Are you the hopeless romantic in search of her one true love?"

Tori throws her head back and laughs . . . and laughs . . . and laughs. Eventually, she realizes everyone's staring at her. "Oh, sorry. It's just . . ." She glances at me. "Never mind." Then she shovels a heaping forkful of rice into her mouth.

"No, no. I'd love to hear Eva's take on love and relationships," Anthony prods.

"This isn't about me," I say.

"Well, since you made it about me, let's make it about
you now." He takes a sip of his wine. When he's done,
he licks his top lip with his forked tongue—okay, maybe
he's not evil incarnate—and then he winks at me—okay,
yeah, he is. It's a shame, really. All that rugged sexiness
is wasted on him.

And even *knowing* he plays mind games, I'm tempted
to tell him that I'd be open to the type of no-strings arrangement he claims to prefer—or a round two. Well,
technically, a round four since that one night *was* long,
and his stamina is otherworldly. I need a way to save
me from myself, obviously. Which is precisely why
I'm going to tell a lie that will ensure I never hook up
with Anthony Castillo ever again: "If you must know,
Anthony, I think sexual intimacy clouds my ability to
develop meaningful relationships with my partners, so
I recently made the decision to abstain from sex until I
get married."

Forget stunt training; improv might be my true
calling.

Chapter Nine

Anthony

NOT WHAT I was expecting her to say. Not even close.

It's cool, of course. And honestly, a huge relief. It means there's no possibility of another hookup between us, and more importantly, no threat of a monumental fuckup on my part. Her self-imposed abstinence—in anticipation of marriage, no less—firmly places us in the incompatible zone. And that's a good development. Because it frees me to engage without worrying about sending mixed signals.

The truth is, if a guy marries her sex unseen, he'll probably want to renew his vows even before the wedding night's over. Shit, I toyed with the idea of getting on bended knee after the first orgasm. Which means her theory has merit: Sex clouds your judgment.

"Explain your thinking," I tell her.

Gabe shifts in his seat. Seems like a nice guy.

"When you say you're abstaining from sex, what do you mean exactly?" he asks.

Is this guy for real? How is that an appropriate

question? Ever. *"Eres un malcriado,"* is what my father would say.

She whips her head in his direction, so I can't see her expression, but her words come out in a staccato beat. "The. Particulars. Aren't. Relevant."

"Sorry, you're right," Gabe says, blushing.

To his credit, he looks sufficiently embarrassed and contrite about his dumbass outburst.

"The fact is, good sex messes with your brain," Eva says with a haughty lift of her chin.

Does she include our one night together in that description? Does she, does she? When I realize my legs are bouncing under the table, I force myself to remain still. Jesus, I'm a puppy begging for Eva's crumbs.

"It's happened to me time and again," she continues. "A guy with zero conversation skills suddenly seems like a Shakespearean scholar if he uses an SAT word. Someone who doesn't forget to lower the toilet seat is the most thoughtful person in the world. And a guy who doesn't call is stressed and overworked when the reality is, he's most definitely ghosting me. So I've decided that if I'm going to build a quality relationship with someone, I need to remove sex from the equation."

Tori looks so confused she might be developing a unibrow over there, but I can't concentrate on more than one person when Eva's near. So I turn back to the woman who makes everyone else fade into the background. "But isn't good sex part of the equation?"

Eva shakes her head. "No, a romantic relationship doesn't require sex." Then she tilts her head and surveys me, a wry grin bringing her pretty lips into focus. "Just like sex doesn't require a romantic relationship, a truth you should be all too familiar with."

The pointed look she gives me lands like a clip on the chin. Ouch. There's a conversation within a conversation happening here, and I'm kind of enjoying it. "Let me rephrase. Isn't good sex part of *your* relationship equation?"

"Well, sure. But if the attraction is there, even bad sex can become good sex over time. Believe me, there are quite a few women—and a man or two, I'd venture to guess—who have me to thank for their partner's superior skills in bed."

I'd bet. But it's not like I can say that out loud. "Well, now who's the one being full of themselves?"

She shrugs. "Confidence is only arrogance if you can't back it up."

Carter, who's sitting next to Tori, reaches across the table and pretends to fist bump her. "That's what I always say."

"You should stop saying it," Tori suggests flatly.

"Exactly," Anthony says. "Someone can have justifiable confidence and still be a jerk about it."

"Just like someone can change a subject and hope no one notices," Eva says, sliding me a knowing look.

Tou-the-fucking-ché. She's a delectable mess of woman who knows just what to say when I need to hear it. If I'm being honest, I kinda want to replace Tori as her best friend. And if she were still living in Philly, I might even be begging her to take me home tonight. Which reminds me that I'm in absolutely no place to argue with her reasoning. So I don't. "Let's plan another dinner in a few months. Would love an update on your search for a meaningful relationship."

She grins. "Let's."

Ashley falls back against her chair and fans herself with a cloth napkin. "Wow, that was something to watch. You two should take this routine on the road." Then she stretches her arms out wide and yawns, the exaggerated move about as convincing as John Travolta's hairpiece. "We hate to eat and run, but I'm teaching guitar in the morning, and Julian has a meeting."

Tori pouts at them and turns to Julian. "You schedule meetings on Saturdays?"

He nods as he rises. "I agree to meetings when people make themselves available." He sighs. "An agent never rests."

"Aww, sweetie," Ashley says, massaging his shoulders, her mouth hovering over his ear, "are you being worked too hard?"

He pulls her into his arms. "I'm being worked perfectly."

Whoa. They're at the *we're not going to make it to the bedroom* stage of the evening. *Get a wall, mi gente.*

With that public display of sexual tension behind

us, everyone else stands, too, and the small talk that goes along with people saying their good-byes begins. Eva excuses herself to use the restroom. Gabe, for his part, fidgets as he pretends not to be waiting for her to return, until Carter takes pity on him and offers to walk him out.

I give Tori a quick kiss on the cheek, hoping I can orchestrate a fast exit, too, but she stops me with a firm hand at my shoulder.

"*Esperaté*," she says. "I have something for you from my mother." Then she wiggles her eyebrows. "*Pasteles*."

I spin around and follow her to the kitchen, rubbing my hands in anticipation. Tía Lourdes is one of the best cooks I know, second only to my own father, who taught her what *she* knows, and *pasteles* are my absolute favorite food. Succulent pork in an adobo sauce of garlic, oregano, pepper, and vinegar, and too many more ingredients to name that sits inside this soft shell made from plantains and *yautia*. And all of that is wrapped in a banana leaf. Damn, I'm licking my lips just thinking about them. They're difficult to make, too, so Papi only makes them for the holidays and stores the leftovers in the freezer for months. This feels like Christmas in September.

I eye the prize as Tori removes the *pasteles* from the fridge and places them in a shopping bag.

"She said to tell you not to overcook them. Defrost and boil for no more than thirty minutes. *Tú sabes*."

Eva waltzes in and her eyes double in size. "Oh my gosh, are those *pasteles*? Do you have more? If not, I'll fight you for them, Anthony."

Tori and I laugh at her enthusiasm.

"No need for violence," Tori says. "Mami sent some for you, too."

Well, damn. And here I thought I was special. Apparently, Eva's wormed her way into Tía Lourdes's heart and snagged a spot on her list of people to receive her food care packages. I shouldn't be surprised. People gravitate to Eva's unbounded energy. She's like a human power source; spend some time with her and you'll be recharged in no time.

As Eva grabs her stash and places it in her handbag, she says, "This reminds me, I've been scoping out restaurants to try. Where do I get good Puerto Rican food in LA?"

Tori and I look at each other.

Eva catches the exchange. "What?"

"Well, the thing is," Tori begins, hesitation in her voice. "There really isn't a Puerto Rican community *per se*, so you're not going to find a bunch of places like you would in North Philly."

"I did find a place in North Hollywood a few years back," I tell them. "I pick up lunch from there every once and a while."

Eva raises a fist in the air. "This is an outrage. I'm so used to buying—"

"*Eating for free,*" Tori says.

"*Eating for free* at Mi Casita," Eva continues, not arguing with Tori's amendment. "What will I do to get my fix of Puerto Rican food now?"

The genuine worry in her eyes makes me grin. "The place I mentioned, Mofongos, is pretty good. And there's always the Puerto Rico Loves Cali Festival in Long Beach. It's this weekend, in fact."

Eva places her hands on Tori's shoulders and shakes her playfully. "Take me, Tori. Please."

"*Lo siento, chica,* but Carter and I have plans."

I sense the suggestion even before Tori voices it. She looks between us, and her eyes and jaw settle into a pensive gaze before she widens her eyes and taps my chest with the back of her hand. "Anthony, you should take Eva. If you're free, that is. It would be a great way for her to see her new stomping grounds. Not a date or anything, of course."

"Of course," I emphasize.

"Of course," Eva echoes.

We both glance at each other and return our gazes to Tori. Eva's probably thinking what I'm thinking: Tori doesn't know we slept together, and eventually one of us will need to tell her. My cousin's working with incomplete information, and it feels . . . wrong.

"You guys don't live far from each other, too." Tori continues, unaware of the implications of what she's suggested. "He's in Atwater Village," she says to Eva. To me, she says, "And she's in Silver Lake."

We live less than five miles apart. God's a jokester, isn't he?

"So, sounds good to you two?" Tori asks.

Eva takes a deep breath and smiles. "I think that's a great idea. It would be nice to see another part of the area with a friend. I'm sure it would be fun. No stress. Casual. Right, Anthony?"

If I'm counting correctly, this would be our second truce in a three-month period. Last time we had one, we ended the night in her bed. That won't be happening this time, though, and getting to know each other as friends strikes me as the only logical next step. "Yeah, I agree. And since you're new here, you'll need all the friends you can get."

"Fantastic," Tori says.

"Excellent," Eva says.

Trying to forget what she looks like when she's overcome with pleasure, though?

Useless.

"Pick you up at nine?" I ask her, hoping a constant stream of conversation will give me no space for wicked thoughts.

"That early?" she asks, frowning. "For a festival?"

"Sometimes fun comes at a cost."

She drops her head back and lets out a frustrated sigh. "Ugh. I was hoping to sleep in, but sure, that works." Then she meets my gaze. "Well, let me get out of here, so I can get a decent night's rest. And you might as well forgive me in advance. I'll be groggy and irritable when you pick me up. I don't really hit my stride until ten."

Her self-awareness is another trait I like about her. She never describes her feelings or habits as flaws; they're just quirks, the little things that make her the interesting woman everyone wants to be around. I tap Tori on the side with my elbow, smirking at them both. "Yeah, we both know Eva's not a morning person."

Tori's smile vanishes as she surveys our faces, her piercing gaze swinging between Eva and me. "We *both* do?"

Oh shit. Did I just say that? Out loud? Eva freezes, while I pray for a genie who'll give me three wishes, one of which would be to get me the fuck out of here, no questions asked.

Tori's face opens like a sunflower, her eyes widening and her mouth curving into a gaping grin. Then she slams her hands against my chest and shoves me. Hard. "Shut. Up. You two? When?"

What is up with these women and their super strength? "In Connecticut," I mumble, massaging my chest.

Tori shoves me again. "At our wedding?"

Eva drops her chin and scratches the area above her brow, not meeting anyone's eyes. Then her phone buzzes and she places it in front of her face like she's the most farsighted person on earth. "Oh, my Lyft is here. Gotta go. We'll chat tomorrow, Tori. See you bright and early, Anthony."

She escapes the kitchen like lightning speed is her super power, leaving me to defend the universe on my own.

Traitor.

Chapter Ten

Yes, scientists have confirmed that oysters are
aphrodisiacs, but have you ever experienced
the power of reggaeton?

Eva

SATURDAY MORNING, MY cell phone rings once.

Ten seconds later, it rings twice.

Ten seconds after that, it rings three times.

God, Tori and I haven't used this code since college. Loosely translated, the escalating number of rings
means, *Bitch, I know you're with someone, but pick up
the phone anyway. It's important.*

I open one eye, roll to the right side of my bed, and
pat the nightstand until my hand lands on the offending
object. Jesus, it's 7:00 a.m. I answer on the fourth ring,
my words tumbling out on the heels of a loud yawn.
"I've been in LA less than a week. Why would you think
it's even remotely possible that I'd have a guy over?"

"I didn't think it was remotely possible that you'd

decide to be abstinent and not tell me, so how the hell should I know what's going on with you?"

Oh my. She's leading with that and not the revelation that Anthony and I slept with each other? This is bad. Or maybe it's good. Who the hell knows at this point? Yes, Tori and I share secrets, but we've never pushed each other on when or how much to divulge. It always happens organically. I didn't tell her about discovering my birth control pills in Jason's jacket pocket until I was good and ready, and that took a while because the ugly episode had sucker-punched me in the worst way. But this is different. One, Anthony blurted it out before I could tell her. And two, this secret involves her relative.

I sit up and stuff a pillow between my back and the headboard. "Is that *all* you want to talk about?"

"What else is there to talk about, huh? The weather? LA traffic? The latest episode of *Insecure*? Or are you referring to the fact that you and my cousin had sex a few months ago?"

"It was a one-time thing. For both of us. I thought I'd be in Philly and he'd be in LA. Forever. Your job offer came later."

"That's essentially what he told me."

"See? It's no biggie."

"Ahhh, now I get it," she says, stretching out each word. "*That's* what all the back-and-forth last night was about. Unresolved tension."

She's wrong. Yesterday's verbal duel was about Anthony's manipulative take on relationships. Tori's aware this is a pet peeve of mine. She more than anyone should know how I'd react to his ridiculous sexual manifesto. "Oh, c'mon, Tori, you were there. I mean, I know he's your cousin, but you can't deny that whole never-gonna-date-never-gonna-marry-never-gonna-be-monagamous-never-gonna-have-kids policy is a total scam." Oof, it's a fucking mouthful, too. "And by the way, I'm not abstaining from sex. I just said that last night because Anthony was pissing me off with his never-have-I-ever bullshit."

Tori's rarely at a loss for words, so the silence that follows surprises me. "Tori?"

"Thinking," she says.

"Think faster."

"Okay, okay. You're such a pain in the ass. Here's the deal. It's not bullshit. Anthony doesn't date, and I believe him when he says he doesn't want to do any of those things."

What I need to remember here is that Anthony can do no wrong in her eyes. He's the brother she always wished to have. Tori might never admit this, but I suspect she loves him more than she loves her sister, Bianca. In her mind, his quest for perpetual bachelorhood must be sincere; otherwise he's not the person she thinks he is. So her defense of him should be taken with a mountain of salt. "It's understandable that you have such confidence in your cousin, but I'm not buying it. I mean, I'm not interested in dating anyone, either, but I'm not tattooing that fact over my entire body."

"Tori, in all the years I've known him, I know of only one woman he dated. That was years ago."

Oooh, I'm super interested to know if this woman's the reason for his stance. "So is she the reason he's anti-everything? What's the story there?"

"Not my tale to tell, *chica*."

Well, in that case, I'm working with what I *do* know, and I've seen this male composite before: single, attractive male with no desire to be pinned down. Snore. Is this movie over yet? "Trust me, your cousin knows his unavailability attracts people who see him as a challenge."

Tori sighs heavily. "That may be, but I don't think he's trying to manipulate anyone. Just give him a break, okay? For me?"

I mimic her heavy sigh because that's what we do. "Well, you're no fun. Should I come clean to him, then?"

"What?" she asks, her voice rising an octave. "Why would you?"

"Oh, I don't know, Tori, because it's deceitful."

"It was deceitful when the words came out of your mouth. Backtracking isn't going to change that. Plus, how would you do it? Are you planning to announce that you're open to having sex again? If, as you say, the hookup was a one-time thing, why would that even come up? Riddle me that, Batman."

She's right. It wouldn't. Even I can admit a conversation like that would be awkward. He'd probably construe it as an invitation and decline it. "Okay, I see your point. I'll fly my freak flag in secret."

Tori giggles. And then I hear Carter's voice in the background. Which makes me realize she's not giggling at me; she's cavorting with her new husband. My time's up, apparently. "Go handle your man, Tori. I need to get dressed for the festival. Anthony's picking me up at nine."

"Have fun. Wait. But don't have too much fun. I suggested the festival so you could convince Anthony you're a perfect fit for the program. Be friendly—but keep it professional. Lay the groundwork for getting him to see you as a potential colleague."

"Right, right. Got it. See you next week."

Be friendly. Keep it professional. That should be easy enough.

ANTHONY TAPS MY shoulder, forcing me to open my eyes.

"I'm not your chauffer, you know," he says, placing his hand back on the wheel of his black Ford F-150. "And we're almost at the park."

I sit up and stretch my arms out in front of me. "Sorry. I went to sleep late, and I'm paying for it today."

"Binge-watching your favorite shows?"

"Actually, I was unpacking and organizing . . . okay, yes, and binge-watching *Black-ish* because Tracee Ellis Ross is my imaginary friend. She's going to be a bridesmaid at my wedding someday. So anyway, after all that work, I looked up and it was after midnight. If I never see a cardboard box again it will be too soon."

"Well, I guarantee you'll be fully awake in no time. This festival is loud enough to flow through your bloodstream like three shots of espresso."

My eyes follow the veins in his hand and forearm as he taps the steering wheel to the beat of the salsa music playing on the radio. He's so damn chipper sitting there in his cute baseball cap with the Puerto Rican flag stitched into the front panel, the curly ends of his hair peeking out the back. Within the confines of the cab of his truck, he's bigger, more intense, more handsome, as if the space forces me to notice the details I wish I could ignore. "Is there a reason we had to come so early?"

"For sure," he replies, nodding thoughtfully. "A primo location. See, there's a main stage, and if we want to have a good chance of enjoying the performances, we need to grab a spot to park our chairs. After that, we can walk around, but staking our claim to a resting place is key. Puerto Ricans can be a territorial bunch."

I snort. "Pun intended, right?"

He gives me a blank look, but the moment he gets it, his mouth widens until his smile reaches his eyes, adorable crinkles at the corners and all. "Good one."

"Did you spend any part of your childhood there?"

"In PR?" he asks.

I nod.

"Nah. I wish I had, but I grew up in New York. Spanish Harlem, born and raised. And you're a Philly native, right?"

"Yep. Northwest. Mount Airy, to be exact. That's where my mom grew up. My dad's family is from Atlanta."

He turns and glances at me before he flips the turn signal. "This is a huge change for you, then. Living on a different coast."

That's an understatement, now that I think about it. Because that's largely what I've been doing—*not* thinking about it. As though the enormity of the move will be easier to handle if I pretend I've simply relocated across town. "Yeah, I try not to focus on that part. Makes it easier to digest. And you have experience doing the same thing, don't you?"

"I do," he says, nodding.

"And I've been dying to ask you about that. How *did* you end up here?"

He doesn't answer immediately, but when he does, his voice is smaller, less confident than it usually is. "To be honest, when I was living in New York, I felt like every person had their shit together except me. Granted, I was in my early twenties, so I shouldn't have been so hard on myself. Still, that was my thinking at the time. Every day, I boarded a train and watched people headed to work, manila folders in their laps, newspapers in their hands, cell phones at their ears, or whatever, and I was the first-generation community college graduate with a messenger bag slung across my shoulder, balancing a bike on its back tire."

Goodness, maybe his career was preordained. "You

survived being a bike messenger in New York? No wonder you're a stunt performer."

"Exactly," he says, a faraway smile suggesting the switch is as surprising to him as it is to me. "But I wasn't thinking about stunt work then. In my head, LA was a place for people in limbo, a place where I could fit in, not because I planned to be an actor but because I wasn't settled, and if there's one thing LA is known for, it's people who are chasing dreams—the busboys and waiters, the valets, the people trying to get into the business and working the side hustle. I didn't have a dream yet, but I was hoping to find one. I had an inkling that this town might be a better fit, and it was."

"But a bike messenger turned stunt person? How'd you even get into this? It's not the kind of job you'd come across at a career fair."

With his gaze still trained on the road, he cocks his head to the side, as though he's recalling a pleasant memory. "Yeah, you're right. It all started the day I made a delivery to the same warehouse where Kurt and I still train. When I got there, he was backing out of a parking space and didn't see me. Luckily for me, I had all kinds of experience dodging careless drivers in New York. Let's just say Kurt was impressed with my agility. My second delivery there, I ventured inside. He invited me to stay, and after a while I started coming after work just to watch what was going on. Eventually, Kurt let me try some of the equipment."

"Did you take the course?"

"Yeah. Kurt didn't charge me, though. By then, he knew a little about my story. Knew I was struggling, and I think he saw an opportunity to mentor me. So here we are seven years later. He's my boss, but he's my friend, too."

Anthony drives through the park's main entrance and maneuvers the car into one of the few remaining parking spaces in this section of the lot. The crowd's already thick, so I know his plan to arrive early was a wise one.

"Got any tips for me?" I ask. "Anything I should know before we go in?"

He pulls the visor down and unclips his sunglasses, putting them on as he speaks. "If you want to fit in, call me a *papi chulo* at least a dozen times while we're there."

Ha. I've probably said *papi chulo* more times in my life than he has. "Nice try, but no." Not that he isn't an attractive man, but he doesn't need me to further inflate his ego.

"Okay, okay, be prepared to yell '¡Wepa!' throughout the concert."

"Do I look like a novice to you? Of course I'll be shouting '¡Wepa!' at the top of my lungs."

"And there will be reggaeton."

I dance in my seat, my hands swaying above my head. "I'd be disappointed if there wasn't reggaeton."

"Then you're all set," he says, reaching for the door handle.

We grab the two camping chairs from the back of his

truck and join the sea of adults and kids strolling from the parking lot to the festival grounds. The crowd is diverse, the familiar sounds of people speaking in Spanish reminding me of the many times Tori and I visited her parents' restaurant in North Philly.

The air is pulsing with positive vibes and excitement, and the music coming from huge speakers in various spots on the lawn is fire. Absolute fire. I don't know the name of the song, but I know it's merengue, and I can't help shimmying my shoulders as we make our way to the area in front of the stage. Anthony's leading the way, blocking me from most of the jostling as people try to reach the same place.

I tug on the back of his T-shirt to get his attention. "I know this song. I've heard it a million times at Tori's, but I don't know the name."

Anthony's laughter travels through the air. "'Suavamente,' one of the greatest merengue songs of all time. If you're curious, look up the video on YouTube. It's the greatest wreck of played-out graphics you'll ever see."

"That bad?" I shout over the music.

"Yes, that bad." He stops on a patch of grass and takes his chair out of the sleeve. "Here's good."

We make quick work of unfolding and positioning the chairs, and then a flurry of activity on the stage grabs our attention. It's fascinating to watch. People removing instruments from their cases, backup singers adjusting microphones and crop tops, and stage hands taping wires to the floor. Around us, festival goers continue to dance to the merengue booming from the speakers. A minute or so later, an emcee takes the stage and welcomes the crowd. He speaks in both English and Spanish, switching between the two with ease as he tells everyone to enjoy themselves.

Anthony hops on the tips of his toes. "Man, this is unreal."

"What's going on?"

He shakes his head and points at the stage. "That's El Gran Combo de Puerto Rico. They're legendary."

More than a dozen men, all in three-piece suits, wait for their cue to begin, and before they do, the crowd cheers wildly. When the emcee announces them, I cover my ears to drown out the shouts and shrieks that follow. And once they begin, Anthony and I are doing our best to dance near each other without getting trampled on by the people around us. We drift apart in the middle of the song, and before I know it, a dozen dancers and feet separate us.

His response is swift. I watch him weave around several people, and then he snakes out a hand, wrapping it around my waist, and pulling me to his side. His touch isn't rough, but it isn't gentle, either. It's . . . sure, and I'll confess to enjoying his hands on me, although on his end he's probably just concerned about losing me in the crowd.

An elderly woman leans over and whispers in my ear. "*Su novio es muy guapo.*"

A teenaged girl dancing nearby yelps, a horrified

expression on her face. "Grandma, you're so *embarrassing*." She stomps off; her grandmother grins as she watches her granddaughter leave.

Goodness. Anthony reels them in no matter the age. I'm not dignifying her comment with an answer, so I pretend not to understand. "Oh, I don't speak Spanish very well. *Como?*"

She takes this as an opportunity to speak directly to Anthony. "I was telling her that her boyfriend is cute." Then she winks at him as though the words coming out of her mouth weren't clear enough. *Get it, abuela.*

Anthony's cheeks redden. "*Y ella es hermosa, ¿verdad?*"

"*Seguro,*" the woman replies as she dances away.

I tug on his T-shirt sleeve. "What was that about?"

"She said your boyfriend was cute, and I told her my girlfriend was beautiful." He shrugs. "It was easier than explaining that we're only friends."

I pin him with a dubious expression. "*Solos somos amigos*, that's all you had to say."

Again, he shrugs. "Like I said, it was easier to let her think I'm your boyfriend. And if you know Spanish so well, why not correct her yourself?"

"I was curious to see how you'd handle it, that's all. And I must say I'm surprised. I thought you were allergic to the word '*boyfriend*.' In fact, your eyes look a little red and puffy. Is that your immune system kicking in?"

"Did you ever consider that I'm allergic to know-it-all people who won't let me live my life the way I want to?"

"Nope."

He chuckles, shaking his head at me like nothing about my response surprises him. "Want to grab some food?"

It's early, but I can always eat. "Yes, please."

The throng is deep enough that we might lose each other if we aren't too careful, so I latch onto his arm as we stroll over to the lawn where the booths are located. He's sturdy. That's the best word to describe him. Like a big ol' tree trunk.

The dishes aren't made to order, no ma'am. They're offering *arroz con gandules*, *pernil*, *maduros*, and a random bread roll on a paper plate. I. Am. Sold. "I'll have one of those, please," I say, pointing to one of five plates on the table.

"You don't want to see what else is available?" Anthony asks, gesturing toward the rows of food tents we haven't explored yet.

"Nope. I'm good here, thanks."

He laughs. "Okay, then. *Dos, por favor.*"

"I'll pay," I tell him, pulling out a wad of cash from my tiny cross-body. "To thank you for bringing me."

He doesn't fuss about it, although I do note a moment's hesitation in putting away his wallet.

"What about something to drink?" he asks.

The vendor lifts a large white cooler filled with soda cans.

"Coco Rico," Anthony exclaims. "I'm definitely having that."

The concept of coconut soda doesn't compute in my brain. "I'll take a Coke, please."

The vendor's nice enough to cover our plates with foil, and we walk back to our spot, drinks and plastic utensils in one hand and our plates of food in the other. We wolf our food down, content to eat in silence and people-watch. Then we toss our lunchware in a nearby trash bin and rejoin the people dancing on the parquet floor.

The air is warm, but not oppressive. Now that I've been moving my body in the sun for more than an hour, though, my skin is sticky with sweat. Anthony switches the front of his baseball cap to the back, a sheen of perspiration forming on his temples. As the band breaks down the stage set, the sounds of reggaeton fill the air. To my surprise, the rapper on this song is a woman.

"Told you," Anthony says as he rocks his hips in tune with the song.

I'm unprepared for the feast on my eyes that is Anthony dancing to this fusion of hip-hop, Jamaican dance hall percussion, and the Spanish language. His large body handles the rhythms like they were made for it, the muscles in his well-defined arms flexing as he raises his arms above his head. Am I staring? Why yes, yes I am. And so are most of the women around me. He's going to realize I'm gawking any minute now, and I'm going to be embarrassed beyond words. And of course, when it happens, I freeze, unable to tear my gaze from his. Without a word, he pulls me closer, not relinquishing my hand but instead raising it in the air as he moves into my personal space. "It's just a dance, right? No stress? Casual?"

His meaning is clear: We can enjoy this without reading anything into it. And given how much I love dancing, it's a message I appreciate. So I move my hips from side to side. "Exactly."

The artist's words are sharp, her voice gritty, but the lyrics sit on a bed of percussion that is so sensual, my mind can only focus on the way our movements mimic lovemaking. We're not touching, but we're close enough that I can feel his body heat. Somehow I don't think this is what Tori meant when she issued those marching orders this morning. Professional? No. Friendly? Very.

He twirls me around with just our pinkies linked, and then he's behind me, his broad chest serving as a resting place for my head. A few beats later, his arms circle my waist and he splays his hands on my belly, his touch light and achingly heavy all at once.

"You okay?" he asks.

"Definitely," I reply.

And it's true. I'm definitely enjoying this. I'm definitely okay. And I'm definitely screwed.

Chapter Eleven

Anthony

TEMPTATION, THY NAME is Eva. Anthony, thy name is Jackass.

Eva's compact body is pressed against mine, the sweet vanilla fragrance in her hair flooding my nostrils. How am I supposed to suppress my attraction to her when she smells like freshly baked sugar cookies? The urge to nibble on her ear and nuzzle her jaw staggers me, it's so strong. But the reality is, if I don't fight it, I'll become the very asshole I'm trying not to be. Making her think I want more when I don't.

"We need to get going," I mumble.

She spins around and stands on her tiptoes, leaning in to hear me better. "What?"

I turn my face away to avoid inhaling her sweet scent. Her hair is up today, those springy curls sitting on top of her head like an intricate crown. My fingers itch to dive into that thickness and massage her scalp, tugging her head back to bring her luscious mouth to mine. Fucking reggaeton is lethal. "I said we should head out. To avoid the rush out of the park."

If she's an observant woman, she'll notice the park is brimming with people, laughing, dancing, drinking from conspicuously unmarked bottles, and no one's scrambling toward the exits. No, the way the emcee's hyping up the crowd, this party's likely to continue well into the evening.

Biting on her bottom lip as she surveys her surroundings, she sees it, too. And maybe I'm imagining this, but I think I can pinpoint the moment she realizes I'm trying to bring our time together to an end: a flare of awareness in her eyes that dulls slowly, her expression going slack before she pastes on a sleepy smile.

"That's a good idea," she says. "The sun's sapping my energy anyway."

"You? Depleted?" I make a big show of looking around me. "Where's a camera crew when you need one? This is breaking news."

We laugh together. The emcee interrupts the moment, though, speaking unintelligible words into the microphone that cause a stir around us. Then several men rush through the crowd, pointing their index fingers at people and gesturing for them to follow.

A man wearing a T-shirt with the word *STAFF* on the front sidles up to Eva and me, a big, seedy smile on his face. "*Vamanos, amigos. Concurso de baile reggae-*

ton." He motions us forward while three couples climb the steps to the stage.

Eva shakes my shoulders, bouncing as she asks, "They want us to dance up there?"

"Worse," I say. "It's a couples dance contest."

She tugs on the sleeve of my T-shirt. "Let's do it, Anthony. It'll be fun."

"Not my thing."

And it really isn't. I'll happily crash through a cement wall. Sign me the fuck up for some crazy shit like that. I'd even serenade someone in a crowded square. Badly. But getting on a stage in front of hundreds of people and shaking my ass suggestively—c'mon, that's what reggaeton requires—sounds like a nightmare come to life.

She pouts at me. "Oh, c'mon. It's a stage. And there's dancing. This was made for me."

"*For you*, is the operative phrase," I say, pointing at her face.

"*For us*. It wouldn't be all that different from what we've been doing down here." She pulls on the bottom of my T-shirt and looks up at me with her doe eyes. "It's just dancing. Anthony. I'm not asking you to marry me, you know. Please?"

Okay, she smells like freshly baked cookies, and now she's pleading for me to dance with her? I'm smart enough to know when resistance is futile. "Fine. But just one dance."

She snaps her fingers and shimmies backward, watching me with a triumphant expression as I trudge to the stage.

"You look like I'm escorting you to the guillotine," she notes.

"Sounds about right."

As she climbs the steps, she hesitates and loses her footing. I shoot forward to place my body between her and the ground, but she rights herself without my help. Breathless, she asks, "Does anyone ever fall around you?"

"Not on my watch, no."

Maybe it's the lack of enthusiasm in my voice, but something about my demeanor stops her from taking another step. She shakes her head, her shoulders slumped. "This was a silly idea, and I can tell you're not into it. Let's forget it."

A minute ago, her smile was bright enough to light up this park, but now she looks like a kid who's lost her favorite stuffed animal. Just because I'm wary of sending mixed signals doesn't mean I need to be a damn stuffed shirt. "If having me twerk my way across this stage is going to take that sad look off your face, I'll do it."

"It will," she says, her bright smile returning. "Watch." She swipes a hand in front of her face and frowns. "No dance." Then she swipes again and gives me a wide smile. "Dance."

I circle my finger in the air, motioning for her to turn

her sweet behind around. "Get up there before I change my mind."

She claps and sprints up the steps.

I refuse to look at the audience, but the murmurs, laughter, and cheers leave no doubt that we're in the spotlight. Two minutes into the emcee's explanation of how this contest is going to work, I'm swearing under my breath, knowing I've made a grave mistake. I thought we'd all be dancing at the same time, with the audience choosing its favorite pair at the end. But no. This is worse. Each couple will dance alone, and the audience will choose the winner by a round of applause, or more likely, given the state of the crowd, by a round of hoots, shouts, whistles, and *wepas*.

Eva's turned into the winningest coach in NCAA history, her body close to mine as she talks up to me, her hands poised like a conductor as she emphasizes her various points of strategy. "Okay, so if we don't go first or second, we'll volunteer to go last. The crowd will be bored by the third one, and it'll be up to us to re-energize them."

"Did you compete in team sports when you were young?" I ask her.

"Swim team at Drexel. Why?"

I squeeze my eyes shut. Someone save me. "Just curious."

"Another thing. Crowds love it when we surprise them. I'll handle that piece."

Wait a minute now. Coming from Eva, that sounds frightening. "What kind of surprise?"

She wags her eyebrows. "I'll surprise you, too. That way, your reaction will be totally authentic."

I make the sign of the cross and leave it in God's hands. We watch the first couple, a middle-aged man and a woman who seem to think salsa dancing pairs well with reggaeton. Even the emcee's confused. Next, a young couple saunters onto the stage, bravado in his steps, sultriness in hers. He's licking his lips like she's his meal, and all I want to do is pass my man a Chap-Stick. They're selling sex, and the crowd's buying it.

Eva nudges me with her shoulder. "That's our competition."

I just wanted to get her to stop pouting. Now I'm trapped in a dance battle. Can't fault her on her prediction, though. The crowd does in fact lose interest in the third and fourth couples, and their cheers resume when the emcee introduces the last couple in the contest: us.

He points the mic at Eva. "*¿Tú nombre, querida?*"

"Eva," she says, waving to everyone.

"*¿Y tú hermano?*"

"Anthony," I say, waving at no one.

"*Un fuerte aplauso para Eva y Antonio.*"

The crowd cheers as Eva leads me to the center of the stage, her hips already swaying to the song's slow, sensual tempo. Why am I doing this, again? Oh, right. Because Eva's the kind of person I don't want to disappoint. She's fun and full of life—even when she's annoyed with me—so interfering with her vibe makes me feel like I've registered for anti-fun camp. Me. Of all people. That's unheard of in these parts.

She trails her fingers up my back, her touch feather-light, and then she rests her clasped hands around my neck, tugging me closer. "You look unsure. Where's your trademark confidence? I need you to be an equal participant in this if we're going to win."

"Hard to figure out where to put my hands. I don't want to get popped in the mouth."

"We're dancing. On a stage." She winks at me. "Just go with it. If I don't like where things are headed, I'll body-slam you."

I'd like to see her try.

No, really. I'd like to see her try. And that's the problem. I wouldn't mind one bit if we wrestled each other to the ground. It's that image that prompts me to place my hands on her hips, directing them from side to side. She releases me and leans back, a sliver of her firm belly peeking out from underneath her top and her arms falling to her sides. The crowd loves it, loves us. My body syncs with the song's steady drumbeat, and she turns around, rubbing her ass against me. I bend my knees slightly so she's grinding right where I want her, and if I'm not mistaken, she gasps before she throws her head forward and sinks into the move.

She's intending to surprise me, but suddenly I'm the one who wants to do the surprising. Unequal partici-pant, my ass. I slip off my T-shirt while she's still bent over, grasp it with both hands, and bring it over my head and across her waist, using it to raise her torso and bring her back against my bare chest. The crowd loses it. Shit, maybe I'm losing it. What the fuck is happening right now?

Not to be outdone, Eva twirls around and places her hands on my pecs. Her heavy-lidded gaze pierces me, tells me she knows this is no longer about a contest, but about enjoying ourselves in the moment. Then, in what can't be more than a tenth of a second, she drops into a split, her face landing directly in front of my crotch. Holy shit. A sea of arms go up in the crowd. The audience cheers. And one guy charges back and forth across the area in front of the stage, a hand on his head and his mouth gaping in disbelief.

They're not the only ones affected, though. My mind is taking me places that should be cordoned off with caution tape.

Like I said, she's temptation, and I'm a jackass.

Chapter Twelve

Thou shall not shake your booty during a professional interview.

Eva

ANTHONY DOESN'T SAY much as we walk back to his truck, but the small trophy I'm holding is picking up the slack and mocking me to no end. I imagine its beady eyes judging me, the small handle on each side of the topper representing a hand cocked on a hip. Oh, wait. The trophy has long curly hair, attitude to spare, and bears a striking resemblance to my best friend.

How's Anthony going to take you seriously after that performance, missy?

Was it necessary to grind your ass against him?

And what about the way you brazenly caressed his chest and stomach?

Goodness, Tori's judgy. And she's far from done.

You enjoyed it, didn't you?

Too much, perhaps?

I thought you said Anthony's a manipulator with a capital M. Why would you even be thinking about him in that way?

"I'm *not*," I say.

"What's that?" Anthony asks.

"Oh, nothing," I say, grimacing at my own outburst. "Just thinking out loud." *Say something else, Eva. This isn't only on him.* "So that was wild, huh?"

He chuckles, but his laughter is subdued, petering out at the end as though he's testing out how enthusiastic his response should be and wants to tone it down. "Definitely memorable."

"Right? There's no way I'll ever forget my first weekend in LA."

"I'm glad."

Blowing out a long, frustrated breath, I toss the camping chair onto the bed of his pickup and slide into the passenger seat. He's been giving me these one- or two-word responses since we left the stage. I want to channel Cher in *Moonstruck* and tell him to snap out of it, point out that we were just dancing. But I suspect that's not entirely true. We were releasing sexual tension *under the guise* of dancing. And now he's in a mood. He's probably just frustrated that I'm damn near irresistible and "saving" myself for marriage. Bahaha. Serves him right.

He tosses his cap between us as he climbs into the cab. Then he attacks the seat belt, his range of motion sharp and controlled as he tugs the shoulder strap across his body and clicks the latch into place.

CRASHING INTO HER 137

"I'm glad we did this," I say, staring straight ahead, my voice airy and light and my hands tucked between my thighs. "It wasn't awkward at all. Nuh-uh. No, sir. Not one bit."

He turns to look at me and barks out a laugh. "I was thinking the same thing."

"What is *wrong* with us?"

His lips twitch, and then he says, "We're a goddamn mess, is what it is."

Okay, he's not hopeless after all. What we need is a come-to-Jesus moment. "Permission to clear the air?" I ask, twisting my torso to face him.

His expression sobers. "Permission definitely granted."

"Here's what I think is going on. We're obviously attracted to each other. Connecticut was proof of that. Today is further proof of that. But neither one of us is interested in being in a relationship. I'm taking a well-deserved break from dating and you're . . . uh . . . not interested in dating ever?"

"So far, so good," he says, nodding.

"And we enjoy each other's company. Agreed?"

"Wholeheartedly," he says with a smile.

Ignoring the little flutter in my belly when I hear his answer, I grin and tilt my head at him. "Awww. Anyway, I think with a little work and maturity on both our parts, we can be friends. Good friends, even. And I'm willing to try, assuming you are, too."

His chest rises as he takes a big, cleansing breath.

"That's exactly what I was hoping for. It's like you reached into my brain and stole my thoughts."

I clap my hands together. "Okay, perfect. We'll be friends on three. One, two, three."

Then we stare at each other, our faces blank, as though we're playing the no-blinking game. He snorts first. I follow within seconds of him cracking. And then we're both howling with laughter, my eyes damp with tears.

Still chuckling, he turns on the ignition and backs out of the parking space, while I settle in for the ride home.

"So tell me about Elite Stunt Training's program," I say.

He straightens in his seat, his hands resting comfortably on the wheel as he steers. "I'm proud to be a part of it. Mostly because we're not a shady outfit."

"Shady how?"

"Every few years, a stunt school will pop up in a random warehouse," he says. "More often than not, it's a scam designed to take advantage of a naïve person. They'll get you into the business, they claim. You'll make thousands, they say. All to entice you to spend thousands of dollars on stunt training. Months later, the warehouse is empty, and the trainers have taken a bunch of people's money and their dreams with them."

That's awful. When I researched stunt work a few days ago, there weren't that many programs to begin with. And I quickly ruled out a few based on their web-sites alone. Threadbare and outdated, the sites gave me little confidence that the people representing the busi-ness knew how to run one. "So how's EST different?"

"Well, we're not scamming anyone. In fact, we pride ourselves on telling it to you straight."

I smirk at him. "Discourage people, you mean?"

He glances at me, a smile dancing on his lips as the trucks slows. "I like to think of it as helping people go into it with their eyes open."

His vehicle's sitting idly at a red light, the ramp to the freeway coming up on the left, and here is where he takes his first opportunity to look my way. For a few uncomfortable seconds, he peers at me with laser-like focus, as if he wants to strip my top layer and investigate what's underneath. When the light changes to green, he trains his eyes back on the road and asks, "Why the sudden interest in stunt training?"

I give him a halfhearted shrug, unsure if it's in my best interest to talk about my father. "I could use the extra money."

"That's a flimsy reason to get into a dangerous pro-fession like mine. You could drive a Lyft for extra cash."

It figures he'd stumble upon that particular sore spot. "I don't have a car."

"Get a job as a restaurant server, then."

I snap my head in his direction. "C'mon, can you imagine me as a restaurant server? Before you answer, remember that the job requires patience and a willingness to assume the customer is always right, and comes with a well-documented risk of sexual harassment."

He opens his mouth to speak, but I jump in to tell him the most important disqualifier: "Also, I'm predisposed to throat-punch anyone who pisses me off."

A ghost of a smile appears in his profile. "Okay, no restaurant work for you. But why not something less drastic?"

Interesting choice of words there, Anthony. "Why do you consider it drastic?"

"Because it's unpredictable. And dangerous. And it could get you killed."

"Only if you're not properly trained, right?"

"*Even* if you're properly trained."

"So why the hell do you do it?"

He frowns. "This isn't about me."

"I disagree. Something about *you* is interfering with my ability to take your class. And bear in mind that at this point, that's all I want to do. It's entirely possible that I won't enjoy it or I won't be any good at it."

He doesn't speak for the length of a city block. I'm seconds away from resigning myself to a silent car ride for the rest of the trip when he asks, "Why do you really want to do this? Talk to me. Pretend I'm your friend."

I blow out a raspberry, knowing he wants me to dig deeper. "Okay, okay. It's not the money. Not primarily. I'd definitely love some extra cash in my pocket . . . for a car, perhaps. But really, I came to LA to stretch myself, to find my passion."

He wrinkles his nose. "Fitness isn't your passion?"

I sigh. "It is and it isn't. Don't get me wrong. I enjoy it, but I wonder if I should be doing more, and I'm trying to figure out what that more could be."

"And stunt work might be it?"

"Could be," I say, nodding. "I've always been a physical person. I was the kid who never sat on the couch. Who always wanted to play outside. Sitting at a desk to do my homework felt like punishment. That didn't change in college, either. I tried to combat my boredom by joining the swim team. Worked for a while, until my father convinced me that I needed to concentrate on my coursework."

"So, what? He didn't want you on the swim team?"

"Essentially, yes. My father's very practical. When my grades started to slip, he pointed out that I was in college to get a degree, not swim."

He nods knowingly. "So you quit the team."

When he lays it out like that, it sounds like I just gave up. But really, I didn't want to squander the opportunity to graduate and land on solid ground. "Yeah. I mean, it wasn't like I was going to the Olympics or anything like that."

"Hmm."

Ugh. He's Tori's cousin, all right. That *hmm* is a defined term in their vocabulary. It means, *I'm not sure I agree with your thinking, but I'm not prepared to say so.*

"My father's not a bad guy. You have to understand,

when my parents split up, he was the one who cared for me while my mother was in school. And when I went off to college, his one wish for me was that I build a stable career, something with growth potential. He just doesn't think fitness fits that profile."

"And some part of you wonders if he's right."

"God, yes. A big part of me hopes he's wrong, though."

Damn, Anthony's so skilled at getting to the heart of a matter that I don't have time to think about my answers. With him, I lose the ability to dress up my thoughts, make them pretty and palatable. They're just there for him—and me—to absorb.

"So yeah, there's some fear," I continue. "But apart from that, I never gave much consideration to other things I could be doing. When Kurt mentioned the training school, it was like a lightbulb went off. 'Why not that?' I thought. 'Why not take all of my skills and use them in a position with the potential for extra money and prestige?'"

"Something your father would approve of."

"I'm not looking for his approval, if that's what you're thinking."

"Hmm," he says, maneuvering his truck into a space across the street from my apartment complex.

I release the seat belt and twist my body to face him. He does the same.

"I just want to show him that I haven't been as short-sighted as he thinks I've been."

Anthony nods repeatedly as he reflects on what I've said. "I'm not sure there's much prestige in stunt work within the industry. But you're right that people outside the industry think it's impressive." Rolling his eyes, he flashes his hands. "Exciting. And sure, you can make good money. But just like anything else in this business, it's a roller coaster. One minute you're turning down projects. The next minute you're begging to get even one. And it's not easy to get into the Screen Actors Guild."

"I read about an easier way to do it. Being Taft-Hartleyed, whatever that means. Could Kurt arrange that for me?"

He draws back and tilts his head to the side. "I see someone's been doing her research."

"There's a page on Elite's website about that."

"I'm impressed. Being Taft-Hartleyed just means you're a nonunion actor hired to work on a SAG production, either as a principal or a background performer. It can get complicated, but yes, that's an option, although again, like anything else, there are no guarantees."

"I don't need guarantees, I need opportunities."

He sighs, his fingers tapping the steering wheel. "Then apply for the boot camp. We'll make space for you in the next session if you want it."

"Really?" I'm so excited by the news, I reach over and hug him, but he doesn't reciprocate. Oh, wrong move. *Be professional, Eva.* I slip on my cross-body to busy myself while I studiously avoid meeting his gaze. "But what about the interview? The website says every applicant must make themselves available for one."

"You just had it."

I want to flail, but I manage to temper my reaction, beaming at him instead. "Anthony, I can't thank you enough for the chance."

"Don't expect any special treatment because you know me."

"I *don't* know you, so that shouldn't be a problem."

He gives me his version of side-eye, and it's the most glorious thing ever. Those dark eyes, along with that kissable smirk, are enough to make me regret the impossibility of a minor fling with him. If I'm not careful, I'll forget Anthony possesses a penchant for playing with women's hearts.

"You'll need a physical."

"Got one before I left Philly."

"It won't be easy," he warns. "Classes are all day on Sundays and on Wednesday evenings, and the first session starts this week."

That's okay. It's better to sign up now when I'm not teaching a full schedule at the studio. The midweek class will be tough to make, though. "Damn, my last class on Wednesday ends at six."

"If you want it badly enough, you'll make it work."

I narrow my eyes at him. "You're going to be a hard-ass about everything, aren't you?"

"It's what I do best," he says smugly.

"Well, before we become mortal enemies, let me tell you that I had a great time today."

His expression softens, a half smile appearing like the perfect end to the day. "Me, too."

There's nothing else to say, is there? Okay, I should leave the car.

Perhaps sensing my hesitation, he helps me along and sends me on my way. "Take care, Eva."

"You, too, Anthony." I'm partly out of the car when I turn around to meet his eyes. "You won't regret this."

I swing the door shut. Before it closes, though, he says, "I already do."

Chapter Thirteen

Anthony

WHEN I GET home, I open the door to find my father sitting up in his recliner, yelling and cursing at the television. *"Ese cabrón, gran hijo de puta, él está mintiendo."*

Which can mean only one thing: My father's favorite Spanish-language show, *Caso Cerrado*, is on. There's no point in fighting it, so I join him, taking a seat on the couch. "What did I tell you about watching this show? It's not good for your blood pressure."

"I can't help it. It's like watching a train wreck."

As if on cue, two security guards in the studio rush forward to separate the parties in the "case," a dispute between a woman and her cheating husband. "No, it's worse than a train wreck. This is like watching the spawn of *The Jerry Springer Show* and *Judge Judy*."

He sits back and reaches for his beer can, bringing it to his lips with a satisfied grin. If I took a photo of him right now, I'd caption it "Single Middle-Aged Man Enjoying Life." Maybe this is enough for him, but I wish he had more.

"No plans to go out with the guys tonight?" I ask, hoping to inspire him.

"Nah." He waves the beer can in the air as though his friends are buzzing around him. "All they want to do is play poker. I'm not good at it." He takes another swig of his beer, eyeing me while he does. When he's done, he raises his chin. "What about you? It's Saturday. Shouldn't you be out with a lady friend or something?"

My mind immediately wanders to my day with Eva, but that's not what he's asking about. She's a friend. Not a *lady friend* in the sense that he's using the term. "The answer is, 'Or something.' And relaxing here counts as something."

He doesn't speak again until the show breaks for commercials, prefacing his question by clearing his throat several times. "Why aren't you dating anyone, *mijo*?"

I give him a blank stare. "What do you mean?"

"You know what I'm talking about," he says with a dismissive wave of his hand. "Isn't there a woman you're spending time with? Or someone you want to bring over for some . . ." He makes a crude motion with his fingers.

I twist my face in distaste. Fuck, this is ridiculous. "Stop. No, there's nobody like that in my life, but I'm not lacking in that department, if that's what you want to know."

His eyes bounce around the room before he speaks again. "Are you seeing a man or something?"

Okay, what the hell is going on here? This isn't like

Papi at all. We kid around all the time. We talk about politics. We discuss whether I've been cutting the grass too low or what meals he should make for the week. But we *don't* discuss my sex life. Ever. "Are you asking me if I'm gay? Bi?"

Beer still in hand, he points at me. "Hey, don't be offended. There's a lot of stuff I don't understand, but I know it's a thing. Berta says you might be exploring your sex."

It's a thing? Exploring my sex? Christ, this is painful. "I'm not offended. I'm just shocked those words are coming out of your mouth . . . And uh, who the hell is Berta?"

"She's a friend."

"A lady friend?" I tease.

A muscle in his jaw twitches. "Just a friend. You know me better than that."

He's right. I *do* know him. And Berta's existence is a monumental deal. As far as I know, my father hasn't dated or spent time with any woman outside our family since he and my mother separated. Until recently, he was still clinging to the hope they'd reconcile. "So let me see if I have this right. You've been discussing my sexuality with your new friend?"

He avoids my gaze. "Maybe."

Shit, now I'm curious about this Berta, but I don't want to push too much or too soon. I'll let him enlighten me when he's ready. "Well, to answer your question, I'm straight."

He still doesn't meet my gaze, focusing his attention on the TV screen instead. "Look, we've never talked about this, but Berta pointed out that maybe you don't date because I'm around. And I never thought about it like that. You're a single guy, in his prime, she says. You should be out there dating or something. Your mother and I were married and had you by the time we were your age."

Okay, so apparently we're glossing over what that relationship did to him. The way he tried his best to make my mother fall back in love with him but failed. The way she left us when she could no longer "hold on." The way he didn't know what to do with himself for *years* after she was gone. The way he still doesn't smile nearly as broadly as he did before they split up. "Dating is overrated. Romance isn't the end game for everyone. And my life is fine the way it is. What about you?"

Maybe that supposedly perfect photo is masking his discontent. If it is, I'd like to know.

"I'm fine," he says, a few seconds too late. "I just worry about you. Sometimes I wonder if you're living *my* life when you should be living your own. Berta says I need to give you room to grow."

Who the fuck is this Berta? And what other stuff is she putting in my father's head? She doesn't know me. Doesn't know that I tried to love someone. God, when I think of *how hard* I tried to make things work with Melissa—how badly I wanted it to work—my stomach cramps.

Melissa, my first and only serious girlfriend, and the woman who broke my heart. She was a receptionist at the bike messenger company where I worked when I first came here. Before dating, we'd flirted with each other, Melissa mostly teasing me about being the incorrigible office heartthrob, until I asked her out. Weeks later, we were inseparable. And it was great for a while. But as we grew serious, things got bumpy. The more I told her I loved her, the less she believed me. I had to be stepping out on her, she accused. *Had* to be. And the pain she felt about an imagined indiscretion devastated me.

"Do you remember when you first came to LA, and I was seeing that woman from my job? Melissa? Did you know we had talked about marriage?"

His eyes widen in interest as he leans forward. "Yeah?"

"Yeah," I say, nodding. "Planned the wedding in our heads and everything. But she couldn't wrap her head around the idea that I'd be faithful to her. And I did my best to prove to her that there was nothing to her fears, but she didn't believe me. Fact is, I loved her more than she loved me."

Just like my father loved my mother more than she loved him.

My father draws back. "How do you know that?"

"*She* left me, Pop. Not because I'd actually cheated, but because one day I would." I rise from the sofa and sit on the arm of his recliner, nudging him with my shoulder. "So you see, Pop, I tried. I tried so hard I didn't recognize myself. And I *still* ended up causing someone pain. I'm just not willing to do that again. But don't worry about me. I have a roof over my head, interesting work to keep me busy, and I get to eat your food most nights."

That's enough for me. It has to be.

Later that night, I lie in bed thinking back on my day with Eva. Winning first place in a reggaeton contest is not an achievement I'd ever thought I'd reach, and I didn't expect to enjoy dancing on a stage in front of hundreds of people. But that's Eva for you. She brings the party with her and sweeps you into the celebration. After that drive home, though, I now realize she's a softie inside, too, vulnerable in a way she lets few people see. I like that she exposed that side of herself to me.

The dancing, as hot as it was, must be forgotten. I can't think about the way we pressed against each other, our bodies bumping and grinding in the afternoon heat, the thump of the heavy bass thrumming through me. I can't picture the way her supple skin glowed in the sun, her smooth legs dipping to the music as her hands caressed my chest. And I'd be a fool to take it a step further and recall the memory of the way she gasped, her eyes fluttering closed, the first time I sank inside her in that hotel room.

With these images fresh in my mind, it would be *so* easy to slip my hand under the sheet and give myself the relief I need. I want to. But Eva and I are friends now and friends don't make friends come—not when they're trying to be platonic, at least. So I take my frustration out on my pillow and pound on it, getting it situated how I like it. Then I flip over onto my stomach, anticipating a restless night—the first of many probably. *Puñeta*.

Chapter Fourteen

When in doubt, make a joke.

Eva

I NEED A T-shirt that says I Survived LA's Metro System.

Twenty-five. That's the number of bus stops I suffer through—on two different bus lines, no less—before I get to Elite Stunt Training's facility in downtown LA. On a Wednesday. After work. And according to this itinerary, I still need to walk half a mile to get to my destination.

Jesus, be a Lyft driver.

I readjust my backpack and mentally prepare myself for the trek. Imagine what it's like for the people with no other option, the ones who rely on public transportation to get them to work every day? There *must* be a better way for people without cars to get here, but whatever it is, it can't be found through a simple Google search. I make a mental note to ask Anthony about it after class.

The neighborhood itself is showing signs of neglect—

too many boarded-up houses, for one—but there are plenty of people walking around and lots of business activity. It's comforting. Reminds me of North Philly, where the structures aren't shiny and new, but the heart and determination of its residents are etched into every crack in the concrete and every inspirational mural on the sides of its buildings.

When I arrive at the address, I see a small professional sign on a steel door. The sign's no larger than a legal-sized document, with the letters EST on it and nothing more. I'm going to take a wild guess and say I've reached the correct place.

My first try pushing the door open fails, so I back up and throw my shoulder into the effort. Because my strength sometimes reaches Wonder Woman levels when I put my mind to it, I fly through the threshold and come skidding to a halt in a room that's larger than all the rooms in Tori's studio combined.

It's surprisingly bright in here, which makes the room's deficiencies more apparent. Dust moves freely in the rays of light that bisect the space, and the walls are riddled with scuff marks, some of them resembling tire treads. What the . . . ? On the walls?

My gaze bounces around the warehouse, finally settling on the bald white guy sitting atop a table by the window, his fingers separating the blinds so he can peek outside. Too many tattoos for my comfort. When they cover most of your body, they're less about the art and more about the message. His tats, a patchwork of skulls, crows, and snakes, say, *Fuck you very much*. I silently pray I won't need to partner with him during the training.

Everyone else is sitting cross-legged or draped across the large mats in different areas of the room. Well, this is a motley crew if ever there was one, and although I can't pinpoint why, it feels absolutely 100 percent right to be a part of it.

I count only one other woman. Blonde, statuesque, and sporting a physique that screams "female professional wrestler," she sits up when she sees me and gives me a shy wave. We shall be friends, I declare in my head—once I suss out whether she's "good people," that is.

Next to her, a wiry guy with pale skin and bloodshot eyes picks at his sneaker laces. He doesn't look a day over eighteen. That one's going to get hurt. He's going to sleep through the program and miss all the safety warnings. In the farthest corner from where I'm standing, two men around my age—one white, the other black—stare at the black man's phone, the muted sound of conversation coming from it suggesting they're watching a video. Now, these guys fit the vision of stuntmen I had in my head: good-looking and brawny.

Kurt and Anthony enter the room, both taking matching long strides that bring them to the center of the space. The students all shuffle to their feet as though our superior officers have arrived, and for some reason, they gather behind me like we're about to break out into the dueling dance sequence in Michael Jackson's "Beat It" video.

"Welcome, everyone," Kurt says. "Thank you for trusting us with your safety and your careers. My name's Kurt Magnus, and I'll be one of two instructors during this six-week training course." He points to Anthony. "And this is Anthony Castillo, my lead instructor and right-hand man. Want to say a few words?"

Anthony nods at us in greeting, and then places his hands behind his back. He has yet to look at me, but I can't help scoping him out. The drill sergeant demeanor, the way his cargo pants stretch snugly against the tops of his thighs, the way his pecs are visible underneath his T-shirt, it's all a bit too much. I hate my new friend.

"I won't lie, this is going to be intense," he says, his expression serious. "Your mental and physical strength will be tested, mostly because you'll be relying on them if you're ever fortunate enough to find yourself on a production set."

Finally, he acknowledges me with a quick scan from my head to my sneaker-clad feet. "If at any point you decide the course is too challenging, though, just let us know. There's no shame in realizing this isn't for you."

Oh, is that a dig directed at me? It's a timely reminder that in this class, he's not my friend. And from now on, I'll address him as Mr. Castillo in here.

Mr. Castillo—shit, I can't do it in my head, though. Thinking of him that way is too weird. *Anthony* continues to recite his opening spiel. "The course will cover a number of dynamic stunts that make up a stunt person's bag of skills: high falls, the air ram, ratchet work, combat, martial arts, stair falls, climbing, and more. We'll go over each skill in detail, and you'll be gaining hands-on experience performing each of them. Sometimes we'll work in groups, other times in teams or one-on-one. It all depends on how you do and the skill in question."

Kurt taps Anthony on the arm. "Why don't we get in a round of introductions before we go further."

Anthony shakes his head as though the notion of introducing ourselves never occurred to him. "Oh, sure. Let's do that."

We fan out in a semicircle so we can see each other, and then Anthony points at the human wall of graffiti. "Why don't we start with you."

"My name's Dexter," my tattooed classmate says in the raspiest voice I've ever heard. "When I'm not doing this, I'm a school custodian."

Dammit. I was hoping his name was Richard or Bartholomew, but no luck. He's a serial killer, for sure. "Dexter, any chance you knit?" I ask.

He smiles, displaying an entire bottom row of gold teeth and an upper row of white teeth that are frighteningly perfect. "No, but I can make you a friendship bracelet."

"Seriously?"

He points at his wrist, and yes, what I thought was a bunch of rags tied around it is a set of friendship bracelets. "My favorite colors are blue and gray," I tell him. "I'll expect my bracelet next week."

Dexter gives me a toothy smile. "Consider it done."

"Are you two finished?" Anthony asks, his expression stern.

I bite the inside of my cheek before I respond. "Sorry to interrupt, Mr. Castillo."

Anthony's eyes narrow, and so do mine. What I wouldn't do for the power to ricochet bullets off my chest and at his head. Spoilsport.

"Would you like to go next?" he asks me.

I curtsy and give him a wide smile. "Oh, sure, I'm Eva. I'm new to LA, and I'm a fitness instructor."

"A black belt in tae kwon do, too," Anthony adds.

I grimace at him. "Yeah. That. But it's been a while."

"Could've fooled me," he mutters.

Oh snap, is someone getting sassy with me? I gesture like a cat scratching at him. "Meow."

I catch his smile before he spins around to hide it.

Turning to the other woman in the class, he says, "And you?"

"I'm Megan. I'm a public school teacher."

Whoa. I was way off.

"Also a lesbian," Megan adds.

Anthony steps forward. "You don't need to give us that much detail about your personal life—"

"With these two in the class," she says, pointing at the burly guys joined at the hip, "yes, I do."

I love her. It's that simple. And I'm relieved I won't be

the only woman or black person in the class. I mean, it's not a position I'm unfamiliar with, but being "the only one" in a group setting can be exhausting and uncomfortable. Given that the class will already tax me physically and mentally, I'd prefer not to add that particular headache to the mix.

We continue going around the room. Thin guy is Wills, black brawny guy (Frick) is Damian, and white brawny guy (Frack) is Brett. Frick and Frack are in love with themselves and also nurturing a bromance. Wills is in a goth phase, I think.

Anthony circles the group as he speaks. "We have several assistants you'll meet soon. They'll work with you on specific stretches geared toward the skills you're learning. They'll also help us with simulation exercises. Before we get to anything else, though, we need to adjust your expectations."

"You might want to sit down for this," Kurt says. "Today's all about giving you an overview and showing you the equipment."

We drop onto the mats, Dexter taking the spot closest to me. Megan gives him a sharp look, as though he's displaced her as my new buddy, and given that he makes friendship bracelets, it's safe to say he has.

Anthony's pacing now, his long stride taking him across the room quickly. "Stunt performing is not an easy profession. It's not for thrill seekers, daredevils or risk takers. In fact, those types of people are exactly who we *don't* want to train. It's a dangerous business, and there are safer ways to make a living. Speaking of pay, it's not guaranteed. Yes, you can make a quick thousand for a day's work, but it isn't steady income, and when it's *really* good pay, they're probably asking you to literally set yourself on fire."

So why does he do it? Does he truly love it, or was this what he fell into because he was looking to do more? Each time I see him, he piques my curiosity. Also, I have zero interest in setting myself on fire.

"Let's talk about attire," he continues. "Everyone should wear long pants. Otherwise, those cuts and scrapes will take a toll on your knees and legs. No jeans, though. And your shirts should be comfortable but not too loose. We don't want your clothing to snag on anything and trip you up. No jewelry, either. And sneakers are a must. Any questions on that?"

"Are tennis shoes okay?" I ask.

"Tennis shoes are good, too."

Finally, he cracks a smile, and an annoying flutter—strikingly similar to the one I felt when he said he wholeheartedly enjoyed my company after the festival—dances across my belly. Maybe I need to get that checked out, but otherwise I have no concerns about how we're interacting. I'm already handling Anthony—just as I said I would. Not sure what Tori was so worried about.

Chapter Fifteen

Anthony

"So, what do you think of this group?" Kurt asks at the end of our first session.

The new trainees are standing around getting to know one another, while Kurt and I talk in the corner of the warehouse. "Feeling good about the different skill sets they bring to the table." I point my chin in Damian and Brett's direction. "We're going to need to separate those two middle schoolers, though."

Kurt laughs. "I have no doubt you'll keep them in line." Then he slaps me on the back. "I'm going to head out. You'll lock up?"

"Of course."

My gaze immediately falls on Eva, who's talking with her entire body—animated as usual and using her mouth, hands, and eyes to convey what she wants to say. Before I can glance away and act like I'm scanning the group, she spots me staring at her and gestures for me to join them.

The trainees disperse as I walk over, like I'm a school principal clearing the halls of loitering students.

"What's up?" I ask when I reach her.

She clasps her hands in front of her and makes a pleading motion, her face contorted in fake agony. "Would you mind giving me a ride home? I don't think I can brave the Metro bus after the trauma of this evening's commute. Please?"

Begging isn't necessary, not when we live so close to each other. I'll even take her home after each class if that's what she wants. "Sure, let me grab my stuff from the office. I'll be ready in a few."

She collapses onto a side chair and closes her eyes. "I'll wait here."

"Can't hang?"

She opens one eye. "On the contrary, my stamina is legendary."

I'm tempted to say, *So's mine*, but as of today she's a trainee, and I should lay off the sexual innuendo for the foreseeable future. Problem is, Eva and I appear to have taken an AP course in Sexual Innuendo as a Second Language—and we both aced it. Instead, I adopt the safest approach and pretend not to hear her.

After grabbing my bag and shutting down my computer, I return to find Eva still lounging where I left her. "Ready?"

She sits up and pats her cheeks. "Ready."

Outside, the pavement is wet, and the air is pungent with the typical city scents after a warm day and a recent rain shower—hot asphalt, roasting coffee, and weed. It's a welcome change from the dust that fills my nostrils when I'm in the warehouse all day. The truck's parked a few feet away from the entrance, and after I unlock it, we silently climb into the cab and fasten our seat belts.

"Do you get Sirius XM in here?"

"Yeah."

"May I?" she asks, pointing at the radio dial.

"Do you promise to use your privileges responsibly?"

She smirks at me, already pressing a few buttons, and after scrolling through a few stations, she lands on "September" by Earth, Wind & Fire. "Now *that's* the only version I recognize."

I purse my lips, unsure what she means. "There's another version?"

"Taylor Swift tried it," she says, her face flat and unamused.

"Oh, that's unfortunate."

"You know the song?" she says, surprise in her voice.

Spanish Harlem was and still is largely a mix of African Americans, Latinx people, and Italians, with smaller African and Caribbean immigrant populations thrown in, too. "I grew up in New York. I probably heard this song at least once a year."

"I did, too," she says with a wistful smile. Abruptly, she pulls out her phone. "Give me a sec. I'm just going to jump online and order takeout from Grubhub so it can be delivered when I get home. I didn't eat before class, and I'm *starving*." She places an index finger over her mouth. "Shhh, don't tell Tori, but I found a place that makes fried catfish and hush puppies almost as good as the ones my grandmother made. This app is going to be a lifesaver."

"Hang on," I say. "Before you do that, let me check something."

She ate every grain of rice in her meal at the Puerto Rico Loves Cali Festival, so I know she enjoyed it. And if she thought that was good, she needs to experience Pop's food. I send him a quick text to make sure it's okay:

Me: Hey, Pop. Would you mind if I invited a friend to have dinner with us?

My phone starts ringing immediately. He refuses to answer texts. "Antonio, no problem. Bring him by whenever. We have plenty of food. I made *piononos*."

I hold the phone away from my mouth as I speak to Eva. "Interested in a Puerto Rican home-cooked meal?"

Her eyes go wide and she nods repeatedly. "Yes. What kind of question is that?" She looks down at herself and cringes. "I'm not dressed for dinner, though."

"It's okay," I mouth to her. To him, I say, "All right, Papi. We'll be there in less than a half hour. See you soon."

I turn on the ignition and place the car in Drive. "Get ready to meet my father."

She claps her hands repeatedly, her bright eyes sparkling. "I can't wait."

And I can't wait to see what Papi thinks of her. Knowing Eva, she'll have a new admirer within an hour.

Right now, though, I'm interested in finding out if she has any qualms about training. "So, what did you think of your first session?"

She's distracted by the passing scenery, but I can see the corner of a smile in her profile. "As challenging as I think it's going to be, I'm looking forward to it. Kind of feels like we're a bunch of adults on a playground. And I think I'm going to learn some stuff that's useful outside of stunt work. Like how to land after jumping off a platform."

"I don't mean to scare you, but it won't be all fun and games. And you should expect some bumps and bruises before we're done."

"You don't have to worry about that. Bumps and bruises don't scare me."

Not a shock at all. I suspect when she sidelined me in the studio last week, she didn't give a single thought to what would happen next. I could have responded instinctually. Knocked her to the ground and hurt her by mistake. But she just reacted, potentially placing her body in harm's way, fearless in her effort to protect herself and kick my ass. "Does anything scare you?"

"Spiders," she says stressing the word with a hiss. "You?"

"Snakes," I say, doing the same.

She cringes, wrinkling her nose in a way I shouldn't find so cute. "Oh no. Dexter's tattoos must be terrifying for you."

"I can handle pictures of them. *Real* snakes are the

problem. But let's get back to the class. You feeling good about the people in it?"

They'll be working together, simulating combat among other things, so it helps if they get along. Each boot camp's success depends on the group's compatibility. I've never asked a trainee these questions before, but then again, I've never trained someone who I've slept or danced with before, either. Eva's in her own category—even if it's not in our best interests for her to lay claim to that distinction.

"Megan's a sweetie," she says, smiling, "and I think I'm already in love with Dexter."

"What about Brett and Damian?"

"Frick and Frack, you mean." Her gaze is pensive as she considers the question. "The jury's still out on them, but I'll tell you my verdict after I get to know them a little better. So far no alarms are going off."

A Michael Jackson song comes on and she gets lost in the music, lifting her arms in the air and swinging her torso from side to side, her voice loud enough to drown out MJ's. "'Human Nature' is one of my favorite Michael Jackson songs."

"'Man in the Mirror' is mine."

She drops her arms and draws back. "You keep surprising me."

"What? You thought I only listened to salsa and merengue?"

Covering her mouth to hide her grin, she says, "And Coldplay." Looking out the window again, she says,

"You know, I used to tell my mother a man could never be my soul mate unless he loved MJ as much as I do."

"Well, it's a good thing I don't love him at all."

She whips her head in my direction and meets my gaze, trying valiantly to fight the smile tugging at her lips. After a few seconds, she breaks her silence, laughter in her voice when she says, "You're such a jerk. And you're right, that *is* a good thing."

We're so easy together, you'd think we've known each other for much longer than we have. I enjoy spending time with her. Enjoy her, period. She's the kind of woman I'd love to know like the back of my hand. The person I could share inside jokes with because her brain works a lot like mine does. And if I find myself thinking about her when I'm in bed from time to time, well, I'll shut it down as best I can. I'm not going there with her—not again. Never mind that I get an uncomfortable ache in my chest when I think about her going there with someone else.

Chapter Sixteen

The quickest way to my heart? Crack my chest
open, duh. Okay, okay, food works, too.

Eva

I'M EXPERIENCING NEIGHBORHOOD envy. "But really,
how many bakeries and cafés does one community
need?"

Anthony smiles as he turns his truck onto a two-way
street. "You're one to talk. Your neighborhood's known
for a surplus of them, too. In Atwater, though, you don't
have to be a card-carrying member of the cool crowd
like you do in Silver Lake. At least not yet."

"Let's not get snarky about my neighborhood, okay.
It's too soon for me to get into a turf war. Besides, no
one's denying Atwater's appeal. I even thought about
living here. Unluckily for me, there aren't many apartment complexes, and I wasn't comfortable renting a
home by myself. When things go bump in the night, I

need to know I can run across the hall and bang on a neighbor's door."

"Yeah, Atwater's mostly single-family homes. We rent the one we're in. Kurt's older sister, Linda, owns the house and gave us the hookup. Pop and I can't afford to buy a home here, not with the skyrocketing prices."

"Do you mind my asking what he does?"

"Trucking. But he's semi-retired, and he only drives across the state. Spends a lot of time at home these days."

He maneuvers the car onto a small driveway and turns off the engine. It's an older home with three large windows facing the street and pale blue siding. Some-one's been taking meticulous care of the shrubbery that dots the perimeter. "Who mows the lawn?"

"I do. And he takes care of the cooking. That's our deal."

It's hard to picture Anthony bringing a woman here. It doesn't scream *bachelor pad* at all. Plus, he lives with his father. But I suppose you don't need to bring anyone home if you're aiming for no-strings sex. Why am I even thinking about this?

He checks the mailbox, finds it empty, and jogs up the front steps. Whistling, he fits the key into the lock and opens the door with a flourish, motioning for me to come inside. "Welcome to our humble abode."

We walk down a short hall with dark wood floors and a small console table decorated with figurines but no pictures. There's nothing on the walls; it's just a neat passageway to get to the rest of the home. "The floors are gorgeous."

"That's the one update my father and I did when we moved in. With Linda's permission, of course."

"You did a fantastic job. I'm impressed you're so handy. Or is it handsy? I always get those two confused."

"Eva, stop," he says on a laugh. "Not now."

"What?" I ask, feigning ignorance that I've said anything inappropriate.

Our inner twelve-year-olds are giggling in the hall when Anthony's father calls out, "Is that you, Antonio?"

"No, Pop," Anthony replies. "It's the boogeyman."

I love that he jokes around with his father. Puts me at ease immediately. Because if Anthony's father is anything like him, I'm in for a real treat.

"Tú eres un malcriado," his father yells back.

I tug on Anthony's shirt sleeve. "What does that mean? I bet that'll be useful one day."

"It's kind of like saying I'm a spoiled brat," he whispers.

"Oooh, that's good. He's right, too."

Anthony pinches me on my arm, and I yelp at the unexpected attack. In fact, I'm so surprised by it that I can't stop laughing, and when we enter the living room, I'm wiping away my tears.

Standing behind the kitchen counter, Anthony's dad finishes drying his hands on a dish towel and looks up. He tips his head to the side when he sees me.

Meanwhile, I freeze, realizing he's shocked by my arrival, his eyes now wide open. Anthony favors his father, mirroring even the smallest details, like the way the corners of his eyes crinkle when he's thinking hard—like he's doing now. Well, this is awkward.

Anthony's voice cuts through the silence. "Dad, this is Eva, a friend of mine. She's actually Tori's best friend."

"But . . . but you're a woman."

I snort and glance at Anthony, whose cheeks are turning a lovely shade of parental embarrassment. I put out my hand. "Good to meet you . . ."

He shakes himself clear of the fog. "Luis. Sorry, Eva. It's just . . . he's never—"

Anthony claps his hands together and rubs them. "Now that everyone's been introduced, where are the *piononos*?"

I glance at Luis, who's wearing an amused expression as he watches his son inspect the stove top. At this point, I can already predict this evening's going to be fun.

Anthony washes his hands, throws on a pair of mitts, and pulls a baking dish from the oven. Angling the dish so I can see what's inside, he starts dancing from side to side. "Now this? This is going to put you out for the night. Guaranteed food coma."

"What is it?" I ask.

"It's plantains wrapped around picadillo and topped with cheese," Luis says. He looks at Anthony. "How do you explain *picadillo*?"

"It's just ground beef in a tomato-based sauce. Loads of seasonings, too."

"I don't mean to be rude, but can we eat?" I ask. "It sounds delicious."

Smiling, Luis points his finger at me. "I like her, Antonio. She's got spunk."

"She's got something, all right," Anthony says under his breath.

"I heard that, *malcriado*," I say.

They both laugh at what I hope was a totally appropriate use of the word. Then Anthony rounds the counter and places the dish on the dining table while Luis brings a bowl of yellow rice over. The small table is already set for three people, and a glass pitcher is sitting in the center.

"May I wash my hands somewhere?" I ask.

Luis points down the hall. "Bathroom is on the left."

"Thanks."

When I return, both men are whispering as they wash their hands in the kitchen sink.

"Are you talking about me over there?"

They respond at the same time and give contradictory answers. Luis says yes; Anthony says no. I'm inclined to believe Luis, but I decide not to give Anthony a hard time about it. I'd like the mood of the evening to remain exactly as is—light and easy. "Thanks so much for letting me crash your dinner. I hope it wasn't too much trouble."

Luis waves my thanks away. "No problem. I always make extra."

We sit at the table, with Anthony to my right and Luis across from me. Anthony immediately puts two *piononos* on my plate and passes the bowl of rice to me, effortlessly making me a part of their dinner rituals, including a short blessing of the food.

"How do I eat this?" I ask. "With a fork? Pick it up?"

"Whatever's comfortable," Anthony says. "I like to pick them up."

I pick up the *pionono* and bite into it. "Oh, my gosh. This is *sooo* good. It's salty and sweet and the meat is seasoned to perfection."

Luis preens like a peacock as I shower him with compliments.

"So, Luis, how do I make this yummy dish for myself?"

"I can give you the recipe. The most important thing is to make your own *sofrito*. We have a cousin who insists on using that store-bought *porqueria*. She's not allowed to cook for any of our parties."

"Yeah, that's like my family and sides dishes for a cookout. Mess up the potato salad and you will *never* recover from the bad-mouthing. And you'll never get a second chance if it's not yellow. My cousin brought white potato salad to a family picnic once. She's been responsible for bringing the beverages ever since."

I bite into the *pionono* again, rolling my eyes in pleasure. "These should be called pio-yes-yes."

Luis barks out a laugh. "You can come eat my food any time. Even when Anthony isn't around."

"Pop, are you making a move on my girl . . ." He flushes and coughs into his closed hand.

I slap him on the back. "You okay there, *friend*?"

He shifts away from me, declining my help. "I'm fine, girl who happens to be my friend. Girl. Friend."

We both know it was a slip of the tongue—there's no point in reading anything more into it—so of course I'm going to needle him about it. "How ya' doin' over there? Allergies kicking in again?"

"Cute," he says, winking at me.

He gets my meaning, and he isn't upset about it. Because we're just hanging out and having fun; it doesn't need to be any more complicated than that. In fact, since neither of us is interested in a relationship, I'm thinking the universe wanted us to find each other.

"You two are funny together, you know that?" Luis says.

In unison, we say, "We know."

What's not as funny? As much as I'd like to pretend otherwise, the moment Anthony almost called me his girlfriend, a tiny, silly part of me liked the sound of that. But it's so miniscule it doesn't even matter.

Anthony

EVA AND I are working side by side cleaning up the kitchen when my father reappears.

With suds dripping from her forearms, Eva turns her head in his direction and whistles. "Luis, you're going out tonight?"

"I am, Eva. A friend invited me to see a movie."

He plants himself in front of the mirror and inspects his reflection, smoothing the hair at the nape of his neck. He's wearing what he calls his "church shirt" and a pair of gray slacks with—hmm, that's not good—a hint of sheen. *Rico. Suave.*

"A lady friend?" Eva asks.

I expect him to say no, but he doesn't say anything at all. His cheeks grow rosy, though, and he chews on his lip as though he's trying to figure out how much to reveal. "Yes, her name's Berta. Real nice woman. We talk sometimes."

Berta? That's the same woman he mentioned the other day. Interesting that he didn't even want to admit she was a lady friend when I asked him myself.

"Is she your *girlfriend*?" Eva asks, a teasing inflection in her voice.

Shit. She doesn't know this, but certain subjects aren't laughing matters to my father. Not surprisingly, he stills, his face falling as he stares at himself in the mirror. "No, I don't have girlfriends." He points at me. "His mother was my wife. The only one I'll ever have."

Eva's stricken face is hard to watch. She's smart enough to know she walked into something none of us was prepared to discuss. When she begins to speak again, my heart thrums as I wait to hear how she'll handle my father's pronouncement.

"Well, I must say, if that's the case, it's great that you

have someone like Berta to spend time with. I'm sure she's a wonderful woman."

My father visibly relaxes, his features softening. "She is." After a last look in the mirror, he grabs his keys off the table and shuffles to the door. "Have fun, you two." And then he's gone, leaving Eva and me alone. Together. In my house.

I can't help thinking my father's giving us space. He probably assumes Eva and I want it. Nothing could be further from the truth, though. I was comfortable bringing her here because I knew my father would be the perfect buffer. Now that he's gone, I'm tense again, worried that I'll do or say something to ruin the good rapport we're developing.

Eva shuts off the faucet, gives me the last plate, and dries her hands on the kitchen towel. "Your dad's sweet."

"He can be a pain in the ass, too, but he's also my best friend." I look around. "You want something else to drink?"

"More of the iced tea your father made would be great."

Grateful for the distraction, I stride to the refrigerator and remove the pitcher from the top shelf. Eva saunters into the living room as she studies the framed photographs on the walls. She points at one. "That's Tori as a little girl. I'd recognize her anywhere."

I nod, handing her a glass of tea. "You mean you'd recognize her hair anywhere."

She smiles and takes a sip, while I do everything in

my power not to stare at the long column of her neck and the way her lips are pressed against the glass. But a wicked force encourages me to do just that. Damn, *maldito*'s back. I mentally brush him off my shoulder and follow her gaze, which is focused on a picture of Papi and me.

"Any pictures of your mother?" she asks.

"No."

She walks over to the couch and takes a seat, sipping her tea while patting the cushion with her free hand to indicate that I should join her. When I sit, she angles her body to face me and tucks her right leg under her left. "Your parents' breakup . . . was it bad?"

My pulse quickens. I hate talking about this shit, but I don't want to be rude and tell her so. It's not her fault that the Castillo men obviously have unresolved issues. And maybe it won't be terrible to say it out loud. "It wasn't messy or anything like that. She decided to leave him, announced her intentions, and bounced. He tried to convince her that it was just a phase, that they could rekindle the feelings that led them to marry, but the more he wanted to hold on to her, the less she wanted to be held on to. She just didn't love him anymore, and he couldn't do anything to change her mind."

She scoots a little closer, her voice soothing. "How'd your father handle it?"

"Not well," I say, shaking my head. "For months, he didn't do much of anything other than work and sleep. I was eighteen, going to school, stressed about him.

Eventually, he started engaging again, with me, with his friends in the neighborhood, but if you want to get a sense of how far he's come, I can tell you that they're still legally married."

Eva reaches for my hand, threading her fingers through mine. "And how'd you take it?"

I draw back. "Me? I was fine. Angry at her for hurting him, but fine otherwise."

She squeezes my hand, sympathy in her eyes. "That's the reason you're no longer close?"

"That's part of it."

"And when she left for PR, she chose to leave you, too. That's the other part?"

"Yeah, I guess. I was the one who had to clean up her mess."

The connection is comforting, her buttery-soft hand contrasting with my callused skin, but I don't need to be consoled about anything, and I don't know what else to say. We sit there in silence, until I slip my hand from hers and stand, signaling the conversation's end. "So, you must be tired. Let me get you home."

She doesn't say anything for a moment. Just watches me under the veil of her thick lashes as she finishes her drink. Then she rises to her feet and says, "Thanks for inviting me. It's been eye-opening."

Eye-opening? God, that wasn't the goal at all. I just wanted to show her some hospitality. I can't imagine what she thinks she's learned tonight. A lot about Papi, I hope.

After I set her glass in the sink, we leave the house and get on the road for the short drive to her apartment.

"Please thank your father again for me and tell him I'll be hounding him for his *piononos* recipe soon."

I easily picture Papi giving Eva cooking tips as she looks on, asking questions and taste-testing. "He'd love that." I'd love it, too, actually. Even if I was just in the background, watching them make a meal together. Papi wouldn't turn down a chance to share his joy of cooking with someone. "Eva, are you and your father close?"

She sighs. "We were close when I was young. As I got older, we clashed more, mostly about the decisions I was making. What to do for a career, where to live, even small stuff like whether I should buy a car in the city. It can be suffocating at times."

"Is that why you moved to LA?"

Pressing her finger against the passenger window, she traces circles against it. "I think I moved to LA for him as much as I did for me. His life shouldn't revolve around worrying about me anymore, but as long as I'm close, that's his MO. It's habit, I think."

"And your mother?"

"My mother's a blast. Wanda is fun and fun-loving. Works hard and plays even harder. Unlike my father, she lets me be. Doesn't feel the need to orchestrate anything in my life. Just wants me to be a good person, happy and fulfilled. And she's perpetually annoyed with my dad for meddling." She groans in frustration. "You know, if

I could just stop the men in my life from trying to make me their puppet, life would be so much easier."

Oh, now we're getting somewhere. She almost ripped me a new one when I told her I don't date, and I'd love some insight into why she reacted so strongly. "The men in your life. They've been puppeteers?"

She looks up, rolling her eyes. "My high school boyfriend tried to pressure me to only apply to the same colleges he was applying to. My first serious boyfriend after college tried to hide my birth control pills. And most recently, my boss, who, admittedly, I shouldn't have been sleeping with, wouldn't let me out of my employment contract early so I could move here." A pointed finger enters my peripheral vision. "And don't say I chose poorly. Their asshattery was all on them."

Damn. It's impressive that she even speaks to men given the shit they've pulled with her in the past. And it does help me understand her better: If you try to tell her what to do, she'll come out swinging. "C'mon, I'd never blame you like that. But what now? No more relationships for you, either?"

"Well, if I met my perfect match, I wouldn't shut him out. In the meantime, though, I'd say I'm on a relationship sabbatical. I need to step away a bit, recharge before I can jump back into the fray. I've got too much on my mind anyway. The move. My new classes at Every Body. And now stunt training. It's exciting, and I just want to focus on getting my shit right."

"I understand that sentiment completely."

It's a comfortable conversation, and when I turn the car onto her street, I'm inclined to keep driving right past her building. But I don't. Because that would be kidnapping.

Before she exits the truck, she places a hand on my thigh. "You're a cool guy, Anthony. Although there are times when I want to strangle you, I'm glad we're friends."

"Good, because I feel exactly the same way."

When she's gone, though, I sit there staring at the spot on my thigh where she casually rested her hand. That simple act yanked me out of our buddy-buddy moment like I'd been doused with cold water. And I know what that means: There's trouble ahead.

Chapter Seventeen

If it's the little things in life that matter, why
are they ever considered little things?

Eva

TORI STROLLS INTO the staff room Wednesday afternoon and stops short when she finds me sitting near
the door. "Hey, woman. You're here early." Yawning, she
glides to the water dispenser and fiddles with it.

"It's the Metro," I explain. "I haven't figured out what
to expect from my commute yet, so my timing's been
way off." I'm nursing a pomegranate smoothie from the
café next door and checking my voice mail messages
before my five o'clock Zumba class. My father's left three
messages, none of them urgent.

"Damn, that sucks," she says, holding down the Cold
faucet.

"It's not as bad as the manspreading. Good Lord, is
there something in the water that gives LA men over-
sized junk? Because they all sit like they're smuggling

anacondas onto the bus by stuffing them in their pants."

"Stop," she says on a snort, holding out her hand with her back to me.

"Anyway, since I'm already here," I say, rising from my chair, "I figured I'd go say hi to Anthony during the break in his self-defense class."

She spins around, water in hand, her eyebrows squished together. "That's . . . cordial of you, but Kurt's covering for him today. Anthony's off doing some kind of commercial work."

"Oh," I say, sitting back down. "He never mentioned that."

She takes a sip of her water, and then she hides behind the cup and studies me. "You could say hi to Kurt, though."

"Nah, that's okay. I can use the time to return my father's call."

Still sipping her water—or, more accurately, still hiding behind her cup—she joins me at the table. "I was going to ask how things were going with you two, with the class and all, but if you're seeking him out here, things must be going just fine."

"Better than fine, actually. I even met his father the other day. His *piononos* were delicious."

"He took you to meet Tío Luis? And you ate *piononos*?"

She's wearing this odd expression—eyebrows raised, mouth agape—as though I've shared a mind-boggling fact. "Yeah. Last Sunday. After class."

"Hmm."

I sigh and shake my head, knowing where she's going with this. "We're friends, Tori."

She shrugs. "I didn't say anything."

"You didn't have to. That 'hmm' spoke for you."

She sits up straight and puckers her lips, mock snootiness dripping from her pores. "Well, I'll just tell you this, then. Tío Luis complains that Anthony never brings people to the house. Says he's worried that Anthony doesn't ever do anything fun. Works and works out, that's it. And now you're hanging out at his place eating *piononos*."

"Nothing you just said undermines my original point. We're. Friends. Okay?"

In truth, it's precisely *because* we're friends that Anthony invited me over to his house. Otherwise he'd be violating his own no-dating rules. As much as Tori would like to attach significance to a simple dinner invitation, the fact is, eating at Anthony's fits within the parameters of the platonic relationship we agreed to. So there.

Tori throws up her hands. "Okay, don't bite my head off. Besides, you have a more pressing issue to deal with today."

"What kind of issue?" I ask, my mouth going dry. "Is it the class?"

She nods. "Sort of." Wearing an evil grin, she hunches over, leans in, and whispers, "I have it on good authority that Ashley's planning to take your class today."

Oh, *that* I can handle. A complaint about my class this early in the session? Not so much. "What? Is she a terrible dancer?"

"I'm not sure, to be honest. But she FaceTimed me earlier and I saw a preview of the outfit. It was very *Flashdance*. You know, with the off-the-shoulder shredded sweatshirt and leg warmers?"

"*Some* would say that's retro."

"Then *some* would be lying," she says, her eyes wide. "Anyway, I'm not sure what she's expecting, but I wanted to give you a heads-up. She seemed a little nervous. So maybe you could work your magic and help her thrive? I adore her so much and I want her to love it."

Anyone who thinks in-laws only fake getting along hasn't met Tori and Ashley. They're sickeningly sweet to each other. And I get why Tori has a sister crush on Ash. She's a walking ray of sunshine with a filthy mind and no filter. My kind of people, indeed. "Don't worry about Ashley. I'll make sure she enjoys herself. It's my job."

Tori nods and stands. "Good. I'll be at the front desk if you need me."

After Tori leaves, I try to reach my father but the call goes straight to voice mail. I send him a short text telling him I'm doing well, but I know he won't be satisfied until he speaks with me directly. I broke our telephone chain by not calling him sooner, so I'm sure by now my mother's told him that I've started stunt training. I'm happy to delay that conversation indefinitely.

Twenty minutes later, I stroll to Studio B and stumble to a halt when I see dozens of people hanging around outside the room. Tori's directing everyone to line up against the wall.

"What's going on?" I ask, raising my voice to cut through the laughter and chatter.

"It appears word's gotten out that your class is not to be missed, so we've got a bit of a traffic jam here. The room's capacity is forty people. We're going to need to turn some folks away. First come, first served." She leans over and whispers in my ear. "The other instructors are going to hate you."

I'm a little breathless from the adrenaline rush coursing through me. I can't believe what I'm hearing. All these people are here to take my class? I never got this type of reaction in Philly, and I don't know why it's different in LA, but I'll take it. Goddamn it, I'll take it and run like the wind with it.

Tori's busy counting out the students entering the studio, while I search for Ashley. A minute later, I find her in the line, waving her hands at me in a happy greeting. She's added a headband to the outfit, and I must admit, Tori's right that none of it is retro.

"I'm excited and nervous and ready to go," she says breathlessly.

"Ashley, I think you're building this up in your head. It's just Zumba."

She looks around her, taking in the people bustling around. "Then how do you explain all this? Doesn't look like 'just Zumba' to me. I think you're selling yourself short and I don't know why, maybe it's the confident way you carry yourself, but I never expected that from you."

Tori ushers her to move forward before I can respond. "Made it just in time, Ash. The person after you is the last one." She turns to me. "Now go teach, *chica*. I'm going to think about adding more classes to your schedule despite probation. Demand for a specific instructor is an exception I can live with."

Ashley's soft-spoken admonition's still rattling in my head. I don't think I belittle my work the way she's suggesting, but maybe I should be more attuned to how I speak about what I do. Starting now. So when I enter the classroom, I set the music player to Ciara's "Gimme Dat" and clap my hands to get everyone's attention. "Thanks for coming, everyone. In case you didn't know it, this is Advanced Fucking Zumba. Get ready to dance your asses off and have a good time."

Everyone laughs and shouts their approval. I'm so pumped about teaching that I'm jumping to the music even before I find my spot on stage. Advanced Fucking Zumba, indeed.

Anthony

"ALL RIGHT, GENTLEMEN, they'd like you on set now."

The production assistant walks away without a backward glance, one of his hands pressed against the earpiece that warns everyone he's got shit to do and no time for us.

A simple job involving a twenty-second fight sequence, today's work coincides perfectly with this evening's training class on hand-to-hand combat. The commercial itself is clever, too. In it, a bunch of football fans at a game taunt the fans of the losing team, but they're seemingly unaffected by the insults, which get increasingly antagonistic, until someone throws a beer and it's revealed that the fans for the losing team are wearing cordless noise-canceling headphones—and the guys are huge. That's when the fight begins. I'm on the losing team's side, so I get to knock some heads. Heh.

We've been practicing all morning, and I'm relieved that I know a few of my co-actors. It alleviates some of the stress of wondering whether someone's lacking the necessary experience to ensure a relatively uncomplicated job remains injury-free. No one's talking. It's an unwritten rule among stunt professionals that the minutes before an action sequence are best spent getting your head in the game. Focus is essential in this business.

The stadium isn't a stadium at all; it's a simulated scene in the corner lot of a huge film studio. Eighteen men and various extras shuffle to the set and get in position, ready to perform the scene we mapped out in rehearsal. Two separate camera crews prepare their equipment, while the producer and director fire off instructions to assistants and the director of photography. The gaffer, who I'm surprised to see is a woman, makes last-minute adjustments to the lighting.

I'm supposed to throw a punch, duck when my opponent (a guy I've worked with before) tries to return the favor, and spin his body around so I can put him in a headlock. If I'm lucky, Bobby won't act on instinct and elbow me in my chest like Eva did during defense class.

The memory makes me laugh. Eva's something else.

Bobby pats me on the arm, his eyebrows raised in a question. "You okay? I'm not used to dealing with anything but your mean mug on set."

I shake off the loss of concentration. "Yeah, yeah, I'm fine. Just thought of something funny."

The director calls standby on the set and everyone quiets. The first take is cut when an actor flubs his lines. The second take is cut when the same actor flubs a different set of lines. In my head, I can picture Eva asking, "Can we give someone else the fucking lines, then?" And I'm grinning at the thought before I realize we're in the middle of the third take and I'm supposed to take a swing. Somehow I manage to time it perfectly despite my momentary disorientation, but then I forget to duck and get popped in the mouth.

Fuck, that stings. So when Eva's on the brain, I get hurt. That must be a metaphor for something, right?

I'M STILL PISSED about my subpar performance when I get to EST a few hours later. In my line of work, being distracted isn't inconvenient, it's dangerous. But I don't have much time to think about it because tonight's training session begins in ten minutes, and I still need to change my clothes—and get a cold compress for my lip.

"Hey, what do you think of Eva?"

I immediately recognize Damian's voice when I push the restroom door open.

"Shit, I'd tap that ass in a hot minute."

That's Brett. The pretty boy with a thick neck and even thicker arms.

I slow down before I come into view, hoping to eavesdrop some more. I'm classy as hell that way.

"Megan, too," Brett continues. "At the same time."

They roar with laughter and exchange pounds—I didn't even hear them wash their hands—and we pass one another on their way out.

"Oh, hey, Mr. Castillo. Looking forward to class."

This from Damian. Although I'm seething inside, I keep it professional. "Call me Anthony."

"Cool," Brett says.

I stop them before they can leave, blocking the passageway with my body. "Listen, fellas, this is a place of business, and your reputation in this industry begins here. As early as today. We don't want to make this an uncomfortable environment for anyone in the class. And it goes without saying that discrimination and sexual harassment are grounds for removal from the course. At a minimum. So keep your thoughts to yourself and treat everyone with respect, okay?"

Brett's eyes go wide, and Damian clears his throat.

"Okay," they say in unison. And then they bolt out of the restroom.

It's a wonder the towel dispenser doesn't come crashing to the ground given the abuse I put it through when I'm done washing my hands. I'd like to think I'm upset because the guys were being sexist assholes, but that's only part of it. I'm incensed because they were talking about Eva that way. And I'm ashamed to admit that I probably wouldn't have reacted this strongly had they been talking about Megan only. Sure, I still would have curbed their language, but I would have done it because it's the right thing to do. I wouldn't have been seconds away from knocking Brett out. That's a problem. On several levels. And my earlier slipup on set only compounds my concerns about it.

I'm still thinking about my reaction when I walk out the restroom and see Brett and Eva talking in a corner. Eva's expression is open and friendly, and Brett's giving off a vibe of mild interest, his shoulder and tilted head resting against the wall as he looks down at her with a half smile. Jesus. This is like standing at a high school locker, watching the jock flirt with the pretty girl.

My teeth aren't clenched because I'm jealous. That's not my style. I'm concerned for her, that's all. But I'm not going to do anything about it—not yet. Instead, I'm going to focus on teaching hand-to-hand combat, and I know exactly who my first volunteer will be.

Chapter Eighteen

Is there an aspirin specifically formulated for
sexual tension headaches?

Eva

UGH. THAT FUCKING shirt Anthony's wearing is going
to be the death of me.

Although the dark gray compression tank leaves
only his sculpted arms exposed, it clings to his body not
like it's a second skin, but like it *is* his skin, highlighting
his barrel chest and taut stomach. I detest that garment
with the fiery passion of a thousand suns and just as
many ghost peppers. It's making me notice Anthony the
man, when I should be paying attention to the person
who's both my friend outside the training room and Mr.
Castillo in here.

He begins to pace in front of us. Well, in my mind, it's
more like a strut, the roundness of his firm ass visible in
profile. "Today's class is all about filming a fight scene."

Mother of mercy, now that he's walked past me, I can

see the dips and planes of his well-defined back. I'm so weak it's embarrassing.

Megan leans into me and whispers in my ear. "You okay, Eva?"

I tap my head with the side of my hand, trying unsuccessfully to knock some sense into it. "What?"

"Thought I heard you moan. Do you have a belly ache or something?"

"No, I'm fine," I say. Smacking my pasty lips, I struggle to come up with an excuse for my inadvertent outburst. "Just remembering what I had for dinner last night. It was so good."

"What did you have?" Megan asks.

"A salad."

"Must have been *some* salad." She gives me a conspiratorial smile. "Finding it hard to focus?"

I finally meet her gaze and see the humor in her eyes. "*Yes*, goddamn it, *yes*."

We both share a laugh, until Anthony plants his feet in front of us, his lips pursed and his neutral gaze settled on me—and *only* me.

"Eva, what are the five tenets of tae kwon do?"

The question evokes a Pavlovian response—but my mouth's still dry when I recite them. "Courtesy, integrity, perseverance, self-control, and . . . indomitable spirit." I bite down on my lip to stop myself from ending with *Sir*. Shit, the way he's looking at me, *Daddy* might be appropriate here, too. Okay, no, that's not happening.

"What's that first one again?" he asks, cupping his ear.

"Courtesy." I narrow my eyes at him. "Understood, Mr. Castillo."

He nods and resumes his insufferable pacing. "Good."

The desire to stick my tongue out at him is strong. So very strong. Why didn't he call Megan out, too? I wasn't the only one laughing. And why am I kind of turned on by the way he took control of his classroom? I drop my head in shame.

"Fight scenes don't reflect actual combat, of course," he continues. "It's a combination of acting, throw kills, sound effects, and camera angles. Think of it as a dance between the two fighters with the sound effects serving as the song you're dancing to. If even one step in the choreography is off, the whole sequence just looks bad. Google 'terrible fight scenes' to see some examples."

"Actually, just Google '*Gymkata*,'" I add.

I can't help it. When there are good points to be made, I make them. But he just chastised me for being discourteous, so I give him a reluctant smile and mouth, "Sorry."

To my surprise, Anthony's eyes brighten. "You've seen that one, too?"

I answer immediately, psyched that he's willing to engage with me about this. "Oh my God, yes. It's awful. What person thought it was a good idea to build an entire movie around an Olympic gymnast with no acting experience?"

Anthony's answering chuckle is loud and uninhibited, the deep rumble sparking a different kind of vibration in my own body. I want to hear it again and again and again. Wait. No, I'm better than this. These aren't the types of thoughts we agreed to. I'm calling foul on myself.

"Exactly," he says, thrusting out his hands in a yes-you-get-me gesture. "He spends the entire movie flipping through the air and conveniently finding ancient structures that look a lot like gym equipment."

I slap away my traitorous thoughts and try to recall as much as I can about the film, my smile broadening when I remember a particularly ridiculous scene. "The pommel horse in the middle of the village square. Do you remember that one? Genius."

Anthony holds his chest and falls over. "That one's the worst. It was made of stone."

"Don't forget it had handles, perfectly spaced for him to do flairs."

Megan clears her throat. "Sounds hilarious. I'll definitely Google it *later*."

Anthony straightens when she emphasizes the word *later*. I scan the faces of my classmates and confirm what I already suspected: They're utterly bored with my and Anthony's conversation. Okay, then. I'll shut up now.

"Right, everyone," Anthony says, back in serious instructor mode. "Sorry, we got off track there. Today, we're going to start out with one of the easiest fight sequences and a personal favorite of mine, the punch. Everyone stand up and find a partner."

Megan and I look at each other briefly and shake our heads. No, it's not a good idea for us to pair up all the time; that's the fastest way for us to be dismissed as nothing other than "the girls" in the class.

I point at Dexter. "Want me to knock you out?"

He grins, bearing the orthodontist-perfected teeth I'll never get used to. "I thought you'd never ask."

Frick and Frack pair off, leaving Megan and Wills together. Wills has said maybe five words since the first class. I'm starting to wonder if *he's* the serial killer.

Anthony, still standing in front of us, twerkable pecs and all, says, "I'm going to demonstrate the fight sequence using one of you as the person receiving the punch. Brett? Why don't you come up and join me?"

It's not really a question. We all know this. So Brett activates his megawatt smile and jogs to the front, throwing fake punches in the air like Rocky.

"Okay," Anthony says. "There are a couple of key components to throwing a good fake punch. First, the thrower should be aiming to swing across the recipient's face just around eye level. This is important for creating a realistic camera shot. At that angle, viewers will think the fist truly connected with the target. Second, the recipient—for now, that'll be me—should react to the punch by showing impact and recoil. Impact is reflected in your expression, recoil is the physical response to the punch. Brett, which is your dominant hand?"

"My right," he says.

"Okay, put that one out by your hip at a forty-five-degree angle. When you punch, you're going to pull back and throw straight across, aiming to sweep your hand along my eye level. Try it."

Brett throws a fake punch. Anthony's snaps his head back, a dazed expression on his face, and then he snarls, stiffening into a fighting stance. The sequence unfolds in less than two seconds. Enthralled by its authenticity, I yelp at the end. Everyone looks at me.

"What? It looked real, okay?"

Anthony tries to hide his grin, but I see it anyway.

"Again," he tells Brett. "Keep doing the same thing until I tell you to stop."

They run through the sequence a few more times.

"Okay, let's switch roles," Anthony says to Brett, "so you can get a sense of how to react." Addressing everyone, he explains a few finer points. "As the thrower, you want your expression to reflect whatever emotion has prompted you to throw the punch. Are you jealous of this person? Angry? Scared and defending yourself? Feel disrespected? Feel like the person's disrespected others? Get into character and be motivated by it. But don't get so carried away that you lose sight of the camera. If you do this correctly, you'll convince yourself you're actually punching your opponent when all you're doing is pretending to. It's a great stress-reliever."

Brett and Anthony stare each other down and . . . something's not right. There's an undercurrent, a tension between them I hadn't noticed before. I have no clue when it arose, but I suspect Brett's the first volunteer for a very specific reason. What if Anthony slips and decks him? I cover my eyes, not wanting to watch what happens next. Then I spread my fingers because, dammit, I *must* see what happens next.

He and Brett get into fighting stances again. "Watch the progression of movements and call out suggestions for how Brett can improve. We'll keep doing this until you no longer have any advice for him. And take mental notes so you can execute your own sequences later."

Anthony throws a swift punch, grunting to emphasize the force of it. Brett throws his head back, recoiling like Anthony instructed.

"Too early," Megan says.

Anthony throws another punch, the muscles in his arms bunching and flexing as he uses his full range of motion to execute the action.

"Try to time the snap to happen when the fist lands," Dexter says, one hand covering his mouth as he shifts from side to side.

Each time Anthony punches and Brett reacts, we make suggestions for improvement, the latter grunting and rolling his eyes because he's unable to take criticism well.

"Do something with your face, man," Damian offers. "You look lifeless."

"What would you do to protect your body?" I ask.

"Think back to any actual fights you've had. Would you leave yourself open that way?"

Brett is panting between each sequence, and his hair is getting less polished with each snap of his head. Anthony, meanwhile, glares at Brett and throws another punch. He's zoned in on the task, no longer commenting on his or Brett's technique.

Wills finally speaks. "Widen your stance, dude. A punch like that isn't going to allow you to remain steady on your feet. Stumble back a bit. You're going to be surprised by that hit. After the recoil, shake it out, look a little dazed. But get back into your fighting stance quickly. And turn your body a little more toward the spot where his fist connects. The camera will get a better view of your reaction that way."

Everyone stares at Wills, our mouths hanging.

"What?" he asks, looking around at us.

"I didn't think you talked," I say.

Everyone nods, plainly thinking the same thing.

He shrugs. "I only talk when I have something to say."

Anthony straightens and shakes out his fists. "All right, everyone. Try it yourselves. Brett, take a break and get some water. I'll work with Damian for now."

Well, that was something to watch. We disperse to different corners of the room to practice, but my mind is still on Anthony's obvious need to relieve stress of some kind and to specifically use Brett to do it.

When we break for the night, I approach him near the water fountain, seconds after he takes a sip of water and wipes his face with a hand towel.

"Is everything okay?" I ask him. "Earlier, I thought maybe you were getting a little *too* into pretending to beat the crap out of Brett. Did something happen between you two?"

Avoiding my gaze, he waves away the suggestion. "Everything's fine. I'm just frustrated about something, and like I said, simulated fighting is an excellent way to let off some steam."

"I'm sorry. Is there anything I can do to help?"

He drops his chin and shakes his head, a hint of a smile trying to break free. "Eva, you've done enough." Then he blows out a slow breath, as though he is in fact trying to calm himself down. "Do you need a ride home?"

"No, Megan's going to drop me off. We're grabbing something to eat first."

"Great," he says, the cloudiness in his features lifting as he wipes the sweat off his arms.

Relief. That's what I see. He's relieved that he won't be taking me home—and I'm hurt that he feels that way. I thought he enjoyed my company. Thought we were managing our new friendship in a healthy and mature manner. Sure, there have been a few hiccups, such as the unfortunate appearance of the compression shirt he's wearing today, but all in all, I thought our friendship was developing just as we'd planned. Apparently he disagrees.

"You could at least pretend not to be thrilled to get away from me," I say, pinning him with a screw-you glare. "I'll see you next class."

"Eva, wait. I didn't mean—"

"Save it, Mr. Castillo." I turn away and toss a disinterested hand behind me, heading for the door, where Megan's waiting. "We're good."

The man's always muttering under his breath. This time, as he stomps in the opposite direction, I hear him say, "See? I knew this was a bad idea."

Chapter Nineteen

Anthony

WHAT AM I doing here?

So what if I can't sleep. So what if I feel terrible about the way we parted earlier. It's not her job to soothe my butthurt.

I'm sitting here outside her apartment building trying to extinguish this overwhelming need to explain myself, to tell her how I couldn't get her out of my mind when I was filming, to tell her how I acted like an ass in our training session because Brett's comments set me off. What the fuck is she supposed to do with all that information anyway? I don't even know what to do with it myself. I should go. She might not even be back from her dinner with Megan.

The memory of Brett and Damian laughing in the restroom convinces me not to start the truck, though. She should know about Brett's nasty comments, at least. I've seen the way he looks at her. And now I know he'd happily try to get in her bed. Eva's on a different wavelength than he is, though, choosing abstinence in order to get to know someone she could eventually fall in love with. There's no way in hell Brett's that guy. So I pull myself out of the truck and climb the few steps leading to the complex's entrance.

I find her last name in the resident directory and enter her code on the panel.

"Who is it?" she asks, her voice crackling through the intercom.

"Eva, it's Anthony. Can I come up? It'll only take a minute."

There's a brief pause, not long enough to be uncomfortable, thankfully, and then she says, "Okay. I'm in B-202. Walk across the courtyard to the first building on the right and go up one flight of stairs."

"Got it."

I take the stairs by twos and wipe my hands down the front of my pants before ringing the bell. A sign on the door reads, No Negative Energy Allowed. I assume she takes this directive seriously because when she opens the door—in a sports bra and leggings, notably—she's wearing a welcoming smile, no hint that she's still annoyed with me to be found.

"Sorry to disturb you," I say.

"It's not a big deal," she says, stepping back to let me in. "I was about to jump in the shower, but that can wait." She gestures to a textured couch in a color so loud it can only be described as in-your-face blue. Everything else in the space—the overflowing bookshelf, the metal coffee table, the small dining set in the corner—fades into the background. There but not really "there." She's a lot like the couch; wherever she is, she's a lot more interesting than anything or anyone else in the room.

"Sit down and tell me what's going on."

It's hard to concentrate when there's so much skin in my field of vision. Beautiful brown skin with fleshy bits that I could press my face into and smother myself in.

"Anthony?"

"Sorry. I'm just a little out of it today." I take a seat, and she plops down next to me.

"So listen, maybe it's not my place to say anything, but I think of us as friends, and you deserve to know what I overheard."

She and her cleavage—it really is its own beautiful life-form—lean forward. "Oooh, you have tea to spill."

"Not the kind you'd like, though."

She leans back and places a hand on her chest. "Now I'm nervous."

The easiest way to do this is just to rip off that Band-Aid. It'll hurt, but the sooner it's gone, the sooner she can move on from it. "Before today's session, I overheard Brett and Damian talking. I shouldn't have been eavesdropping, but they were in the restroom, and they didn't seem to care that anyone in there could hear what they were talking about."

"Okay . . ."

She's biting her burgundy-painted lip, her white teeth pressing into the fleshy skin and—

"Anthony, wake up."

Focus, pendejo. Focus. "Well, I'm just going to say it. Damian asked Brett what he thought of you, and Brett said he'd tap that ass in a minute. Direct quote."

She shakes her head, seemingly unaffected by what I've just told her. "And?"

"And he said he'd do Megan, too. With you." I throw up my hands. "At the same time."

"Anything else?" she asks.

What? Like that isn't enough? Will I ever understand this woman? Probably not, a voice whispers. "I think that about covers it."

She drops her head to her chest, and not long after, she's shaking—whether in defeat or disgust is unclear. *Coño*, this is bad.

I scoot over and take her hand. "He's an asshole, Eva, but don't let it get you down. Better that you know now."

Finally, she raises her head, and my heart squeezes a little. Her eyes are brimming with tears, and her mouth is curved into . . . a smile?

"What's so funny?" I ask, struggling to understand the humor in the situation.

"Anthony, you just shared that information like you were defending my honor. *Now* I understand why you were so grouchy during combat training. And that's sweet. But there's nothing earth-shattering about what you told me. People can be assholes, and maybe this is a bit egotistical of me, but I assume every hetero or bisexual male wants to tap my ass unless they tell me otherwise. It keeps my skin clear."

I have no idea what to say to that, so all I manage is, "Oh."

But wait. Wouldn't she want to know this? I mean, the guy's been sniffing around her, flashing her those fake-ass smiles, and she's not having sex again until marriage. He'd be a waste of her time if she pursued him. "I just thought you'd want to know. He doesn't sound like the kind of guy who would wait until marriage to . . ."

She snaps her brows together. "To have sex? Why would he have to?"

"Because you're abstaining from sex until marriage. Or did I imagine that conversation at Tori and Carter's place?"

She falls over sideways, roaring with laughter and repeatedly slapping her hand on the cushion.

I hate not understanding the punch line of a joke. "Are you done?"

She sits up and places her folded hands on her lap. "I'm done."

I stand in a daze. "It wasn't my place to say anything. Sorry. I'm going to head out."

She places a hand on my wrist. "Don't go, Anthony. Please sit so I can explain."

I do as she asks, a billion thoughts crashing into each other in my head.

"Confession. I'm not abstaining from sex until marriage. Not on purpose, that is."

"You're not?"

"Noooo. I just said that because I got so annoyed with your 'I never date' stance. I thought I needed a way to . . ."

Her mouth remains open, but words appear to fail her. She swallows hard, her brows knitted in concentration.

I'm trying to turn this over in my brain, but I'm failing to connect the dots. "Needed a way to what?"

"Needed a way to . . . uh . . . to uh . . ." Her eyes widen, and she sits up straight, grimacing. "To stop myself from wanting you, to be perfectly honest. I figured if you thought I wasn't down for sex, you'd lose interest, and I wouldn't be tempted. And then we'd be exactly where we are now. Which is in a good place, right?"

I draw back, tapping a finger against my lips. "You thought I'd lose interest in you if I thought sex was off the table?"

"Exactly," she nods, looking pleased with herself.

"Right. That makes so much sense. You're so fucking extra, you know that?"

"I know." She gives me a wide, cheeky grin. I'm lucky she doesn't have dimples. If she did, I'd be done for. Jesus, now I've got even more information I don't know what to do with in my head. Where the hell we go from here is anyone's guess. One the one hand, I wish I could pretend she didn't come clean about this celibacy bullshit. On the other hand, I wish I could bury my face between her thighs and make her regret she ever lied to me.

And until I can figure this out, she deserves to be as confused as I am. "Well, guess what, genius?"

She sits up straighter, her hands folded in her lap. The playfulness in her eyes is so fucking charming I want to nibble on her neck and tickle her until she laughs *with* me, not *at* me.

"It didn't work."

She frowns. "What didn't work?"

"I'm not sure I should say . . ."

"Say what?" she asks, her eyes narrowing in impatience.

"Permission to speak plainly?"

She smiles, probably remembering that she asked a similar question a while back. "Permission granted."

I lean forward and drop my eyelids to half-mast. "Okay, here's the thing. Your lie didn't make me lose interest in you. In fact, despite my attempts not to, every night, I stroke myself to sleep thinking about our one night together. The way you shattered under me. The way my body trembled over yours. I can't get it out of my head. So if you think we're in a good place, you haven't really been paying attention."

Her mouth falls open and she lets out a soft "Oh."

I wish I had a literal mic right now. If I did, I'd drop it at her feet. But a figurative one will work just as well.

As I stand, I raise my arm perpendicular to the floor and open my closed fist. "Boom."

Then I walk out the door.

Eva

(sings to the tune of "Happy" by Pharrell)
Because I'm crabby
Clap along if you know your annoyance is nothing new
Because I'm crabby
Clap along if you feel like no one else has a clue

I CLEAN WHEN I'm agitated, and I sing when I clean. My neighbors are going to murder me this morning. I'm pulling books from their spaces on the bookshelf and smacking the feather duster across them while belting out my greatest rebooted hits. It's not very effective, but I need to *do* something.

At least I had the good sense not to embark on this cleaning spree last night after Anthony left, although I was tempted to. Boy, was I tempted to. Instead, I spent half the night talking myself out of texting him the universal booty call Bat-Signal: "You up?"

I will *not* be duped by him. Anthony's attitude toward dating and relationships is a nonstarter for me. He claims his painful honesty is a virtue. I think he's just playing games with women's hearts, roping them by dangling what they can never have in front of them. It's one thing to say you're not interested in relationships at this point in your life. It's quite another to say you *never* intend on changing your mind and then wax poetic about not being able to get a woman out of your mind. See? Dangling. I've been blindsided by manipulative men too many times to count. I'm certainly not going to walk right into a situation that's bound to be more of the same.

Too bad I like him too much as a friend to quit him altogether. He's nice, and witty, and hardworking, and funny. So, so funny. And he's a devoted son. Has this great rapport with his father that makes me happy just watching them together. Plus, he's a feast not only for my eyes, but also for other parts of my body. And oh God, hearing him say he regularly strokes himself to sleep thinking of us together just about made me want to dissolve into a shameless puddle of want. Fact is, if I could surgically remove the part of his brain that cooked up his foolish edict on sex, love, and dating, he'd be damn near perfect.

I'm dusting the chandelier above my ridiculously small dining table when it hits me, my heart beginning to thump wildly in my chest to match the base pounding through my Bluetooth speakers.

Oh shit.

No, no, no, no.

How did this happen?

I don't like Anthony as a friend. I'm interested in

him romantically. What that means exactly is beyond my mental capacity to determine at the moment, but regardless, this is all kinds of fucked up for one fundamental reason: Although Anthony probably wouldn't mind if I got up close and personal with his dick, he doesn't want me anywhere near his heart.

I can't deal. Not now. So I set aside my inconvenient feelings and lose myself in the music, singing and dancing around my apartment and using my feather duster as my microphone. When Missy Elliott's "WTF (Where They From)" blasts through the speakers, I pretend I'm one of Missy's backup dancers. And when Pharrell's rap solo begins, I slide across the room—and trip over the coffee table.

A sharp pain travels from my tibia to my knee, and as I awkwardly try to right myself, I twist my left ankle. Wincing from the intense ache that throbs in triple time each time I take a step, I stumble to the couch and collapse onto it in a pathetic heap.

My stomach knots as I inspect my swollen ankle and pray it's not broken or sprained. Dammit, can a sports injury get any more humiliating than this? Does this even qualify as a sports injury? No, this could only be described as a your-stupid-ass-shouldn't-have-tried-it injury. Which is also known as a no-one-will-ever-know-about-this injury.

Le big fucking sigh.

Chapter Twenty

Anthony

I'M SITTING IN EST's office thinking of the sign on Eva's apartment door: No Negative Energy Allowed. That sign's an excellent reminder that I can't control the people around me, but I *can* manage my own reaction to them. People like the irate applicant currently berating me over the phone because he didn't get into the next training session. He's trying my patience, but I'm not going to let him mess with my positive energy.

"I refuse to believe I'm not a good candidate," he says, his voice low and angry. "What am I lacking?"

"Discipline."

"What the hell?" he says. "How can you tell that from my application?"

"You described speed racing on LA's streets as a skill, Mario. Running a red light and avoiding a collision isn't part of a stunt person's regular bag of tricks. You're reckless. That's the *worst* type of person for this kind of training."

"Man, you don't know what you're talking about. This is bullshit."

I sigh, irritated with myself for even indulging this guy after he called me "shit-for-brains." What an asshole. "Look, you're entitled to your opinion, but here's what I *do* know. The stuff you described in your application? It's illegal. Period. So why don't we call it a day and part ways now?"

He yells "fuck you" into the phone and hangs up.

Good riddance, Mario.

I'm in the middle of responding to an email when the phone rings yet again. Maybe I'll get through my inbox someday, but today's not that day. "Elite Stunt Training, how may I help you?"

"Anthony?"

I recognize her voice immediately and sit up straighter. It's been four days of radio silence between us, mostly because I wanted to give her the space to deal with our last conversation in whatever way she saw fit. Apparently, she's choosing not to deal with it at all. "Hey, Eva, everything okay?"

"Yeah, everything's fine. I think I'm coming down with something, though. A cold, maybe?" She coughs to emphasize her point. "So I was just calling to let you know that I'm using my one excused absence. I'll be ready to go again for next Wednesday's class."

A muscle in my jaw twitches as I listen to her flimsy justification for not attending the training session. It makes no sense. A cold? "Eva, this is the third class of the program. We're finishing up air ram work. It's a little early to be taking an excused absence."

"I . . . I thought we could take an excused absence at any point in the program? Kurt never mentioned that we needed to have a certain number of classes under our belt before we could make use of it."

She has a point, and yet I'm still irritated.

"No, no, you're right," I tell her. "But what if something else comes up in the next four weeks? It would make more sense to save your excused absence for a time when you're really sick or something, not just when you have a minor cold or can't be bothered."

She pounces as soon as the words are out of my mouth. "Can't be bothered? Whoa, whoa, whoa. Who said anything about not wanting to be bothered with coming to class?"

This is escalating in a way I never intended, all because I'm in my feelings about her not showing up for one class. It's up to me to deescalate the situation. "You're right. You didn't. I'll make a note that this is your one excused absence. I'll see you next class, okay? Take care."

"Fine . . . bye."

As I sit there going over our conversation in my head, I realize in this instance I'm the negative energy. Biting her head off like that served no good purpose. Shame spirals through me as I clench and unclench my fists, the memory of Eva's confusion intensifying my surly mood. After class, I'll go for a run. That always helps me decompress. Why it's necessary is a question I don't want to answer.

THE FIRST THING I see when I reenter the warehouse after my run is Eva flying like a superhero and landing on the large mat in the center of the room.

Nothing about this woman will ever surprise me.

The door clicks shut behind me, and she scrambles up and hops off the mat. Chest heaving, she closes her eyes and tries to catch her breath. The overheads shine a spotlight on the sheen of sweat on her well-defined arms. When she opens her lids again, her gaze is fierce, determination apparent from the set of her shoulders and the wideness of her stance. She's a warrior goddess in vintage Adidas, and I pray she doesn't use them to kick my ass.

"What are you doing in here?" I ask. "Class is over."

"I'm practicing air ram maneuvers," she says curtly, her eyes narrowed on me in defiance. "*Someone* thinks I'm not taking this course seriously, so I'm trying to apply myself. Is that a problem?"

Oh, *she's* the one bringing the bad energy now. And as much as I'd like to diffuse the situation, I'd be a poor instructor if I didn't point out what's obvious to me. "Eva, you signed a waiver acknowledging the risks associated with stunt training and agreeing not to perform any skills without appropriate supervision. You shouldn't be doing this alone, so yes, it's a problem."

The look she gives me could extinguish a forest fire. I'm fucking frozen on the inside. Wouldn't be at all surprised if my veins had turned into icicles.

"Fine. I was finished anyway, *Mr. Castillo.*"

She says my name like she's relishing the opportunity to be naughty, like I'm her superior but she's looking forward to defying my orders. The way my body reacts to the taunt, you'd think she just whispered dirty words in my ear. I wasn't exaggerating when I told her I couldn't stop thinking about her. Every night before bed, I think about what she looks like when she's aroused, the noises she makes when she comes, what she tastes like. It's my new nighttime routine: shower, brush my teeth, think about Eva, lights out. Now that she's in front of me, her body pulsing with tension and her eyes simmering with annoyance, I want to break the dam that's been building between us.

"Do you need a ride home?" I ask.

"No," she says, her gaze distant and cold.

I shake my head at her, wishing I could revisit our telephone conversation earlier and self-edit like she's suggested. "Eva, c'mon. Let me drive you."

She swipes her hoodie off the floor and heads for the door. "I'll see you next class. I'm taking the bus."

"Eva. Wait."

She stops midstride, but she doesn't turn around.

I hurt her. I can see that plain as day. In the tension in her shoulders. In the dejected way she hangs her head, as though she wants to battle it out with me but is too

exhausted to do anything other than listen. I need to give
her an apology worthy of her time. "I'm sorry I was so
hard on you earlier. I should have been more understanding. I know you've got a lot going on, and I shouldn't have
assumed that you were missing the class for a superficial
reason. I was way out of line and I apologize."

She spins around, her eyes searching mine. "You
were so dismissive. Why?"

I try to weasel out of the truth, not ready to acknowledge it myself, let alone share it with her. "I was just
tired and irritated. It wasn't you specifically."

She narrows her eyes at me, probably because she has
the supernatural power to detect my bullshit from miles
away. We're standing a few feet apart, so this probably
isn't all that challenging to her.

"Try again," she says. "I deserve better."

I blow out a harsh breath. She's right. She does deserve better. But now comes the hard part: Explaining
my reaction even though it exposes me as a self-absorbed
ass. "Okay, here it is. I'd been looking forward to seeing
you, okay? Had a few minor squabbles about equipment
deliveries this morning. A rejected applicant tried to tear
me a new butthole. But I didn't let any of that get to me.
Why? Because I kept thinking about seeing you this afternoon. Then you called to say you wouldn't be coming
to class. There's no other way to describe it. I was disappointed."

I take a few steps toward her, and she takes a corre-
sponding number of steps back, her gaze cloudy.

"You were disappointed in me?" she asks, her head tilted to the side.

The sadness in her voice is like a thousand paper cuts to my chest. I shake my head, hating that she's asking the correct follow-up questions, the ones that leave no place to hide. "No, I was disappointed that I wouldn't be seeing you."

Dios. This is why I don't date. *This* is why I run from relationships. Start fucking around with feelings and someone's bound to get hurt. Emotions aren't static. They ebb and flow for each person. Maybe the person likes me, but not as much as I like them. Maybe I care for them, but caring isn't enough, and they want more. Or maybe the person fools you into falling in love with them, only to snatch that love away because they never fell in love themselves. Like I told Eva before, relationships are messy. My instinct is to take no part in them.

She nods as though she's satisfied with my explanation. "Your disappointment. It scared you, didn't it?"

I stare at my feet when I answer. "Yeah. And I took my frustration out on you. I won't do it again."

She peers at me for several seconds, her expression neutral. "Good." She continues to stare at me, leaving no question that I'm being assessed in some way, although I don't know the parameters of the evaluation. "You know, Anthony. I'm not asking you to change in any way. If you want to remain friends, that's what we'll be. I just want you to be honest with me. So that if there's something to figure out, we can figure it out together. Okay?"

I nod, stunned by this woman's patience. "I like you, Eva. A lot. As a person. As a friend. And I'm attracted to you. My goal here is to not play games. But those are my truths. Anything else would be a lie."

She nods as though she's impressed with my frankness. "Thanks for your candor. I'm still taking the bus, though."

I watch her pivot and stride toward the exit again. This time, though, I notice a limp in her step. "Eva, what's wrong with your leg?"

She waves me away without turning around. "It's nothing. I twisted my ankle. Went to Urgent Care. They took an X-ray and said the same thing."

"Can I see it?"

"No," she says, enunciating that one word with enough authority that it sounds ten syllables long.

"Eva, must you be stubborn about everything?"

I'm almost certain I know how she'll answer this question.

"Yes, I must."

Called it—in my head. I wish I could say I'm disappointed that she's predictable, but honestly, nothing about Eva disappoints me. That's the scariest part about all this. "Will you please let me make sure you're okay?"

She spins around, rolls her eyes, and stomps across the floor, gritting her teeth in discomfort as a testament to her bullheadedness. With a dramatic huff, she stops directly in front of me and pulls up the left leg of her track pants. "See, it's an ankle. A twisted one. I'm fine."

Hell, above her twisted ankle is an orange-sized bruise, a splash of blue and purple that looks like the start of a watercolor painting. "Eva, this isn't itty bitty, but yes, it'll heal on its own. You need compression on that ankle, though, and a couple of painkillers."

"All that's not necessary."

"It is if you want to heal in time for the next class."

Sighing, she pinches the bridge of her nose. "Fine. Take me to your leader."

The office is only twenty feet away. Halfway there, I realize my error. There's not much square footage to it. Eva and I won't function well in a small room like that. It's the same reason I was on edge the few times I've driven her home. The cab of the truck forces us into a space that isn't big enough to let my attraction to her bounce around comfortably. It's confining. Suffocating.

I spin around and put my hand up. "You know what? You shouldn't be walking any more than you need to. Why don't you take a seat over there. I'll bring it to you."

Her eyebrows shoot up. "The office is less than ten feet away. Don't be absurd."

This time, I'm trailing behind her, plodding toward certain doom. I flick the light switch on and search for a bandage, while Eva eases onto my desk and watches me.

Bandage located and in hand, I raise my arm in the air. "Found one." I stand in front of her and reach for her leg. "Let's get this sneaker off you for now. I'll loosen the laces so you can put it back on when I'm done."

"Fair warning. My feet probably stink."

"Probably."

She nudges my thigh with her foot, the hint of a smile fighting to emerge. "You're such a pain."

I remove her sock, revealing her toes. Like the rest of her, they're pretty. "Blue polish suits you."

"It's my favorite," she says with a small smile.

"Put your foot here so I can bandage it."

She slowly lowers her heel onto my thigh, and I meet her unwavering gaze. I know when her foot lands on my thigh only by touch, because our eyes haven't strayed from each other. If we string enough of these small moments together, we might generate enough sexual tension to supply power to a strip club.

When I begin the process of wrapping her foot, however, I'm efficient and focused, my hands turning over in small circles as I wrap the bandage from the top of her foot to above her ankle.

"Your bedside manner leaves a lot to be desired, Dr. Castillo."

"And why's that, Ms. Montgomery?"

I don't hazard a glance at her, choosing instead to remain hunched over, my gaze trained on the task. It doesn't take much for Eva to distract me.

"You're very clinical, I'd say. Detached. As though you want to be done with this as soon as possible."

Damn fucking right. That's *exactly* what I want. "Just trying to do my job, ma'am."

"Get in and get out, huh?"

My head snaps up to her face. She winks at me

and gives me a wicked smile. Nope, not responding to that one.

"I get it," she continues. "Sometimes a quickie really is the best way to go."

It seems Eva has an inner *maldita*, too. "One more comment like that and I'm sending you to the naughty corner."

She sticks her tongue out at me. "Oh, all right. You're no fun. And you're making a big fuss over something that would have healed on its own."

"That may be, but this will help it heal faster."

"It was already healing," she huffs.

"All right, you're all done," I say as soon as the last butterfly clip is in place.

She flutters her eyelashes at me and claps her hands in front of her chest. "You're my hero."

Standing to my full height, I give her a thumbs-up and a wink. "Glad to be of service, ma'am. And tell me this, how'd you twist it anyway? At work? In training?"

She mumbles a couple of words under her breath as she stands.

"What did you say?"

"At home," she says with a lift of her chin. "If you must know, I was cleaning my apartment the other day and tried to reenact Tom Cruise's slide across the floor in *Risky Business*."

I cover my mouth with my fist. She'll probably kick me in the face if I laugh at her. "Were you in a shirt and underwear, too?"

"Of course. That's what gave me the idea. Socks, too. But they had grippers on the bottom, so I couldn't achieve a smooth slide. Hence, the twisted ankle when I tripped over the coffee table."

"Did you use a candle holder as a microphone?"

She smiles. "Feather duster."

"This story gets better the more you talk. Keep going."

She pushes me away, her eyes glistening all of a sudden. "It's not funny, actually."

Her voice breaks on the word *funny* and my gaze flashes to hers. One of the most dynamic women I've ever met is crumbling before me, and I have no idea why. Instinctively, I pull her into my arms, wanting to comfort her as best I can. When I cup her cheeks, sweeping my thumbs under her eyes to dry them, she leans into my touch, all soft and vulnerable.

"Hey, hey, baby," I say. "Talk to me. Why the tears?"

Eva

I LOOK UP at Anthony, not caring that I'm a blubbering mess. The warmth of his body is a balm that calms me like a magic cure for a colicky baby. Closing my eyes, I press my cheek against his chest and slow my breathing to match his. "I didn't come to class today because . . . because I didn't think my ankle could . . . handle the impact. And I canceled my Friday class at the studio be-cause . . . I knew I wouldn't be able to handle that, either.

And all I kept thinking about, worrying about, was the possibility that my father's right. An injury sidelined me and I couldn't do my job, couldn't train." I lift my head and blink up at him, my stupid lower lip quivering. "What the hell am I doing, Anthony?"

He inches forward, pulling me deeper into his embrace, tightening his arms around me like a cocoon. "Ah Eva, don't do this to yourself. You're being human, and that means you're going to trip and fall from time to time. We all do. Don't give it more meaning than you need to. You're stressed. And you're in mild pain. You've got a lot going on. I doubt this is the best time for introspection."

With not a hint of self-consciousness, I press my face into his chest, breathing him in, listening to the hollow thump of his heartbeat. "Yeah, I'm sure you're right."

I can count the number of people who have seen me cry on one hand. They include my parents; my second grade teacher, Mrs. Potts, who refused to let me leave the classroom to pee when I had to go badly (I ruined her shoes that day); Tori (but only during gut-wrenching dramas like *The Color Purple* or epic love stories, never in sadness); and now this man.

Anthony, who just called me baby and probably doesn't even realize it. Anthony, who'd likely swear up and down that the endearment was nothing more than a slip of the tongue.

"You know what you need?" he says, pulling me out of my musings.

"What's that?"

He takes my hand. "To get out of your head and enjoy the evening. Forget about everything and appreciate what this town has to offer. I could take you to the Chinese Theatre or the Walk of Fame. You know, the touristy stuff. We could just drive past them if you're not up for walking. Whatever you want to do." He shrugs, pulling at the collar of his hoodie as he waits for me to respond to the idea. "We could grab dinner after. Not a . . ." Grimacing, he swallows hard.

I draw back and pinch the skin under my bottom lip as I consider him. Oh, this is fascinating. "You can't say it, can you?"

He frowns at me. "Can't say what?"

"The *D* word."

"*Dick?* I say it all the time. Dick. Dick. Dick. Dick."

I reach over and poke him in the stomach. "Enough. You're such a goofball. I meant the other *D* word."

He scrubs a hand over his face like he's transforming his expression into a serious one with just a swipe. "Eva, will you hang out with me tonight? Not a *date* or anything."

"I'd love to go on a non-date with you," I tell him with a smile. Then I inspect his face. "And no apparent allergic reaction from saying the word *date*, either. You're making progress."

He waggles his eyebrows at me. "I aim to please."

"If that's the case, then take me to one of your favorite spots. Doesn't have to be touristy."

He answers immediately. "I know the perfect spot, then. I think you'll love it."

"I'm sure I will."

So this is adulting, huh? We talked openly and honestly about our feelings and concerns, and we're still enjoying each other's company. I could get used to this new normal.

Chapter Twenty-One

Anthony

"ARE YOU SURE I'm not underdressed? I don't know where we're going, so I was at a disadvantage when I changed."

I keep my eyes on the road and suppress a smile. "Eva, what you're wearing is perfect. I said casual. Look at me, I'm wearing jeans."

She shakes her head and shoves a hand in her purse. "That's not saying much. Most guys think every occasion either calls for T-shirts and jeans or a tuxedo. They have no concept of anything in between."

Out of the corner of my eye, I catch her peering at me. "You don't like surprises. Is that it?"

She pulls out a tube of lipstick, lowers the visor to access the vanity mirror, and applies her makeup as she speaks. A woman's never done that in my car. When she puckers and pops her lips, I shift in the driver's seat, trying to convince my brain that putting on lipstick isn't foreplay. Then she licks her lips. Oh, yes, the fuck it is.

"It's not that I don't like surprises," she says. "I just

like hints, too. Thinking about the clues helps me pass the time. Makes me less nervous about it."

"So you want a clue."

"Yes, that would be nice."

"Black latex."

She tugs on the sleeve of my sweater, a touch of indignation in her voice. "Oh my God, are you taking me to a sex club?"

"No, I'm not."

"Confession. I'm disappointed."

"I'll bear that in mind for future dates." Dates. *Future* dates. How the hell did I let that slip out? Oh, I know. Eva crashed into my life and upended it in the best way. I'm not that guy. Haven't been that guy in a long time. But I'm finding it hard not to be that guy with her. "You know what I mean. I'll keep it in mind when we hang out next time."

"Oh, yes, Anthony, I know what you mean."

The surprise location isn't far from where I live. I make a left turn onto Fletcher Drive and half a mile later another left onto San Fernando Road.

"You're taking me to a park? At night?"

Her voice doesn't betray anything other than curiosity.

"I am."

The road is hugged on both sides by a canopy of trees that add to the mystery. I couldn't have planned a better route to our destination. The car hits a patch of gravel, and then we enter a clearing.

"A drive-in movie?" she asks.

Her voice is high, a note of laughter in her question.

"Yeah, is that cool with you?"

"More than cool. I *love* this surprise."

She's grinning from ear-to-ear and taking in the sight of the rows and rows of cars already parked on the grounds. The people who aren't watching from their cars are sitting in their own chairs and on blankets on the lawn in front of the large projector screen, which for now, only shows a digital clock counting down to the start of the movie. Eleven minutes to go.

The attendant waves us into a space, but it's front and center, and that's not where I'd like to be. Too far from the restrooms.

I lower the driver's side window. "Hey, we're probably going to head out before the movie ends. Where's the best place to put us?"

The attendant looks around and points his traffic baton at a space in the last row. "There should be good. When you're ready to leave, just make a left here and get on the exit road."

I park the truck and turn off the engine. The bag between us holds a bottle of wine for her, a few bottles of water for us both, mini-sandwiches courtesy of the deli across the street from EST, and a few fleece blankets. "Ready to jump in the back?"

"My ass will be raw by the time the movie's over."

I laugh. "I've got a cushion and plenty of blankets. Your ass will be fine."

She eases out of the car and smoothes her bottoms,

a heather-gray skirt that ends above her ankles and resembles sweat pants without legs. A sweatskirt is how she described it when she first got in the car. The way her ass and hips look in it, I'd say the name is accurate; I'm sweating just thinking about the loveliness underneath.

The ankle wrap reminds me that she shouldn't be hopping around, though. "Need help getting up there?"

She shakes her head in exasperation. "I'm fine, Anthony. I can handle the climb. I'll be careful. Promise." Sure enough, she sits on the truck bed and scoots backward, slowly shifting around to get into her desired position. "So what's the feature film?"

I place the bag inside and climb in behind her. "*The Matrix*."

"That's what you meant by black spandex. Trinity's outfit."

"Right. Kind of hard to forget it."

"I saw the second film first."

My mouth drops open. "You watched them out of order?" I place my hands over my chest in a fake display of outrage. "How could you?"

She laughs at my reaction. "I was ten when the first one came out. I knew it was out there, but my parents wouldn't let me see it. Had to wait until four years later. Watched it during a sleepover at a friend's. Now I understand that it was groundbreaking, but back then I just wanted to be a badass like Trinity or Niobe."

"It *was* groundbreaking. I can see its influence on the movies I've worked on, too."

"Can you watch without analyzing the action sequences?"

"Nope. That's mostly what I do. Figure out what's special effects, what's stunt. It's a totally different movie experience. Now that I'm a stunt performer, I can't go back to be being blissfully unaware of what's happening behind the scenes. It'll happen to you, too."

I pull out our goodies, watching her face to see if she's okay with her options. She sits back as I unwrap the sandwiches. For a second, she grimaces.

Groaning, I pause and consider the obvious. "Don't tell me. You're not a fan of sandwiches, right? I ordered tuna, ham, corned beef, and roasted veggie, but I didn't think about getting something without bread. Sorry, I should have—"

"No, no," she says, gently placing her hand on my arm. "It's not the food. And I don't mean to be high maintenance"—she points to the back of the bed—"but this isn't the most comfortable way to sit."

I slide the platter of sandwiches within arm's reach and crawl over to her. "That's a problem I can solve if you want." I lean on the back of the bed and pat my chest. "Use me as a pillow."

Her gaze drops to my chest, and her lips part.

Fuck. I'm doing it again, aren't I? Making it awkward between us. "Hey, but we can prop up some of the extra blankets, too. Here." I refold the blankets and hand them to her. "See?"

She looks at the stack. "No, it's okay. I'm going to need those to keep warm. It's chillier than I expected out here. Just don't think about getting frisky, okay? Unlike the women in your class, I do know how to split a man's balls in half."

I shake my head at her. "Woman, if you want my chest, take it. But don't threaten me with bodily harm for offering you some comfort."

She throws a blanket at me and turns around, grabbing a roasted veggie sandwich. I spread my legs to give her space to recline, and then she falls back against me. Humming softly, she holds the sandwich in the air while she uses the other hand to spread the blanket over us. It's cozy. *Too* cozy. And the smell of sugar cookies fills my nose.

"What's the stuff that smells delicious? Is that in your hair?"

"It's my deep conditioning treatment. Why? Is it bothering you?"

I take a deep breath and realize my error as soon as her head moves with my chest. The scent is intoxicating. "No, it smells good."

She enjoys her food as I try to remain unaffected by the way her body's draped against mine.

"Thanks for getting the food, Anthony. This really is perfect."

"I'm glad you like it. You're not too cold, though?"

She shakes her head. "It's great under here. No complaints at all. Oooh, the previews are starting."

For some unknown reason, I'm ridiculously happy that she's content. Maybe it's because I know she's experiencing big changes in her life and she's worried about whether it's going to work out. Maybe it's because she's a vibrant woman who makes me laugh and I want to give her back a little of the happiness she's given me. Whatever it is, I'm glad I could give her this evening.

Eva

ANTHONY'S CHEST IS the best pillow I've ever had the pleasure to rest my head on. It'll be a miracle if I'm able to stay awake for the movie. Every breath he takes calms me. It's like I'm out on a lake and the water is lapping gently against my kayak.

"The sandwich is delicious, by the way." I lift the remaining half behind me and toward him. "Want a bite?"

He dips his face down and sinks his teeth into it. Is this too intimate? Yeah, this is too intimate. But then why does it feel so right? Trying not to overthink as usual, I focus on finishing the sandwich during the theater's rundown of its upcoming season. "*Shrek* in September. We should come back to see that."

"Not something on my watch list, but for you, sure."

For you, sure. Now that Anthony's clarified his feelings, I don't need to guess what he means. He cares about me, yes, but that doesn't mean he's going to change for me, either. I don't have time to wallow in my conflicted feelings, though, because the film's starting, and the first scene has a killer action sequence. Pun intended.

He leans in close, speaking near my ear. "See there? When she looks like she's running across the wall. That's a wire-harness."

I try my best to appear unaffected by the warmth of his breath against my skin. "Right." I clear my throat. "But she does a flip, too, so there's some work beyond the harness."

"Yeah. And it looks like she did that herself."

"That ambitious wench needs to step aside and give someone else a job."

He chuckles against my ear. "This movie employed plenty of people in the stunt industry. No need to be outraged on our behalf." He points at the screen. "See there. That jump across the roof?"

"Wire-harness again, right?"

"In a warehouse somewhere with a green screen. She's landing on a big stunt pad."

I turn my head to the side and look up at him. For a moment, it's as though we're both frozen in place.

"What's wrong?" he asks.

"Nothing's wrong exactly. I'm just wondering if you're going to ruin the entire movie for me this way."

He pinches my hip, causing me to yelp. Someone in the car to our right whispers for us to be quiet. I turn into Anthony, burying my face in his chest to stem the laughter that's bubbling up inside me.

"Sorry," he whispers, moving his hand off my hip. "I shouldn't have pinched you."

"It's okay," I whisper in reply.

And then, because once again, it just feels right, I reach for his hand and return it to my hip. His heart is beating so hard and fast I can feel it at the base of my neck. My heart is beating so hard and fast I'm afraid I might pass out. But it's okay. I don't think I'm alone in this. I *want* him to move his hand against my hip. If I had kinetic abilities, I'd try to will him to do it. He won't, though. Because that's not Anthony's way, and I'm glad for that.

So I thread my fingers with his, and now we're both resting our hands on my left hip. Slowly, so very slowly that I'm worried it'll take forever, I move my hand and his along with it. In circles. Slow, torturous circles.

"Eva," he whispers in a low groan. "Friends shouldn't do this."

My mind agrees, but my body wants the relief it knows he can give me. I feel compressed on all sides, enfolded in his warmth and consumed by the need to release the tension building in me. "I know. I do. But I don't care."

He takes a fortifying breath, but he doesn't speak or move. My chest collapses when I realize he's not willing to go further, but then a few seconds later, his other hand lands against my right hip and I gasp in relief.

"Is this okay?" he asks, his voice whisper soft.

My mouth's dry now, so I nod.

"Use your words, Eva."

I smile at that directive. "It's okay. It's better than

okay. So okay that I wish you would do okay things to me all night."

His chest vibrates under me. How can he laugh at a moment like this?

"When you say 'okay things,' what exactly do you mean?"

"I'd like you to touch me. Everywhere. Anywhere. Just . . . I don't know."

"Would you like me to raise your skirt and slip my fingers inside your panties? Is that what you mean?"

I raise my hand to my mouth, needing to stem the moans that are desperate to escape it. "Yes, that's exactly what I mean."

He leans down and nips at my ear. "Keep watching the movie, and don't make a sound. I'll see what I can do for you."

On the screen, Neo's on a ship. There's talking. *So* much talking. But none of it makes any sense. And the pounding in my ears isn't helping to clarify it.

Behind me, under the cover of three blankets, Anthony's hands are raising my skirt inch by delicious inch, his fingers leaving a blaze of heat across my skin as they travel up my thighs. My ass refuses to stay put. I'm squirming in an embarrassing display of ultra-heightened arousal.

"How does this feel so far?" he asks.

"Really nice, but I wish you'd hurry up a bit."

He pulls my skirt up to my waist before I take my next breath. "Spread your legs for me, Eva."

I point my toes, stretching them like a world-class ballerina, the swelling in my ankle long forgotten, and then I slide my legs open so my outer thighs are pressed against his inner thighs.

"I wish I could see you, but for now feeling you is going to have to be enough," he says. The palm of his right hand slides from my hip to the crotch of my panties. He traces a single finger up my slit, pressing the fabric inside me. "Oh fuck. You're already wet."

I don't recognize his voice. It's low and ragged, as though he's struggling to make any sound at all. I'm not even going to try to recall enough of the English language to form a coherent sentence. Heavy breathing and whimpers will need to suffice. And to make matters worse—no, better, this makes it better—his erection is straining against his pants and announcing its presence along my lower back.

"Can I come in?" he asks.

The answer is a resounding yes. In fact, it's so much a yes that I'm teary with the anticipation of it. "Please. Touch me."

He doesn't waste any more time and dips inside my panties with a deft hand, the back of it brushing against my mound. "Almost bare. Just like I remembered. Feels nice. Plump."

"Anthony, please."

He slips a finger inside, and I nearly combust from the heat spreading through me.

"More?" he asks.

My hands are grasping at his jeans, as though my neediness will spur him to do more. But he's made clear he needs to hear the words, so I manage to say what needs to be said. "Yes, more."

He adds a second digit. "I could do this all night. Just touch you. Am I making you feel good?"

"You are. Yes. But I need you to move your fingers a bit."

"Over your clit?"

"Yes."

He slides his body down a bit, raising his knees for leverage and placing his lips against my temple. "Tell me when it feels perfect." Then he makes a light pass over my clit, barely touching it, and I'm so desperate for his touch that I chase it.

"Your clit is firm," he says. "Feels nice against my fingers."

I moan in frustration, wanting more than the fleeting sensation of his digits dancing over my achy nerve endings. "Abstinence makes the clit grow harder, you know."

His chest vibrates under me. "Stop that. You're breaking my concentration."

He dances over it again.

"Not perfect," I tell him. "That's cruel."

He puts his free arm over my chest and cages me in. "I'm sorry. I'll do better, I promise." Then he does just that, circling my pussy to draw its juices up over my folds. And with exquisite care, he centers two fingers on my clit and rubs it at a torturously slow pace.

"Oh, that's perfect, Anthony. Keep doing that." I glance up at the movie, registering the green code raining down on the screen. Then I squeeze my eyes shut because I can't possibly focus on anything else but the intense throbbing between my legs.

"God, I want you to come so hard. I want that so badly for you. And tonight, when I'm back at home and in my bed, I'll stroke myself to the memory of your sweet pussy swallowing my fingers and making them slippery."

His words trip something inside me, like a circuit reaching its limit and overloading. "Please do it faster. Anthony, I'm so close . . . I'm almost there." His fingers are rubbing fast and tight now. Tiny circles directly on my nub. And then his free hand travels back across my chest and into my hair at the nape of my neck. He massages my scalp. And he isn't gentle.

"Yes, keep doing that," I urge. "Yes, more of that."

"Shhh," he whispers against my ear. "You're getting louder."

I blink my eyes open. Someone could see us, I suppose, but I'm so close to the peak I don't care. I shut my eyes because I don't want to know if someone's watching. I don't want anything to stop me from reaching the orgasm that's been simmering for what feels like hours.

"Would it help if you imagine my cock inside you?" he says with a low growl.

That does it. He circles two more times and I fly the fuck apart, clutching his thigh as I shudder in a state of complete and wanton bliss. I pull on his sweater, hiding my face in it as the orgasm rocks me, and I don't let go as I regain my bearings. If anything, I tighten my hold on it, likely ruining its natural shape. Oh. My. God. That was frustrating, and naughty, and everything I needed it to be.

Beneath the blanket, Anthony removes his hand from my panties and strokes my thigh. "You okay?"

I nod, although my head wobbles from the effort. "I'm so much better than okay." I lift my chin to study him. His eyes are glossy, his lips are red—as if he bit into them as he touched me—and his face is flushed. He looks so fucking primed to tear me apart that I wish we weren't in public. "Are *you* okay?"

He smiles. "I'm so much better than okay, too."

With that, I think a piece of my heart jumped out of my chest and latched onto his. That wasn't supposed to happen, but it's true, nonetheless. *Nice going, Eva. If leaving yourself open to heartbreak were a class, you'd get an A+.*

Chapter Twenty-Two

Anthony

"IT HAPPENED. DON'T *freak out on me, okay? We don't have to make a big deal about it. Thanks for a great night. See you Wednesday.*"

Eva's parting words have been running on a continuous loop in my mind since our non-date on Sunday. Unfortunately, that loop's been interspersed with images and memories of that evening: the way she gripped my thigh as I touched her; the way her moans rose with each stroke; the way she buried her face in my chest as the orgasm slammed into her. I'm supposed to forget how she fell apart in my arms? *Chacho*, what a fucking joke.

I look down at the invoices in front of me. Have I reviewed any of them yet? I have no clue. I'm tempted to pick up the entire stack and throw it in the trash.

Kurt breezes into the office, his face ruddy and cheerful. "How's it going, young man."

Shit. Kurt got some this morning. The fucking whistling is a big tell. "Must you make it so obvious you had good sex recently?"

He looks at me dreamily as he settles into his chair. "Is it obvious? How do you know?"

"Because you look like you're blowing bubbles as you walk through a field of flowers, that's how."

He frowns at me. "And that upsets you, why? Not getting any lately?"

I drop my head onto the desk. "You don't have to rub my face in your active sex life, okay?"

His chair squeaks as he rises from it. Oh, damn. God save me if he's feeling fatherly. Sure enough, he rounds my desk and puts a hand on my shoulder. "Chin up, kid. What's got you so down? And what can't be corrected with one of the random hookups you used to enjoy so much?"

He'd be shocked to know I haven't had one of those in months—since my night with Eva after Tori's wedding. Although even I must admit that encounter doesn't count as a random hookup anymore. I throw off his hand and sit up. "You make a good point, actually. I'm in a weird mood, but it isn't anything I can't resolve with the right attitude."

"There's the Anthony I know and love." He lumbers back to his chair. "So, you ready for today?"

I give him a confident nod. "Ready."

"More importantly, do you think the trainees are ready?"

It's our job to make sure they are. "I think so. We'll start off easy and work our way up. If I get a whiff of any fear that might interfere with anyone's ability to perform a high fall, I'll take them out of the practice rotation."

He clasps his hands in front of him, his elbows resting on the desk. "I knew you'd have everything under control. Plus, I'll be there for backup, along with the rest of the crew. It's not all on you."

"I know. I just don't want anyone to get hurt on my watch."

"Someone could," he warns.

"No one has so far, and I'd like to keep it that way."

He studies me in silence for more seconds than I'm comfortable with. Kurt's never been a contemplative guy, so this is uncharacteristic of him.

"What?" I ask.

He shakes his head to clear it. "I'm just noticing how you've come into your own recently. Not sure exactly when it happened, but you're talking like someone with a serious stake in this business. I'm proud of you."

All that's missing from this heartwarming moment is for Kurt to slap me on the back and hand me a cup of cocoa. Mistletoe above us would be good, too. Still, I'm gratified that he's finally seeing me as a potential partner. It means I'm moving in the right direction in his eyes. "Thanks, Kurt." I hold both of my hands over my heart. "I'm touched."

He waves me away. "Get the fuck out of here with that bullshit."

The warehouse door slams, and then excited voices fill the air. The trainees are beginning to arrive. After straightening the stack of invoices—as well as a dozen other items on my desk—I slowly rise from my chair.

One thing's for sure, I'll be taking my cues from Eva today. As hard as it would be to pretend nothing happened, if that's what she wants, that's how it'll be. She knows where I stand; what she does with that information is her choice.

I cross the room and study the trainees through the office window. When Eva walks in, I draw in a fortifying breath, mentally preparing myself for the challenge of forgetting for the next few hours that she's someone more to me than just another participant in this boot camp. She surveys the room and everyone in it, and then she glances at me through the window. Her smile builds the longer we stare at each other, until she gives me a tentative wave. She doesn't wait for me to return the greeting, though. Instead, she power walks past her classmates and settles onto a mat to perform her stretches.

Just three days ago, her legs were trembling as I stroked her. Just three days ago, I would have risked life and limb to be inside her if she'd said she wanted that, too. Still, Eva's a level-headed woman, and apparently she concluded it was better not to entangle herself with someone who won't give her what she needs. Maybe that's for the best.

I put on my game face. For now, she's a trainee, and I'll treat her as such. With my clipboard in hand, I march out of the office and stride to the center of the room. "Gather around, everyone."

They shuffle over and wait for my instructions.

"Today's a big day," I tell them. "We're working on high falls. Here's what you need to know. One, high falls are among the most dangerous stunts in a stunt performer's toolbox. You can die performing a high fall. That's just a fact. Two, the *really* high falls, sixty feet and above, are done by people with years of experience. Years. Your goal is to be able to handle a twenty-five-foot fall and work your way up from there. Over years. Years. Is that clear?"

The trainees nod. One of them looks a little green, though. "You okay, Megan?"

She wipes her brow and gulps. "I'm fine. Totally."

Megan's not fine, but I'll deal with that discreetly. "The ability to do a high fall isn't a prerequisite to being a stunt person. In fact, your inability to do one type of stunt is rarely disqualifying. But as a new performer, it behooves you to figure out what you're comfortable with. Questions about any of that?"

Brett raises his hand.

"Go ahead, Brett."

"What about you? Ever done a free fall?"

"Yeah, several. My latest was from fifty-five feet, for a new cop drama. It was a jump from one rooftop to another, so not a vertical fall, and a bit more complicated than what we're doing here. Kurt's trying to convince me to put my hat in the ring for a high fall at eighty feet, but I don't think I'm ready. The possibility of whiplash is too great. Anyway, know this: A stunt performer recently died performing a fall at twenty-two feet. Things happen. Things we can't predict. This is our craft, and it involves a level of risk most people aren't interested in taking. Figure out before the end of this program whether you're one of those people."

I can't help giving Eva a pointed look. She needs to understand what she's getting herself into. I'd hate for her to injure herself doing something that isn't her passion. But she doesn't appreciate my advice, it seems. Nostrils flaring, she glares at me, and then she focuses on a spot behind my head.

I turn slightly and see Kurt in my peripheral vision.

He slaps a hand on my shoulder and shakes me. "All right, I think we've done enough to make you shit in your pants, people. Let's get going. We're starting inside with a fifteen-foot jump, and then we'll head outside after lunch for a twenty-five-foot jump off the scaffolding."

We spend the next hour discussing the proper way to fall, how to protect your head and neck, the purpose of the various mats around the point of impact, and more.

As expected, everyone handles the fifteen-foot drops relatively well. Except Megan. Off to the side, out of everyone else's earshot, she tells me she just discovered—during today's class, in fact—that she's afraid of heights. Where that leaves her, I don't know, but we have a brief discussion about her comfort level, and she agrees to sit out the remainder of practice.

I gesture for everyone to follow me outside. The sun

is shining, and the air is surprisingly clear and calm. No wind to speak of. Perfect conditions for getting everyone up on the scaffolding. Behind the warehouse, the eight-person crew double-checks the airbags and landing mats.

I turn to the group. "I'm going to climb up and demonstrate a fall. Kurt will narrate what I'm doing. Then we'll get all of you up there. Remember, we're not doing anything fancy here. We're looking for a suicide fall and a landing on your back. Always on your back. Got it?"

They all nod.

Before I even put my foot on the first rung of the tower, Eva's pacing, both of her hands resting on the top of her head. Maybe fifteen feet is manageable to her but twenty-five feet is too daunting? The truth is, she won't step off the platform unless I'm 100 percent certain she's ready for it.

Once I reach the top, I give myself a minute to focus. There's nothing like the rush of a free fall. For those few seconds, you're weightless, your body slicing through the air with nothing holding you back. Experienced jumpers like me don't even feel the sensation of our stomachs dropping anymore.

I give everyone a two-thumbs-up sign, and a crew member uses a megaphone to count off from five. With my arms out, I jump up in the air as I fall, leaning back to go horizontal before I hear the familiar *thwap* when I land in the center of the airbag.

"Dawg, you made that look so easy," Brett exclaims as I roll off the mattress.

Dawg? He needs to cut that shit out.

"What does it feel like from that height?" he asks.

"More of that free-falling sensation you get at fif-teen feet, but there's also a sense of helplessness because you're in the air longer and you're wondering where the hell the airbag is. Ready to try it?"

Brett claps his hands together. "Let's do it."

As Brett climbs the scaffolding, Eva continues to pace, giving herself a pep talk. "I can do this. I can do this. I can do this."

I believe she can, too, but I'm not going to be up there with her, and she needs to be in the right mindset to successfully complete this stunt. "Kurt, keep your eye on Brett. I need to speak with Eva for a minute."

He nods and walks over to the airbags crew, shading his eyes to watch Brett as he ascends to the top.

"You okay?" I ask her.

"I can do this," she repeats, ignoring me and con-tinuing to pace. She's massaging her hands now, her gaze darting from the top of the scaffold to the landing spot.

I fold my arms over my chest, the clipboard serv-ing as my shield in case I need it. "Just because you can doesn't mean you should."

Her head snaps up and she jolts to a stop, giving me a frosty look. "What's that supposed to mean?"

"Oh, now you want to acknowledge me," I say, giving her a little iciness in return. "What I mean is, are you enjoying this? Was your adrenaline pumping through your veins as you fell onto the mat inside? Do you wish you could do it again? Over and over? Is there something else that makes you feel that way?"

Eva narrows her eyes as she considers me. Then she moves closer, so close that I retreat to maintain an appropriate distance between us, her insanely luscious mouth more distracting now that she's only inches away. "Are you asking these questions of the other people in the class?"

Well, damn. I'm not. And viewing it from her perspective, I can understand why that would piss her off. Hands in the air, I take several steps back. "You're right. You ready to try thirty feet?"

She squares her shoulders as though I've issued a challenge. "I sure am."

"Let's do it, then."

Shaking out her limbs and stretching her neck, she bounces in place, alternating between small hops and knee-to-chest high jumps. My gaze never wavers during her short demonstration of power and athleticism. Odds are high Eva the pro wrestler will star in my dreams tonight. "I see your ankle's better."

"I told you it would be," she says without looking at me.

When she places her foot on the first rung of the ladder, I follow behind, ready to climb the scaffolding as well. An invisible hand tugs on my shirt and pulls me back. When I turn around, I see Kurt behind me, shaking his head.

"She can do it on her own," he says. "You can't coddle the women like that. Doesn't look good."

Shit. He's right. But only partially. Because I'm not coddling the women, plural, I'm coddling the woman—*this woman*—singular. It wouldn't be appropriate either way, but in Eva's case, I must admit it's not coming from a purely professional place.

She's now on the fourth rung, watching Kurt and me, although I doubt she heard what he said. Still, I spy her pensive expression and knowing smile before she turns back around and resumes the climb. After a minute or so, she appears at the edge of the platform, feet together and arms out to her sides.

Blowing out a deep breath, she gives everyone a thumbs-up and the count-off begins. On the one hand, I'm inclined not to watch; seeing her fall will be worse than the clawing feeling in my chest as I watch her prepare for the jump. On the other hand, I don't want to take my eyes off her so that if this practice stunt goes wrong, I can help her in any way I can. The moment she's in the air, my heart punches its way up to my throat, making it difficult to breathe.

But my worry is unnecessary. She executes the jump as perfectly as any student could, keeping her arms out and jumping up and back just as I instructed. Her body falls like a rag doll, and seconds later, she lands in the center of the airbag like as if it were a bull's-eye. The class and crew cheer, while I gulp in deep breaths as I rush over to help her with her dismount.

She looks up at me with pride in her eyes. "I did it!"

"You sure did. You're a badass."

Her classmates surround her, celebrating a stunt well done, and I ease out of the circle, relieved that it's over. More relieved than I *should* be under the circumstances. And I know exactly why. It's not because she's a student. It's not *just* because she's a friend. It's because I care about her. Another one of my inconvenient truths that I'm not ready to face.

Kurt slaps me on the back. "You all right? Looking a little pale there."

Dammit. Is it that obvious? "I'm fine. Didn't eat lunch. I think it's finally catching up with me."

"I've got some protein bars in the office," he says. "You're welcome to have one."

A protein bar isn't going to help. My problem goes much deeper than a missed meal: Because, even though I was worried about crossing a physical line with Eva, I hadn't counted on crossing an emotional one, too.

Chapter Twenty-Three

Stalking is not a good look, sure, but who really cares what you look like when you're stalking?

Eva

FRIDAY EVENING, I join Tori and company on an outing to see Ashley perform with her new band, Syntax. Conveniently, we're at Muddy's, a bar and lounge in my neighborhood. Inconveniently, the men here are impersonating alien life-forms encountering people for the first time.

"If one more drunk frat boy steps up to me, I'm going to lose my shit," I tell Tori.

Tori looks at my reflection in the bathroom mirror as she reapplies her lipstick. Tonight, her hair's pinned on top of her head in a cascade of messy curls, and her face is positively glowing. "Yes, the clientele leaves a lot to be desired, but we're here to support Ashley. Lower your expectations and you'll have a better time."

"I wish you had given me a heads-up, though. I wasted an outfit for this."

Yes, I made a few assumptions about the place and the demographics of its patrons—namely, that the men would be older, wiser, and hotter than the guys I've met so far. None of those assumptions was warranted. Instead, I'm pretty sure I'm trapped on the set of *The Unfuckables*. And although I'm not actively searching for a hookup, I wouldn't be averse to spending time with someone who can remind me that Anthony isn't the only man in the universe.

"Speaking of outfits, is Carter going to take that silly disguise off?" I ask.

The man is wearing an obviously fake mustache, a baseball cap, and sunglasses—inside a dark bar.

"Nope," Tori says with an exasperated shake of her head. "He thinks he's fooling everyone. Doesn't seem to understand that my presence next to him is a big clue as well. I've already picked my battles, and that wasn't one of them."

I stand behind her and primp my hair. "Fine. But if he insists on disguising his voice, too, I'm pretending not to know any of you.

"You have my full support on that game plan." She spins around and places her hands on my shoulders. "Look, let's just go out there and make Ashley feel loved."

"Now *that* I can do."

We walk out to the main lounge area, and once my eyes adjust to the dim lighting, I stumble to a halt and pull Tori to a corner where we can't be seen by the guys. "What's Anthony doing at our table?"

Tori follows my gaze and scrunches her face. "I invited him. Is that a problem?"

"No, no, it's fine. I wasn't expecting to see him, that's all."

I haven't seen him since Wednesday's class. In the meantime, I've thought about what he told me: He likes me as a friend and a person and he's also attracted to me. It's an underwhelming summary of his feelings, but I appreciate that he's being straight with me. He just doesn't want to be in a relationship. And given my history, I shouldn't want to be in one, either.

"You two have been getting along, right?" Tori asks.

An image of the way he touched me in the back of his truck flashes in my brain. Oh yeah, we're getting along splendidly. "Of course. He's been great. Even took me to a drive-in movie last week."

"He took you to the movies?"

"Yeah. Last Sunday. I was feeling frustrated about my ankle and he wanted to cheer me up."

She peers at me, a pensive expression on her face.

"It's not like that, Tori." My voice betrays me, likely revealing that I wish it *was* like that.

She gives me a sympathetic smile and slips a hand around my waist. "Fine. I'll just say this. Know what you're getting into and be sure it's what you want."

"I'm not getting *into* anything."

She gives me a smug look. "Okay, *pendeja*."

"Okay, *malcriada*."

Cackling at our ridiculous exchange, we weave through

the rows of tables and chairs until we reach the men. They all stand as we sit. Not surprisingly, Anthony's taken the open seat next to mine. He's wearing jeans and a black V-neck with the sleeves rolled up to reveal his forearms. His only accessory is a blue-faced watch with a brown leather strap. I've never seen it before, and that small detail suggests that although he may not be trying too hard, he did give some thought to what he would wear tonight.

"Damn, I was seconds away from sending a search party," Carter says to Tori. "One of these days I'm going to find out what goes on in the women's restroom, and I bet I'm going to be shocked."

She shakes her head, raising her drink to her lips. "It's really not that deep, sweetie. We're either peeing, complimenting one another, or making plans to smash the patriarchy."

"That explains everything," Julian says.

Anthony leans into me. "How are you, Eva?"

Oh, dear God, his cologne is going to short-circuit my brain. Makes me think of sipping cognac in front of a fireplace. I bet it's called Pheromones. "I'm great. You?"

"Good." His gaze sweeps over the top half of my dress. "That dress looks perfect on you."

I'm not ashamed to agree. It's one of my favorites. A jersey tank that hugs my spectacular backside and emphasizes my small waist and round hips. "Thank you. Is your mind blown by seeing me in a dress for the first time? Admit it, I clean up very well."

"It's not the first time I've seen you in a dress, though.

You wore a dress with pretty little yellow flowers to Tori and Carter's wedding."

Oh, I shouldn't be touched that he remembers, but I am. "Great memory, Mr. Castillo."

"For the things that matter, Ms. Montgomery."

A round of applause and Julian's ear-splitting whistle prevent me from responding. Which is fortunate, because I'm at a loss for words. Is he flirting with me again? And to what end?

I set my cluttered thoughts aside and focus on the stage. Ashley's standing in the center, backed by a drummer, two keyboard players, a bassist, and a sleepy-eyed man with an array of horns at his disposal. Her own acoustic guitar rests against a stand behind her.

"Good evening, everyone. We're Syntax, and this is our first appearance as a band. Be gentle."

She gets the chuckles she was hoping for, and when the crowd quiets down, the band begins playing its first song, a number that's hard to characterize. The bluesy undertones are unmistakable, though, and remind me of Amy Winehouse's music. Ashley's delivery is relaxed, unrushed—and sensual as hell.

I shouldn't want you, but I do
You shouldn't want me, but you do
What are we going to do about it?
Tonight's too soon
Wish I could say what this is
It isn't love and it isn't hate

What are we going to do about it?
Tomorrow's too late

Julian squirms in his seat, his gaze trained on the stage. I look between them, a voyeur to the intimate messages they're sending each other. Ashley's engaging in foreplay and forcing us to watch. Brava, my dear. Bra-va.

Anthony stands abruptly. "The servers aren't coming around. I'm going to order a drink at the bar. Anyone need anything?" He looks at me. "Eva, you want a Cosmo or a Sea Breeze? Something with cranberry?"

Tori whips her head in my direction, her lips pressed together, but she doesn't say anything. She wouldn't with the guys around. Still, she wants *me* to know that *she* noticed that little exchange.

"No, I'm good," I say, ignoring her.

Everyone else declines, too, and he slips away. I try not to follow him with my eyes, but within seconds I'm watching him squeeze his way to the front of the bar. A woman with dark hair and dark jeans edges close to him, and when a man abandons the space next to Anthony, she fills it, turning her face to give him a co-quettish smile. Anthony leans forward to speak with the bartender, and then he angles his body in the woman's direction and says something to her.

I can't watch them flirt with each other.

No, I *must* watch them flirt with each other.

I *need* to see this, if only to be reminded that Anthony's not my person and never will be.

Another round of applause pulls me out of my messy thoughts, and I belatedly—and distractedly—shower Ashley's band with enthusiastic praise. "Woo-hoo! Yes, Ashley!"

Forgive me, Ash. I'll make it up to you.

I'm trying to be as surreptitious about my visual stalking as I possibly can, but the moment I pretend to scan the bar area, Anthony leans into the woman and points at our table. She squints at us, and Anthony waves at me. Not knowing what else to do, I wave back. When they're no longer looking our way, I slide down my chair. My public humiliation is well and truly complete.

Tori reaches across the table and taps me on my hand. "You okay?"

"I'm fine," I say, refusing to look at her when I lie. "Just a little tired."

"Hmm."

My gaze snaps to hers. "Yes, exactly. Hmm." I'm trying my damnedest to focus on Ashley's band, but a part of me wants to go to the bar and watch Anthony up close. I want to hear what he says and how he says it. Is he flirty like he usually is with me, or is he smooth and mysterious in his approach?

I glance at the bar again, and a heavy weight settles in the pit of my stomach. Anthony's walking out of the lounge area, and the dark-haired woman is trailing a few steps behind him. Wow, he works quickly, and he didn't even say good-bye. My throat tightens and my vision blurs, but I try my best to shake it off, sucking on the last of my cocktail and pretending to enjoy the music I can't really hear. It's all white noise at this point.

Kudos to Anthony. He's off somewhere with a woman who wants what he wants, while I'm stuck here with Julian, who's still squirming in his seat; Carter, who's fake-ass disguise is making me cringe; and Tori, who's looking at me like she knows exactly what's going on in my head.

Abruptly, I stand and place a few bills on the table. "Hey, guys. I think I might be coming down with something. I'm going to head out."

"Do you need us to drive you home?" Tori asks.

I raise my phone in the air. "I'll get a Lyft."

"Text me when you get home."

"Will do."

"And Eva?"

"Yeah?"

"Everything happens for a reason."

I meet her troubled gaze and manage a wink to suggest I'm only moderately disappointed by Anthony's departure. "So they say, Tori. So they say."

Chapter Twenty-Four

Anthony

I'VE GOT A finger over one ear, trying to listen to my father explain why the power's out, when Eva appears outside Muddy's in the fucking dress to end all dresses. She can't see me, but I sure as hell can see her.

"Papi, calm down. You probably just tripped a circuit breaker. Go down to the basement and check the panel."

"It's dark down there, *mijo*," he says into the phone. "*Mierda*, my *pastelón* is going to be ruined."

"You won't be able to finish cooking if you don't switch the circuit back on."

He grumbles, but the squeak of the door tells me he's braving it. He'll do anything for his food. If I were being held hostage down there, though, I'd be shit out of luck.

"How are you doing?" I ask him.

"Don't rush me. I'm moving as fast as I can." More grumbling follows. "Got it. You were right."

"As usual."

He hangs up on me.

Laughing at my father's good-natured impatience with me, I shove the phone in my back pocket and walk to the bar's entrance, where Eva's preoccupied with her own phone screen.

"Heading out so soon?" I ask her.

She gasps and recoils, almost getting wiped out by the door when a patron exits the bar. As I pull her down the steps and out of harm's way, she asks, "What are you still doing here?"

"Still? I never left. Got an SOS call from my father, but everything's fine now."

A line appears between her brows. "I thought I saw you leave with the woman you met at the bar."

Ah, the woman. Yes, that would have been an excellent plan. Instead, when she asked me if I was alone, I claimed that I wasn't, pointing to our table and waving at Eva to emphasize my unavailability. The thing is, even though Eva and I aren't together, I wouldn't have felt comfortable leaving the bar with someone else. Worse, I wasn't inclined to anyway. Eva's fitting herself into every nook and cranny in my brain and she has no idea. "Nah, she wasn't feeling me at all. I guess my game wasn't up to par."

"Really?" she says, her pinched expression perfectly matching the strain in her voice. "Because that's not what it looked like from where I was sitting."

"You were watching us?"

She pouts at me as though she's offended by the question. "No."

And there's that trace of vulnerability again. It contrasts starkly with her confident demeanor, and it's that duality that has the capacity to bring me to my knees. It hints that I'm special to her, and being special to Eva is important to me. But I can't be if I'm not vulnerable with her, too. Never mind that the thought of doing that makes me want to jump outside my skin.

I raise her chin. Reluctantly, she meets my gaze.

Focusing on her big, beautiful brown eyes, I gather the courage to tell her the truth. "Let's try this again. The woman was interested. I wasn't. The entire time I was speaking with her, my mind was pulling me in a different direction. Toward you. Now you try."

She licks her lips and swallows. "I'm not sure why I was watching you two, maybe to remind myself that you're looking for one-time hookups and I don't fit the bill. But when I thought you'd left with her, I was disappointed." She sighs. "I don't know what to do with my feelings."

"Neither do I."

She throws her head back, leaving her delectable, kissable neck exposed for my viewing pleasure. "What's the point of honesty if we remain in the same place we've been in since Day One?"

"If you think we're in the same place as Day One, then you're being dishonest with yourself again."

When she lowers her head, I meet her stare, dizzy with the need to kiss her. But I don't advance on her. If Eva and I are taking any more steps, she'll be the one to initiate them.

"You're disappointing me again," she says. "I need you to be as dense about this as I am. Misery loves company, you know."

"Let's get your miserable butt home, then."

She raises her phone in the air. "I requested a Lyft. I'm just ten blocks from here."

"You can cancel it."

"I can but I won't."

I tilt my head and watch her with a smug smile. "Because you don't trust yourself alone with me anymore, right?"

She shoves me away. "What? That's hardly what's going on here."

I pretend not to hear her. "You know, it's really embarrassing how you're always throwing yourself at me. Showing up at my doorstep. Begging me to take you everywhere. Calling all the—"

She rushes forward like she's going to tackle me, but I sidestep the move, scramble behind her, and pull her into my arms, her back to my chest.

"Cancel the Lyft," I whisper in her ear. "There's no strings attached to a ride."

With my arms still around her, she opens her phone, and after a few taps, cancels the ride. "Where's your truck?"

"In the lot out back. I can bring it around."

"No, that's okay. I'll walk with you."

We stroll behind the building, our arms brushing against each other since we're so close. She spots the truck in the far corner of the lot and snorts. "The walk to my apartment is shorter than the distance to your truck."

"Didn't want it to get dinged. Drunk people are destructive assholes. If you'll recall, I did offer to bring it around."

She leans into me and pokes my side. "I'm just giving you a hard time."

"I can always count on you for hard times, Eva."

She walks a few steps before she gets my meaning. Then her eyes go wide, and she shoves me away. "It took me a few seconds to pick up on that one. I'm disappointed in myself."

"I'm disappointed in you, too," I say with a grin.

Eyes twinkling in amusement, she winks at me.

We walk the rest of the way in silence. When we reach the truck, I open the cab door for her and hang on to the frame as she climbs in. She doesn't swing her legs in, though, so I can't close the door. Instead, she places her feet on the running board and scoots to the edge of the seat.

"Something wrong?" I ask.

"Everything's right," she says, grabbing a fistful of my shirt and tugging me close. Her mouth is parted, and her chest is rising and falling like she's just finished a race. "But I don't want to get in this truck with you."

My heart bangs against my chest, thumping wildly to mimic my erratic thoughts. Where did this come from? What does she mean? What should I say? I don't want to misconstrue her signals, but the possibility that she's as weak for me as I am for her makes me light-headed. A wave of heat spreads through me, and my cock hardens against the fabric of my jeans. "What do you want, then?"

Her brown eyes are glossy and soft as she whispers an answer, her voice shaking with need. "I want you to fuck me. Right here. Right now."

I lean over, burying my face in the crook of her neck and groaning at the thought alone. The goddamn sugar cookie scent is back and I'm done for. She takes a deep breath and rubs the back of my head, running her fingers through my hair.

"Someone could see us," I note, trying to be the voice of reason. In reality, the passenger side is facing a multicolored brick wall, so we're unlikely to be disturbed.

She takes my head in her hands and brings our faces close. Chest heaving, she says, "Do I look like I care?"

The urge to devour her in every way possible is tangible, so strong I could reach out and touch it, mold it to my will. This beautiful, sweet, funny woman wants me inside her, and I'll be damned if I deny her, deny myself, the pleasure we both crave. "Panties. Off. Dress. Up."

The words come out like marching orders, but she doesn't seem to mind. She scrambles inside the cab and makes quick work of her underwear. Then she tugs her dress up to the waist, oblivious to how deeply I'm affected by the sight of her. My knees buckle. The neat strip of hair covering her mound does nothing to hide how wet she is. I'm so enthralled by the view that I slow my own efforts to unbuckle my belt.

She snaps her fingers. "Look less. Act more. You can savor later."

"Some help would be nice," I growl, unable to contain my frustration with my current lack of coordination.

With greedy fingers, she dives for my buckle, and I refocus my efforts, pulling the straps of her dress over and down her shoulders.

"This stretchy material is my new best friend," I tell her.

"Jersey knit," she says, pausing her work on my button fly when it's time to slip her hands through the arm holes.

Whatever that means. I pull her dress down to reveal a strapless bra that's barely holding her tits inside. "Oh, fuck me."

She laughs. "That's what I'm trying to do. But you're not understanding that time is of the essence. Condom?"

Reaching behind me, I say a silent thank-you to myself for always keeping two in my wallet and place one on her lap. She pops open the last jeans button, widens her legs, and slides her hands inside my pants, cupping my ass as she pulls me forward. "Damn, you feel good."

"Weren't you just complaining about wasting time? Please feed your ass fetish later."

"Will do," she says, laughing. Then she pulls my jeans down to my thighs, bringing my underwear with them and lowering her gaze to my dick. "Oh, shit, I've missed you, and I'm so fucking happy right now."

My dick jumps at the compliment.

"You've got a live one there."

I bark out a laugh. "Will you put the condom on, please?"

She straightens. "Oh, right." Then she twists around, looking for it. "Where'd it go? Oh, here it is." She rolls it on, clamps her legs around my waist, and guides me inside, so efficiently that I'm struggling to keep up. Inch by inch, she takes me in, her voice rising as I fill her. "Oh, oh, oh, oh, oh God, yes, that's . . . yes."

I grit my teeth as she stretches to accommodate my thickness, and then, at long fucking last, I'm balls-deep inside Eva again. Squeezing my eyes shut, I grasp the cab's frame for support and pump into her like my body's made to do nothing else. I don't know that I'm capable of speech anymore. She's soft in some places, hard in others, and hot and lush everywhere in between. I just want to stay in this position and pass out. "Jesus, Eva, this is going to be quick, but I'll make up for it later."

"There's nothing to make up for," she says between pants, her luscious tits bouncing in time to my thrusts. "This is perfect. Just don't stop, okay?"

I pause to regain my balance, and she hisses.

"Do that again," she whispers.

I jerk my hips, pull out to the tip, and slam my way home. "What? Like that?"

"Yes, please, please, please, do that again."

I repeat the move and her head falls back.

"I'm going to come soon," she says. "Are you close?"

"I've been close since we started."

Wanting to prolong the tingling at the base of my dick but knowing that wouldn't be wise, I slam the middle console up and tip Eva over so her body's splayed across the seat. She raises her left arm over her head and grabs the steering wheel for leverage while I settle over her, bracing my arms on either side of her head.

"How do you feel?" I ask. "Is this okay?"

She moans her approval, adding, "So much more than okay."

I plunge into her again and again, knowing the instant she flexes her muscles around my cock and tightens around me like a vise. "Are you . . . trying . . . to break me?"

Her voice is just as ragged as mine when she responds. "I'm trying . . . to make you . . . feel good."

"Fuck. You're succeeding."

She's writhing beneath me, her cries rising with each passing minute. I try to swallow them, but she twists her head from side to side, until she freezes and then splinters, her spasms strong enough to shake my body, too. "Anthony, yes. It's . . . I . . . don't stop."

"*Dámelo.* Yes, Eva. That. Is. It." One more thrust sends me to the same state, a wave of mind-numbing pleasure coursing through me and snatching my breath. I'm stunned, blinking stupidly, as though I've never had sex before.

In a way, it is new for us. Sex with someone you care

about is entirely different from a hookup. And while I've experienced the latter with Eva, it's only now that I'm experiencing the former with her. I want to bottle it up and carry it around with me like *pique*. "Incredible."

She stretches under me, her features soft and relaxed. "That it was." I'm trying to regulate my breathing when she stills, abruptly sitting up and looking around her. "We should go before someone sees us."

I back off her, removing and tying off the condom in record time. As she struggles into her panties and readjusts the straps of her dress, I pull up my underwear and jeans, not bothering to button my fly. She never meets my gaze, though, and my gut tells me we're back on shaky ground.

I round the front of the truck and climb in, prepared to ask her what's wrong.

But Eva's got other plans. She fastens her seat belt, turns to me, and says, "That was great. Thank you." Then she closes her eyes, a satisfied smile dominating her pretty face. "You don't mind if I take a short nap, do you? I'm wiped out."

"Go right ahead," I say, acknowledging that she could in fact be exhausted given that I'm sleepy as hell, too. Then my dumb ass remembers that she lives ten blocks away, hardly enough time for a nap. No, she's shutting me out—whereas I'm prepared to let her in. Or try to. I'm still considering how to let her know I want more than the occasional hookup when I park the car in front of her apartment complex.

"Eva," I say, tapping her on the shoulder.

She opens her eyes and looks around. "Oh, we're here." She quickly unfastens the seat belt, reaches over, and squeezes my hand. "That was great. Thank you." She's repeating the words she said ten minutes ago like some fucking robot on autopilot. What the hell? Then she climbs out of the car and sprints to the entrance of the complex. As I watch her slip through the doors, an astonishing fact comes to me: We never kissed. Not once.

And now I'm wondering how an amazing evening turned to shit in the span of a few seconds.

Chapter Twenty-Five

Look, guys, a post-sex debriefing isn't necessary. Just grab your shoes and go.

Eva

I'M SCRAMBLING TO get ready for work when my intercom buzzes. "Yes?"

"Eva, it's Anthony."

Crap. I can't do this now. He's probably going to tell me he regrets what happened last night. I couldn't have made it clearer that I was willing to work within the constraints he places on building relationships—I even had sex in public for the first time, for God's sake—but maybe he thinks I need a refresher. I'll pass, thank you.

"Uh, I'm kind of busy. One of the instructors called out sick, so Tori asked me to come in this morning."

"How were you going to get there?"

"Metro."

"What if I drive you to the studio? That'll save you plenty of time. We can talk before you go."

Not a bad compromise. Since he obviously needs to get this off his chest, I should at least get *something* out of it. "Okay, come on up."

A minute later, he's at my apartment, wearing training pants and a V-neck hoodie. V-necks are a staple of his wardrobe, apparently. Oh, and his hair is mussed, as though he rolled out of bed, threw on his clothes, and came to my door. Seeing him this way prompts me to think of what it would be like to wake up in his arms and witness his bedhead first thing in the morning. It's never going to happen, but my imagination doesn't care.

"Good morning," he says carefully, as though he's testing whether I'm receptive to the greeting.

"Morning," I mumble, feeling wary of what comes after it. I wave him in. "So, what's so important that you had to speak to me before 9:00 a.m.?"

He ignores my question and strides inside. "What class are you teaching?"

"Cardio kickboxing."

The corners of his lips quirk up. "You should be excellent at that."

"Oh, yeah?" I say, narrowing my eyes. "Why is that?"

"Cardio kickboxing is all about harnessing your strength and doling it out in quick bursts. It's the perfect mix of power and energy. That's you in a nutshell."

Oh, that's good. He's trying to disarm me. That must be what's going on here. "Anthony, why are you here?"

"I need to speak with you about last night."

Yep, called it. I sigh, knowing from experience how

this conversation will progress. "Fine. We might as well get comfortable for this."

We sit on opposite ends of the couch. I tuck my legs under me and hug my favorite throw pillow, a tacky canary-yellow gem with pom-poms all around the edges.

He leans on his thighs, making a steeple with his fingers and resting it on his chin. Then he slowly turns his head and meets my gaze. "First, I want to tell you that I thought last night was incredible."

"But?"

He smoothes his hands on his thighs. Stalling. "But—"

I'm unable to keep the frustration out of my voice when I ask, "But what, Anthony? But it shouldn't have happened? But it can't happen again?" I park my expression in Neutral, willing myself not to show any distress. It's a challenge, but I'm up for it.

Silently, he considers me as he pokes the inside of his mouth with his tongue. A few seconds later, he sits up and peers at me, his mouth curved into a sexy smile. "Let me start again. Last night was incredible, but I hate that we didn't have enough time to do more. *Much more.*"

He moves an inch closer. "Last night was incredible, but I think you wanted to keep it impersonal, and only after experiencing impersonal did I realize it doesn't fit the way I feel about you."

My heart is hammering against my chest. This isn't

going the way I expected it to. And now I'm feeling all kinds of foolish for assuming he was here to cut me off. If Anthony's taught me anything in the time we've known each other, it's that I should never expect the worst of him.

He moves another inch closer. "And last night was incredible, but I want the chance to show you it can be even better between us. If you can be patient with me."

Now I'm the one scooting toward him, my arm brushing against his.

"Last night was incredible, but I wish we'd kissed," he says. "Can I kiss you now?"

Kissing would be nice, but it doesn't give me answers. "What exactly do you want from me?"

"The better question is, what exactly do you want from me?"

Oh. Wow. No one's ever flipped a question like that to make it about me. Although what I'd really like to do is make it about us. "If I told you I want to build a relationship with you, what would you say?"

He ponders this for more seconds than I like, but eventually he answers. "I'd say I've never been boyfriend material, but I'd like to try with you."

"And what brought on this miraculous change in your no-dating tune?"

"You, Eva. You brought this on." He draws my hand away from the pillow and laces his fingers with mine. "I can't stop thinking about you. You're on my mind more hours than I'll ever admit. I want to laugh and hang out with you. Be the person you wake up with. Give you—

and only you—mind-blowing orgasms on the regular. Hold your hand when we're walking down the street. Let you have your way with me. All of that sounds like dating to me."

"Why have you been fighting this so hard?"

He shifts away from me, taking what appears to be much-needed space, and drops his head.

I place a hand on his thigh and he lifts his chin, giving me a reluctant smile.

Several beats later, he says, "Don't ask me to explain why because I won't be able to, but that simple touch, you placing your hand on my lap, it does something to me. It's . . . I don't know . . . comforting and arousing at the same time."

I squeeze his thigh. "I love everything you just said, but I know when you're trying to divert my attention. Tell me about her. Please."

He returns to his original spot next to me, erasing the small space he created between us. "It's not a long story. I dated a woman about a year into my move here. I'd just moved from Costa Mesa to LA for my job, and she was the receptionist there, at the messenger service I told you about. We were inseparable for a year, but she never really believed that I wanted to be with her exclusively. She'd built me up in her mind as this incorrigible flirt who'd eventually be a player even though I tried to prove otherwise. Looking back, I suspect some of it might have been her own stereotypical beliefs about Latino men. I couldn't be faithful because that's

not what we're known for, is probably how she saw it.
She suggested as much once. And I remember her being
fascinated by the idea that my father cooked, as though
that's not a thing."

I laugh at the ridiculousness of that idea. "Oh, I know
damn well it's a thing. Luis can cook for me anytime."

He smiles and takes my hand, kissing the back of it
before he continues. "Anyway, I was young and in love
and I wanted it to work. And I tried. I really did. But she
was miserable. And in my mind, I'd done that to her."

I get on my knees and pull him to me, wrapping my
arms around him. "Anthony, she did that to herself.
Those were her insecurities playing out."

He leans against me, letting me take his weight. "I
can see that now. But it just turned me against relationships. I didn't want to hurt anyone like that again. I'd
seen what that kind of hurt could do to a person, watching my father turn himself inside out for my mother.
So I figured if I always kept it light, made it clear that
there was no chance of a relationship, there'd also be
no chance that I'd hurt someone like I hurt Melissa, or
how my mother hurt my dad. I just didn't want to *affect*
anyone. Not in that way, at least."

Goodness. I think back to all the things I said to him.
About being manipulative. About playing with woman's hearts. Anthony was doing the opposite of that, but
I couldn't see it. Couldn't get past my own biases to see
the real man underneath. "Anthony, I hate to break it to
you, but you *do* affect people. Your father. Tori. Kurt.

Me. Oh God, how you affect me. In the best way. *Always* in the best way."

He lifts his chin and brushes his lips against my jaw. "We have one problem, though."

I don't like the sound of that. "What is it?"

"Kurt's going to kill me," he says. "As an instructor, I shouldn't be pursuing you, although the reality is, we'd already been together before boot camp started."

I take his shoulders and shake him. "Anthony, it's boot camp. And we have three more weeks to go. Kurt will be fine."

"Yeah, I suppose," he says, though his voice isn't as enthusiastic as it was about everything else.

"Do you think you could promise not to treat me differently?" I ask him.

He hesitates.

"Let me make it easier on you. Do you think you could promise not to undermine me?"

This time he doesn't hesitate. "Of course."

"And can you promise not to give me any advantage over anyone else?"

He nods.

"Then Kurt can mind his own business."

The corner of his eyes crinkle. "I think that's what he's trying to do, Eva."

I throw my head back. "What I mean is, Kurt can stay out of our personal business. It's not like the class will last forever."

He ponders this, which, honestly, makes admire him

even more. He's thoughtful. Wants to do the right thing. "Yeah, you're right that it's not forever. So what now? Want to watch Netflix?"

I'm interested in revisiting what he said earlier. That bit about him wanting to show me how good it could be between us? That, please. I flip my leg over and straddle him. And he's ready, adjusting me to fit comfortably on his lap and pulling me close.

I place my hands on his shoulders. "I want that kiss now."

He obliges, cradling my face and pressing his lips to mine. It's sweet and tender and nothing like what I was expecting. It's . . . fine.

"How was that?" he asks.

"Um, honestly? That was underwhelming. Sorry."

His shoulders shake with laughter. "So what you're saying is you'd like me to improve on that performance?"

"I guess what I'm saying is we both need to up our game."

This time, he sweeps his hands under my hair and massages my neck, his fingers making light circles against the sensitive skin there. His expression, no longer playful but hot and intense, mirrors my own desire. I lean forward, licking the seam of his lips. With a low rumble in his throat, he bridges the distance between my breasts and his chest, crushing me to him as he opens his mouth to let me in. Now *this* is what was missing. What I wanted and needed. This closeness. Breathing his scent and feeling his warmth. I roll my ass against him to match the greedy pace of our kiss.

He drags his mouth away, trailing a line of kisses from one temple down to my jaw, and ending on the other side, all the while cradling my face gently, as though I need to be handled with care. The urge to ask for more is strong. If the press of his erection against my stomach is any guide, he'd happily lower his pants and let me ride him. It would be quick. It would be satisfying. It would be *irresponsible*.

Must. Get. To. Class.

I pull away from him, unwilling to look at him because I know what I'll see. Lust. And I must be vigilant. Untangling myself from his embrace without eye contact isn't easy, but I manage the task—barely.

"Why aren't you looking at me, Eva? Is something wrong?"

I reach inside my purse to make sure my keys and wallet are accounted for. "Nothing's wrong. I just need to leave soon, and I don't want to be distracted by the expression on your face."

He laughs. "What am I? Medusa?"

"Precisely."

"So one look at me and you'll turn to stone?"

"No, one look at you and I'll want to bone."

"I'm ridiculously attracted to the way you speak. You couldn't be more perfect if you tried."

My heart squeezes in my chest. "Stop saying things like that. You're undermining my efforts to get us out of here."

He rises slowly and shakes out his legs to straighten his pants.

I look. Not at his eyes, but at his crotch, where the outline of his stiff erection mocks me. *Dammit, eggplant, stand down. We don't need your services at the moment.* I spin away and shove my hands back in my bag. "Okay, I think I have everything. We should get . . ."

He drapes his arms over my shoulders and pulls me against him. The back of my head settles comfortably against his chest. He's not playing fair, and we both know it. Still, I'm not going anywhere.

"How tall are you?" I ask him.

"Six feet. Why?"

"Just thinking about logistics."

"The possibilities are endless, aren't they?"

I pull him toward the door. "No more talk of possibilities until we're on the road."

"You started it."

"I did. And now I'm ending it."

I'm inches from turning the doorknob, when he places his hand on the door. "Wait."

I spin around to face him, alarmed by the look of uncertainty on his face. "What's going on?

"Nothing. I just . . . Let me take you somewhere tonight. We can dress up a little, maybe listen to some jazz." He shrugs. "Whatever you want to do."

"Say it," I taunt, a hint of humor in my voice.

He rolls his eyes at me. "Let me take you on a date."

"See?" I ask, standing on my toes to kiss his chin. "Was that so hard to say?"

I'm kidding, of course. I know it was hard to say. And it's not lost on me that he's done nothing but show his willingness to try this whole time.

"Will you answer the question?" he asks.

"Will the other *D* word be involved?"

He leans over and whispers his answer close to my ear, his mouth grazing the shell as he speaks. "If you want it to be."

Oh. The promise in those words and the fire in his eyes threaten to make me turn around and drag him to my bedroom. No, focus. "Splendid, then. We're going on a date."

Or so he thinks . . .

Chapter Twenty-Six

Anthony

I'm going on a date. My first one in seven years. Let's hope I don't fuck this up. Blowing out several puffs of breath, I press the buzzer for Eva's apartment, a bouquet of fresh-cut orchids behind my back.

"Who is it?" she asks.

"Eva, it's Anthony. Want me to come up?"

"Sure. I just need a few more minutes. I'll buzz you in."

Nodding at a couple exiting the building, I enter the vestibule and push open the door to the courtyard. A minute later, I clear the second-floor landing and ring Eva's doorbell. An instrumental jazz song plays in her apartment.

Behind the closed door, she invites me in. "Door's open, Anthony."

I turn the knob and peek inside. Eva's relaxing on the couch in nothing but an untied peach silk robe and black heels, her open legs framing her bare pussy like the directional arrows of the most perfect map on the planet. An invisible force snatches the breath out of me. I've done nothing to deserve this, but I'll accept it with pleasure. Unable to draw my eyes away from the image that will forever be seared into my brain, I manage to put one foot in front of the other and lock the door, collapsing against it for support.

Stating the obvious, I say, "You're not dressed."

"You shouldn't be either," she says.

Her sultry tone threatens to make me lose my shaky grasp on remaining upright.

Alarm bells sound in my head despite the enticing picture she makes. She's done this before: narrowing our interaction to a sexual encounter and nothing more. Does she think that's all I want?

"I thought we were going out on a date?" I ask.

She covers her face and peeks through her fingers. Naturally, I'm distracted by the way the cleavage between her perfect breasts materializes.

"Would you be disappointed if I told you I'm not in the mood to go out?" she asks.

Could it be as simple as that? She's just not in the mood? I need to know. "I wanted to take you out." I point to the flowers in my left hand. "Pamper you. Shower you with affection. If you're doing this for me, because you think I only want sex, it's not necessary. I want to be around you. Every second, minute, or hour you're willing to give me."

She drops her hands from her face and places one of them over her heart. "That's sweet, but we've spent plenty of time together. The festival in Long Beach, all the rides home, dinner with your father, Moody's, the drive-in. How could you forget the drive-in?"

My dick swells as I recall that night. "I didn't."

"So you see, it's like we were dating before either of us knew it. And now I'd like to recapture the perfection of that night in Connecticut. Except not in a hotel room."

This is when I realize I'm the ridiculous in a ridiculous situation. A woman I adore and can't possibly be more attracted to is sitting on her couch, openly displaying a dozen signals of her horniness and trying to convince me that her reasons for not wanting to go out are valid. We're staying in. Not only that, I'm making it my night's mission to watch her come so hard she forgets what state she's in.

"So, Mr. Castillo, are you with me?" she asks.

I toss the flowers on a nearby table, sending a few petals flying, and then I stride toward her, removing my jacket as I go. "We should order takeout. It's important to eat and stay hydrated before and after a marathon."

Eva

"STOP RIGHT THERE," I tell him.

Anthony freezes, his jacket hanging from the tip of his index finger.

"You can throw it over there," I say, pointing to the accent chair in the corner of the living room.

He gives me a lazy smile, his eyelids at half-mast. "Let me guess. You want me to strip for you."

I rise from the sofa and saunter toward him. "No, I'd like the pleasure of doing it myself."

The jacket goes flying across the room.

Trailing my fingers across his broad chest, I circle him and admire the three-sixty view of Anthony in a white dress shirt and navy-blue slacks. "No tie?"

He shakes his head, his audible breaths growing louder the more he watches me. "Too constricting."

"That's a shame. I could have used it to keep your hands off me. I'll need to improvise later."

"Can't wait," he says, his voice low and gravelly.

Wearing heels gives me the extra height I need. It allows me to nuzzle his jaw and nibble on his earlobe. I can feel his body vibrating under my touch, as though he's an engine in an idling car waiting for the light to turn green.

"Eva," he whispers, the neediness in his voice unmistakable. "This is torture. Absolute fucking torture."

I make another revolution and stand behind him, reaching around to unbutton his shirt. After unfastening the last button, I draw the shirt out of his slacks and slip it off him, caressing his shoulders and sliding my hands down his back before letting the shirt fall to the floor.

Slowly, I skim my fingers across his torso, making

it my personal Candy Land board. Four spaces to Hard Pecs Forest. Eight spaces to Chiseled Abs Mountain. I will happily die of this sweet tooth.

I press a kiss between his shoulder blades while I unbuckle his belt. "You're very quiet. I'm not used to it."

"I'm trying not to move from this position. Talking would fuck with my concentration."

I slide his belt off. "I admire your commitment to the cause."

"How much longer do you think you'll be at this?" he asks, his voice scratchy like a scouring pad.

"Not sure. Why? In a rush?"

"No, just curious," he says.

The frustration in his voice prompts me to quicken my pace. I'm not the only one being denied the pleasure of moving this along. I unfasten and unzip his pants, reaching inside to stroke his cock through his boxer briefs. He jumps at the contact. The thickness fills my hand and I hold back a moan. I'm shaking from the anticipation of having him inside me again.

His legs dip when I press my breasts to his back and rub myself over him.

"Let me turn around, Eva," he pleads.

"Stay where you are, baby."

He throws his head back, his fists clenched at his sides.

I come around and face him. He slowly lowers his head, pinning me with a stare that promises exquisite retribution. For a moment, I'm rendered speechless by the man in front of me, floored by his fully aroused state. His eyes are soft and unclear, his lips are wet, and his cheeks are flushed. Every visible muscle appears to be stretched to capacity, as though he'll snap from the slightest touch. And all I want to do is bring him the relief he so obviously needs.

I kneel in front of him and pull his pants and boxers down his legs. "Up."

He lifts one foot, then the next, and toes off his slip-on loafers.

"Socks, too," I tell him as I place his shoes to the side. "We're not filming a porno."

"Do it for me," he says.

The gruff command snags my attention and I look up, clumsily falling back on my ass now that his whole body is in my eyeballs.

Big mistake.

Well, big, yes. Mistake, no.

Because a fully erect and wholly naked Anthony could never be a mistake. Good. Lord. "Let's get these socks off you, so we don't mess up the view." I scramble back to my knees and tug his socks off, and then I fall flat on my ass again, because I need to see this as nature intended. "Anthony, your dick deserves its own national appreciation day. Do you see this?"

"I see it every day," he says, amusement returning to his voice.

"I'm jealous."

"Don't be. I'm willing to give you a visitor's pass."

"I'd want nothing less than VIP access."

He chuckles. "No doubt. Ask me what VIP access gets you."

I gulp. "What?"

His eyes burn with need. "First row access. So close you can touch it."

I rise to my knees, cupping his balls with one hand and stroking his length with the other. "Like this?"

He shudders. "Yes."

I want more, though, and I'm sure he does, too, so I sit back on my heels, licking the broad head of his cock before taking him inside my mouth.

He rests his hands on my shoulders, rocking gently to match the rise and fall of my lips over his dick. "Eva, baby, that feels so fucking good. Your mouth is perfect."

His words light something in me, make me greedy for all of him, so I grab his hips and help him pump into me. Above me, he grunts, his hands sliding up to my head, and then he digs his fingers into my scalp as he guides himself between my greedy lips. "Fuck, Eva. Yes."

All too soon, he pulls away. Through gritted teeth, he says, "We have to stop. I need to get my mouth on you, too."

Oh, well, in that case, sure. That's an interruption I can get behind. I stand and draw his face down for a searing kiss, our tongues swirling greedily. Then I take his hand and guide him to my bedroom, where I've already dimmed the lights and pulled back the coverlet.

Behind me, Anthony reaches for the collar of my robe, slipping it off my shoulders and arms in one fluid movement. His arms envelop my body in his warmth, and then he brushes a finger against each nipple, until I'm straining for more of his touch.

"Bend over," he says.

I brace my arms on the bed and fold my body over.

His hands explore my ass like he's worshipping it. "Do you want your shoes off?"

I turn back to look at him. "I kind of like them."

"So do I," he says, still caressing my ass. "Spread your legs."

I do as he asks.

"Can I lick and touch you?"

"Yes, yes, yes."

He runs his finger from my clit to my pussy and pushes a finger inside. "Like this?"

I take a shuddering breath. "Oh, God, yes."

He shifts behind me, lifts one of my legs and guides my knee onto the bed. "Okay?"

I answer with my body, placing my other knee on the bed and pressing my face into the mattress.

"Eva, I wish you could see this. I'm going to combust just thinking about eating this glorious pussy."

"Please Anthony, just do it. Please."

He clucks his tongue, but nothing else happens. The waiting is unbearable.

"Change of plans," he says as he joins me on the bed. He sits up in the center and pulls me up. Then he lies back and utters the sweetest phrase I've ever heard. "Come on up here and ride my face."

I picture myself writhing against him, and the ache in my core intensifies. Dutifully, I crawl up his body and straddle him as requested. Groaning at the view, he places his big hands on my backside and adjusts me just so. It begins with a soft kiss, as if he's thanking me for this honor. That tiny connection causes me to tense, my arms and legs locking in anticipation of what's to come. Then he inhales, burying his face between my thighs, his five o'clock shadow grazing them and creating a delicious friction that makes me sway above him.

"Anthony, please, I need your mouth on me."

In answer, he rubs his lips over my outer folds. I jerk forward, grasping the headboard to keep myself from falling over.

"More," I plead.

"Open yourself up to me," he says. "Show me exactly where you need it."

I drop my arms and slide my hands between my legs, gently separating my folds so my clit is front and center. In doing so, my limbs graze my stiff nipples, and I whimper at the sensation my own touch elicits.

Beneath me, Anthony moans. "I might stay here forever."

"I wouldn't stop you," I manage to say between heavy breaths.

He responds by drawing my clit into his mouth, rolling his tongue over it, and applying the perfect amount of pressure to ignite my senses but not overwhelm them.

"How's that?" he asks.

"Perfect. Keep doing that. For the rest of my days."

I shift above him, hovering over his lips so he can latch on where I need him most, and he doesn't disappoint. With a low growl rumbling in his throat, he kneads my ass and pulls me to his face. Blessedly, he laps at me in a torturous rhythm that alternates between steady flicks at my clit and long, strong licks against the skin surrounding it. My body throbs in response to the onslaught, the sensitive flesh between my legs tingling with each swipe of his tongue. "Yes, Anthony. That. Is. It. I'm so gone. Please . . . just don't stop."

I'm in a daze, quivering from the pleasure he's wringing from me, until I can no longer hold myself open and reach for the headboard again. My breath hitches. Goose bumps dot my sweat-soaked skin. And the familiar throbbing builds and builds and builds, the torment of being *so close* making me cry out. "Baby, I need you inside me."

Blinking to orient myself in the dimly lit room, I climb off him and reach for a condom, one of many I placed on my nightstand before he arrived. He shakes his head as though to clear it and stretches his arms above him, his cock hard as granite.

Opening the packet as I straddle him, I settle myself on his upper thighs and raise the condom in the air. "May I?"

"Yes, you most definitely may," he says, his dark eyes hazy with desire.

I place the condom on and guide him inside me, so slowly it's torture to me, and *must* be torture to him, too. I feel *everything*. The head as it stretches me. The veins along his length as he pushes into my core. The soft hair at the base of his dick.

"Fuck," he says, his voice straining. "Eva, honey, your greedy pussy is so . . . fucking tight . . . around my cock. But I need to kiss you, too. Give me those lips."

I place my hands on his chest, massaging the sprinkle of curls there, and then I lean over, pressing my breasts against him. Our eyes meet for several beats before he closes his and devours my mouth, invading it with firm strokes of his talented tongue, while I remain fully seated on his dick.

After we come up for air, I brace my hands on the side of his head and slowly grind against him. All I want to do is stay here, in this moment, with him inside me.

He chants my name like an invocation. "Eva . . . Eva . . . yes . . . Eva . . . yes, yes, yes. You feel it, yeah?"

I squeeze my eyes shut, wanting to savor his fullness. "Yes, Anthony, I feel it."

We revel in that sweet and slow pace for several minutes, the sounds of slick skin and panting the only soundtrack in the room. When I can't bear it any longer, I beg for him to make me come, my voice matching the neediness powering through me. He lifts his torso slightly, digging his hands into the small of my back. Demonstrating a level of strength I can't fathom, he helps me ride his cock, pounding into me in quick bursts.

My voice is a decibel away from an outright scream as he fucks me furiously. Needing him closer, I crush his face to my chest. He seals my fate by closing his mouth over my nipple and sucking it hard. I detonate, seeing reds and yellows behind my eyes and trembling uncontrollably.

"Eva, I'm going to come, too," he shouts.

I feel him throb inside me, and then a gush of warmth fills my core as he pours himself into the condom.

It takes us several minutes to return to Earth. When we do, Anthony slips out from under me, gently turning me on my back, and climbs out of bed. Pointing behind him, he asks, "Bathroom?"

Basking in my drowsiness, all I can do is nod.

He disappears and not long after returns with a washcloth. "Can I clean you up?"

Again, I nod, opening my legs. He sits beside me and wipes between my legs, his finger teasing me as he makes several passes.

"We're closed," I say. "Come back another time."

He grins at my quip and takes the hint. After disposing of the washcloth, he lies down next to me and pulls me into his arms. I change positions, resting my head on his chest and draping a leg over his.

"Eva, that was like all the best days in my life melded into one."

The sweetness of his words melts me. Boneless and wanting to convey how much he means to me, I kiss his jaw and say, "Same."

"Can I stay the night?" he asks as he caresses my cheek.

"It wouldn't be the best days of my life melded into one if you left."

WEARING A BROAD smile, Anthony places a hand on my table and leans forward. "You called him *what*?"

"Cookie Monster Calvin," I say, trying to keep a straight face.

We're sitting at my dining room table the next morning, enjoying coffee and a fruit plate before he heads home. Moments ago, I inadvertently mentioned an ex-boyfriend by his nickname.

Anthony stares at me, his expression incredulous. "Which means . . . ?"

I lift my mug to my lips so I can hide my face behind it. This is so embarrassing. "Well, you know how the Cookie Monster attacks a cookie. That's how he attacked my vagina. Om nom nom. Me eat pussy!"

He throws his head back and holds his stomach, laughing so hard tears well up in his eyes. "Crumbs flying, too?"

I throw a napkin at him. "Don't mock my poor sexual experiences."

"Me?" he says, placing a hand on his chest. "You're the one who called him Cookie Monster."

"It was apt," I say.

He spears a slice of melon and dangles it near his mouth. "What nickname would you give me?"

I rise from the chair. "No nicknames for you."

He stands as well. "You're no fun."

I tug him toward me and gently bite his arm, breathing in the crisp sea scent he favors on training days. "On the contrary, I'm so much fun, you're still here."

"Can't argue with that, but now I need to go."

Pouting, I place a finger under my eye and draw it down to the apple of my cheek. "Sad face." Then I walk him to the door and hug him at the threshold, not caring that my lipstick is smudged or that my hair is showing the negative effects of skipping my nightly twist-out routine. And we don't say anything. For once, we just let the moment stand, our arms tightly wrapped around each other. Eventually, we separate, and I already miss his touch.

Jacket in hand, he presses a kiss to my forehead. "Okay, I've got to go."

"Call me later?" I ask.

"I'll everything you later. Don't know how I'll do anything else."

He excels at melting my cynical heart. It's his superpower. And I don't mean to be rude, but I wish I could close the door right now, so I can end our time together on this precise and perfect note.

But my wishes aren't granted. Someone's force-ful steps interrupt the mood. Looking past Anthony, I watch as a figure appears on the second-floor landing... a figure that looks suspiciously—and horrifyingly—like my father.

Damn, damn, damn.

Chapter Twenty-Seven

Surprise visits from parental figures are the
worst. No person should experience more than
one in a lifetime.

Eva

"DAD, WHAT ARE you doing here?"

My father swings his gaze between Anthony and
me, no doubt noticing my disheveled appearance
and Anthony's bloodshot eyes. I'm almost thirty years
old, dammit. I refuse to cower under his judgmental
inspection. Okay, no, that's not entirely true. This is
awful. I kind of wished my father never realized I had
sex. Ever.

He shifts to face me, giving Anthony his back. "I received a last-minute invite to speak at a teaching confer-
ence here, something you'd know if you ever returned
my calls. I've been trying to reach you for a week. It isn't
like you to avoid me. And since I was in the area, I decided I'd check on you."

Anthony clears his throat. "I'm going to leave you two to catch up."

I shake my head, clearing myself of the fog. "Sorry, Anthony, I'm a little out of it. Meet my father, Charles Montgomery. Dad, meet Anthony."

"Good to meet you, sir," Anthony says.

"Likewise," my father replies, his expression neutral.

This is *not* how I expected their first meeting to go. Despite the problems between my father and me, I want him to like Anthony. Our relationship is brand new, sure, but who knows where we'll be in a year's time? They're not going to be bosom buddies today, though, or anytime soon for that matter, not after that introduction.

I open the door wider and motion for my father to enter. "Come in, Dad. I'll be inside in a minute."

My father slips past me and I shut the door.

"Well, that was awkward," I tell Anthony, cringing.

He grimaces and mouths, "Yikes."

"Whatever. I can't take anything back now. The man could have texted me instead of leaving vague voicemail messages. And then he shows up unannounced. Who does that?"

Anthony pulls me to him. "Your father does that. Good-looking guy, I must say. I can see where you get it from."

"You haven't met my mother."

He peers at me, his expression turning uncharacteristically serious, before he presses his lips against mine.

When he straightens, he says, "Yet. I haven't met her yet."

There goes that little flutter in my belly again. "Fair enough."

With a wistful smile, he traces the back of his index finger against my cheek. "Talk to your father. We'll see each other soon."

I stamp my foot like a two-year-old. "I don't want to. Don't make me."

He spins me around and gives me a gentle push toward the door. "You got this."

Head and shoulders down, I trudge back inside. My father's studiously inspecting the shelves of my bookcase, no doubt wondering why my favorite romances and mysteries overshadow the classics.

"A friend of yours?" he asks without turning in my direction.

"Yes," is all I want to say about Anthony.

But he's not done. "And you know him how?"

"He's Tori's cousin. I met him at her wedding."

"Didn't know he existed."

What he means is, he wasn't aware that I was dating anyone.

"Well, he exists. And he's really great. Maybe one day we could all go out to dinner and you could get to know him?"

My father nods. "Maybe."

"I'm going to change. I'll be back in a sec. Fresh-squeezed lemonade's in the fridge."

When I return, now in a T-shirt and a pair of yoga pants, my father's sitting on the couch drinking a glass of lemonade as though he's lazing the day away on my grandmother's porch in Atlanta.

Anthony's right: He's a handsome man. Distinguished-looking. The tortoiseshell glasses and his salt-and-pepper hair make it easy to picture him in front of a class of college students. It's a wonder he's not wearing his trademark sweater vest.

I join him on the couch. "So, as you can see, I'm alive and well."

He places his glass on the coffee table and leans forward. "Your mother tells me you're switching gears and becoming a stunt performer, but I told her that couldn't be right. Sounded too nonsensical even for you."

Too nonsensical even for me. Nice. We could have had this conversation over the phone, in which case I'd be pretending we had a bad connection. Maybe that's why he showed up. He knew I wouldn't be able to escape him if he was here in person. "Okay, so Mom isn't exactly right."

"Ah. Figures."

"I'm not switching gears. I'm expanding my skill set. If you know the right people, stunt work can be a lucrative business. Anthony says—"

He furrows his brows. "Anthony? What does he have to do with any of this?"

"He's a stunt performer. Sometimes a coordinator, too. Anyway, I thought you'd be impressed that I'm not putting all of my eggs in one basket." All he does is stare at me. Oof. "I'm still teaching classes," I continue. "They're going great, by the way. Thanks for asking."

He rolls his eyes. "I'm glad I came. Eva, can't you see what's going on here? You're so confused about your life that you're grasping at straws, trying anything to make an unworkable solution work for you. It won't, sweetie. Just come home."

He's wrong. And his insistence that he's right only reinforces my resolve to prove how wrong he is. Just because it doesn't align with his vision for my future doesn't mean it's aimless. I know what I'm doing. When he sees the results, he'll be forced to agree. "Dad, I really need you to just trust me on this, okay? If it matters, the more you speak, the more I'll dig in my heels. I need space to do what I choose to do."

"I'm trying to give you guidance."

"Then guide me. But don't expect me to follow you blindly."

He's poised to respond, his lips parted to challenge me. But then he says nothing. Now I can confidently say miracles do happen.

"Where are you staying?" I ask, hoping to steer the conversation to less sensitive topics.

"I'm at the Queen Mary in Long Beach. Figured I'd enjoy a mini-vacation before the semester gets into full swing."

Now there's a surprise. The history professor tries to

soak in history by staying on a historic ship that's been converted to a hotel. No wonder he can't understand anything that isn't squarely inside the box.

"And you're staying for . . . ?"

He swallows a laugh. "I'm leaving tomorrow. Want to join me for dinner tonight?"

Ah, yes, thank God for excuses. "Sorry, I can't. My training class is an all afternoon and evening affair."

His face falls, and my mood falls with it. He's not a bad man, just an opinionated one. Unfortunately, his most stubborn opinions tend to relate to me. "Have you eaten? I had coffee and fruit, but I could go for a real meal. We could grab brunch somewhere in the neighborhood."

"That sounds nice," he says, eyeing my outfit. "Somewhere casual, I suppose."

"Yes, Dad, somewhere casual. Let me throw a headband on."

A few minutes later, I return with keys and wallet in hand. "Ready?"

He rises from the couch. "Ready." The he looks around the room, nodding as though he's sufficiently impressed with the apartment. "Your place. I like it. But if I could give you one piece of advice?"

It's nice that he asked at least. "Sure, go ahead."

"Don't buy too much stuff just yet. Especially given that you don't have unlimited resources. You wouldn't want to worry about getting all this back to Philly if you decided not to stay."

Damn. I'm going to need a spell to cast the demon out of his body. Satan did not come to play today.

WHEN I RETURN from brunch, two familiar figures hover near the entrance to my apartment building. I groan at yet another unexpected visit on what once had been a Sunday filled with promise. "Well, if it isn't Thelma and Louise lurking in the neighborhood."

Tori and Ashley spin around, both crossing their arms over their chests like I have some explaining to do.

"Why aren't you answering my texts?" Tori asks.

"She was worried about you," Ashley adds. "I wasn't. You're a grown woman, after all. But I did pretend to be worried so I wouldn't have to explain why she was overreacting. Sometimes I'm lazy like that."

Tori elbows her. "Are you listening to yourself?"

Ashley shakes her head as though what she's going to say is regrettable. "Never do, babe. Never do. I kind of just throw everything out there and hope for the best."

"Excuse me," I say, bumping my way between them so I can use my key fob to open the door. Once unlocked, I prop myself against it to let them pass. "Are you coming?"

"Of course," Tori says.

As we walk across the courtyard, Tori peppers me with questions. "What were you doing last night? I texted you like ten times. Called you twice, too. Did you have your phone on silent? Or were you ignoring me?"

I precede them up the stairs. "The phone was the

last thing on my mind last night. And then my father showed up out of nowhere this morning. Sorry about not responding, but I was busy."

"*Getting busy*, perhaps?" Ashley asks, her eyes so-not-innocent wide.

Before I reach the last step, I turn around and give her a sly smile. "Yes, if you must know."

Tori slaps me on the back. "What? With who?"

"You don't want to know," I say.

Tori narrows her eyes. "Yes, I *do* want to know."

I pretend to examine my nails, a bored expression on my face. "I'll give you a minute to figure it out."

"Gabe?" Ashley asks. "I got the sense that he was really into you."

"Definitely not. I haven't seen Gabe since the dinner party."

I open the door for them, and they waltz inside.

Ashley heads straight for the tiny pantry next to the fridge. "Anything sweet?"

"Chocolate chunk cookies," I tell her as I pick up the pillows that were tossed around during last night's festivities.

"Yes!" she says.

I love this. I'm in a new city, and it finally feels like I'm putting down roots, interacting with my people. LA's been good to me so far. I hope that continues to be true.

When I fall back on the couch, I find Tori staring at me, her mind whirring like an engine in overdrive. She already knows Anthony and I hooked up at her wedding, but I wonder if she'll react differently to the news that we're dating. This isn't news I'll be able to keep from her, nor do I want to.

Her eyes widen and her mouth drops. "Anthony?"

The question comes out as a shriek.

Ashley straightens, a cookie that's going to crumble any minute now in her hand. "Say what now?"

"Yes, Anthony," I confirm. "Is that a problem?"

Tori furrows her brows and shakes her head. "It's not a problem. It's a surprise. Especially given our last conversation about this." Then she collapses on the couch and laughs uncontrollably.

I did this to Anthony once, when he told me about Brett and Damian. His response is appropriate here, too. "Are you done?"

"No," she says, continuing to laugh. "Didn't you say he was player? A master manipulator? Trying to control women with his 'I don't date' card?"

A sudden and pressing need to fluff the sofa pillows overtakes me, and I can't look at anything else while I do it. "Turns out he's not like that at all."

"So you were wrong?" she asks.

I don't answer her question. Let her work for that I-told-you-so.

Tori places her index finger under my chin and forces me to look at her, a wicked grin in place. "Say it. You were wrong."

I jerk my head away, sniff, and respond in a haughty

voice, "I was misinformed. And after the morning I've had with my father, it feels nice to know Anthony's a straight shooter. He just wants to be with me, no games and no bullshit. It's refreshing."

"Enjoy it, then," Tori says with a nod. "I'm happy for you."

Ashley flops onto the couch, wedging herself between Tori and me. "I'm rooting for you two. Cumgrats!"

My ears must be clogged. "Did you just say 'cumgrats'?"

She nods, chewing on her third cookie.

I look over to Tori. "Get your sister-in-law."

Tori shakes her head. "Nope, she's hopeless."

For a moment, we're all exchanging glances, and then we're cackling. Everything feels right. My classes at Every Body are going well, I'm expanding my friendship circle, and I'm dating a phenomenal guy, who I get to see—I glance at my watch—very soon.

I rise from the sofa, stretching my arms above my head. "Well, as much as I enjoy spending time with you, ladies, I need to get ready for stunt training."

Ashley sits up. "Oh, that reminds me. I was telling Julian about the training. He said he'd love to speak with you someday about your career goals." She leans over and touches my shoulder with hers. "He knows everyone in Hollywood, and he focuses on representing actors of color, so he'd be a good person to have in your corner."

Who wouldn't want Julian in their corner? The

man's roster is impressive. It's as though the universe is telling me I'm finally making the right decisions. "I'll definitely follow up with him. Thanks, Ash."

"How's the training going, by the way?" Tori asks.

"Interesting. Challenging. A little exhausting. It's fine."

"Just fine?" she asks, studying me closely.

"It's fine. What else do you want me to say? It's going well."

"I'm not asking you to say anything in particular. I was just wondering how your plan to expand your career is going." She shrugs. "I guess it's too early to tell. Never mind."

There's no time to press her on what she isn't telling me. But I'd be willing to bet a year's worth of orgasms it's not anything I want to hear anyway.

Chapter Twenty-Eight

Anthony

I'M WHISTLING AS I enter the house. Good sex will do that to you. No, not just good sex. Incredible, mind-numbing, spine-tingling, ugly-face-while-you-orgasm sex. With a woman I can't stop thinking about. In the past, I'd run from thoughts about Eva; today, I'm telling them, *Come at me, bro.*

Smiling to myself, I round the wall separating the front hall from the living area to find my father sitting at the dining table staring into his cup of *café con leche*. He looks so fucking alone over there. Makes me wish I could fill the house with people, surround him with friends and relatives he could cook for and laugh with. Since he missed Tori and Carter's wedding, maybe I can suggest we host a dinner to celebrate the newlyweds.

"Hey, Papi. Doing okay?"

He looks up at me and smiles. "Hey, *mijo.* I'm doing just fine." His gaze travels from the top of my head to my toes, inspecting me for signs of what kept me out all evening. "Had a good night?"

"A great night," I say as I open the fridge and look for a drink. It's an understatement, of course, but I'm not going to give him a rundown of my evening. No, those memories are all mine.

"With Eva?" he asks.

"Yeah."

He nods knowingly, his mouth curving into a sneaky grin. "I could tell there was something between you two. But I thought you'd fight it."

I *did* fight it. Underestimated my opponent, too; Eva knew just what to do to leave me defenseless and knock me on my ass. "I tried, Papi, but you met Eva. It was a losing battle from the start."

He stirs his coffee and peers at me. "It's serious?"

"Not sure how she'd answer that question, but it's serious for me. What I feel for her, I mean."

"Good," he says, announcing it like a verdict. "I like her."

That means a lot. I want my father and Eva to get along. I can easily picture her dragging him to Grand Central Market, where'd he'd take her to the Latin grocery and share the secret spices he uses in his recipes. And Eva's probably the only person who could convince my father to visit a tourist location. I should drop a hint to make that happen.

I pull out the orange juice. "I'm glad to hear that, Pop. Eva likes you, too."

"Don't drink it from the carton," he says, still watching me.

I take the carton of orange juice to the cupboard, pull out a glass, and pour. "What about you? Did you go out?"

He shakes his head. "We said we were going to watch the Angel Benitez fight on pay-per-view, remember? When you didn't come home, I just decided to watch it alone."

Fuck. In my excitement to spend time with Eva, I forgot about my plans with Papi. He'd never make me feel bad about it, and he doesn't need to. I feel terrible about it all on my own. "Ah, man, *discúlpeme*. It slipped my mind." I take the chair across from him, waffling between wanting to beg for his forgiveness and playing it off like it's no big deal. I go with the latter. "So, who won?"

"Benitez, of course." He jabs in the air, a cheesy grin on his face. "That man's the real deal."

"I'm sorry I missed it."

"Don't be," he says, his expression sobering. "I'm glad you're going out and spending time with someone special. For a long time, I wondered if you ever would. I don't want you to end up like me, you know. Good to see you're not going down that path."

The offhand comment makes my gut twist. *End up like me.* There's the proof that my father isn't happy. But if I'm being honest with myself, I didn't need it; I've always suspected he wasn't happy. How could he be? He thought my mother was the love of his life, and he's never recovered from the reality that he was wrong.

And it's not that he can't move on, he just doesn't want to. But I'd be a shitty son to tell him how to live his life, especially considering that until recently my coping techniques haven't been healthy, either. What we both need is some father-son time. "Hey, how about we watch Sunday Night Baseball?" I waggle my eyebrows at him. "The Yankees are playing."

He rises from the table and rinses his cup in the sink. "Sounds good. I'll make the snacks." Predictably, the prospect of cooking lightens his mood.

"And I'll bring the beer," I say.

This is an important reminder. Although Eva takes up a lot of real estate in my brain, I can't toss my father aside like he's yesterday's listing. He deserves better.

KURT RUSHES INTO the office, drops onto his desk chair, and furiously thumbs through the papers on his desk.

"Where's the fire?" I ask.

"Got an emergency request from Newhart. One of the stunt performers called in sick, and they're all ready to go on an underwater helicopter scene. He's looking for someone ASAP. A woman, if you can believe it. She's trapped and needs to be rescued. How rare is that?"

"Who's the coordinator?"

"Gary."

I press my lips together to avoid saying too much. Gary Simms is an asshole. He does a sloppy job on set and relies on his assistants to clean up his messes. For some unknown reason, Kurt likes the guy. Probably because when Gary's overwhelmed, he asks Kurt to jump in and help on set, claiming he needs extra hands. But all Gary needs is a new brain.

Kurt inspects my face, no doubt noticing the flare of annoyance I can't contain. "I know what you're thinking, Anthony, but you know how this works. We help him, he helps us. Gary mentioned he could also use some people for a few combat scenes. You could join me."

"When's the shooting?"

"Next couple of days. In Irvine. Retakes on Wednesday if needed. You up for it?"

Up for it? It isn't even a question. If there's a job, I'm not passing it up. Every job is extra money in my pocket and another credit on my resume. "Whatever you need, man."

Kurt nods distractedly. A minute later, he sighs and throws the papers in the air. "What am I fucking around with this for?" After scrubbing a hand down his face, he jerks his computer keyboard closer to him and starts typing. "Brenda Little might be a possibility. I'll check with her." He picks up the office phone and punches in a bunch of numbers.

I've never performed an underwater stunt, but I've studied them and watched one performed live. They're terrifying. Granted, a diving team is on hand to release you from your constraints if the stunt goes wrong, but time is of the essence when you're submerged in water, and if the diving team is off even by a second or two, the lack of air combined with the buildup of carbon dioxide in a person's body can lead to disorientation, spasms, and worse. Performing the stunt upside down increases the danger index tenfold because the person is disoriented to begin with.

Kurt covers the phone's mouthpiece and whispers, "You think either of the trainees would be able to do it? Perfect opportunity to Taft-Hartley one of them."

True. If he brings one of them in for this stunt, the person would be able to avoid the red tape required to get into the union. But Megan's out of the question. "Just the other day, Megan said she's afraid of small spaces. Add in her fear of heights and I'm not sure why she's here. What do *you* think?"

"No, no, you're right. That wouldn't work. What about Eva?"

"I don't think—"

"Brenda? Hey, it's Kurt Magnus. Calling about a potential job."

I hope Brenda's available because even the idea of the alternative—getting Eva to do it—makes my heart race and my skin go clammy. Eva's not out of the question, but I want her to be. This is a complicated stunt. Plus, the director's rushing to get it done while he has access to the simulation site. And Gary's at the helm. Not the best circumstances for her first stunt. She'd likely jump at the chance to do it—and Kurt would, too, if he knew about her swimming experience—but my gut tells me it's too risky. And if something happened to her . . . No, I'm not going there. She needs more experience. Period.

Kurt hangs up and shakes his head. "She's out of town and can't get here in time."

"When's the shoot?"

"Tomorrow."

I should tell him about Eva, but an invisible hand is covering my mouth and preventing me from sharing what I know. "It's always nice to get a job we weren't expecting, but if it's not practical or safe to do it, we should just accept that. Why don't you call up Spriggs? His roster is huge."

Kurt sighs. "Don't remind me. Would have been nice to use one of our own, though. But you make a good point, and I'm impressed with your judgment on this. Safety should be our number one concern, right?"

I don't meet his gaze when I respond. "Right." My voice cracks, undermining the confidence I was going for. I try to ignore the thickness in my throat, but it's interfering with my ability to take regular breaths. Scrambling to my feet, I leave the office in search of something to drink. Kurt will get over this missed opportunity. In fact, I'm confident that by this time next week, he won't even remember it.

Chapter Twenty-Nine

Don't assume a person who eats and runs is
rude. Sometimes, they're being very polite,
indeed.

Eva

I AM GOING to rip this man to shreds—in bed.

Oh, maybe I'm being a tad overzealous. It's just that
his demeanor in class today was exactly what I'd hoped
for. He didn't treat me differently. Didn't make a single
suggestive comment. Just treated me like a colleague. It's
a low bar, yes, but after spending all night in his arms, I'll
confess that I entertained my own X-rated fantasies here
and there, so I didn't know what to expect from him.

Apparently, I'm the one who needs to curb her trashy
thoughts. Which is why I turn away as he approaches.
If I watch him stride toward me, on the same powerful
legs that I grasped as I guided him into my mouth last
night, I'll betray my thoughts and whimper for good
measure.

He stops at an appropriate distance for a conversation between an instructor and his trainee. "Eva, would you like a ride home?"

I push the hair away from my face. "Yeah, that would be great."

"I'll meet you out front in five."

"Okay."

My voice, in all its low and breathy glory, broadcasts my desire for him. Surely, he notices, because he stares at me. Longer than he should. And it's the first time this evening that he's acted in a way that hints at something more between us. The subtlety of him looking at me a few seconds too long, the smallness of it, has more impact on me than any overt act could.

He shakes his head. "Right. I'm going now."

Five minutes later, we're headed north on Interstate 110.

"How'd it go with your father?" he asks.

It's not a question I expected him to ask. It doesn't address the most urgent matter between us. Doesn't satisfy my pressing need to dig my fingers into his scalp and pull him close. But if he wants to talk about my father as if the last five hours weren't torture, I'll play along. "He still thinks I'm wasting my time here. I tried to argue otherwise, but he's decided that he's right and I'm wrong."

"But you know better than to believe him, right?"

"Right. I'm just so frustrated with the situation. He was *not* impressed with the news that I'm training for stunt work. 'Nonsensical' is how he described it." That hurts, of course, but I'm not going to let him dissuade me. "He's my father, so I care about his opinion. Still, I'm not giving up."

"Glad to hear it. Because you're talented. Physically strong. Flexible. Skilled. Daring without being reckless. With more training, you'll be one to watch. It doesn't hurt that we're seeing several action movies featuring black women being produced each year."

I cross my hands over my chest. "'Wakanda forever.'"

A bubble of laughter escapes him, and he shakes his head. "What you need are sequels forever. *When more badass black women get work, your chances of landing a job rise, too.* There are no guarantees, though. And you need to keep in mind that as a newcomer, you're coming into it at a disadvantage. Still, you have the same background as many of the women who were cast as doubles for the Dora Milaje in *Black Panther*. Dance, martial arts, gymnastics."

I'm not sure I can adequately describe how much I appreciate his support. He's sharing what he knows about the industry without sugarcoating it, while still encouraging me to meet the challenges I'll undoubtedly face. He has my back, and I'm grateful for that.

"Yeah, when I was doing my research, I read about a woman who was both a main Dora Milaje and the stunt double for Okoye. She said she decided to become a stunt performer after watching a movie with poor acting. She was a college track star, was even on the US bobsled team, had tae kwon do training, too. It felt like I could have been reading my story. Except swimming for me, and yeah, obviously no bobsledding." It's so comfortable being with him like this. I'm tempted to kick off my sneakers and roll off my socks, turn my body toward him and just talk until we can't talk anymore. "What's that face for?"

His eyes are still focused on the road, but he's holding himself in check, thinking about something funny. "Honestly? I'm imagining you bobsledding, and in my head it's hilarious because you're screaming curse words the entire run."

I reach over and pinch his arm. It's our thing.

He flinches, letting out a weak "ow," but he doesn't take his hands off the steering wheel to retaliate. "Questionable bobsledding aside, no one's going to argue that you have the wrong background. It's in line with other stunt performers. Now you just need more training and experience. That takes time."

"Right. I get it. Luckily for me, I'm patient. And obviously I'm not doing this as my main source of income. I know the industry's unpredictable. You've drilled that fact into my head. But it feels like I'm taking steps toward a multidimensional career. One that isn't dictated by my father's opinions." I rest my hand on his thigh. "Thanks for being my sounding board." Yawning, I look out the window to enjoy the city lights. "Shoot. You got off at the wrong exit."

He stares straight ahead when he answers. "No, I

didn't. I'm trying not to scandalize you in your own neighborhood."

Oh, that's intriguing. Also, I see nothing wrong with being scandalized. "What are you up to?"

"I need to kiss you. Badly."

Glad to know he's finally catching up. "I was wondering when you were going to fess up to that. But we could kiss in my apartment, you know. No need for extraordinary measures."

"Unfortunately, we can't. I promised my father we'd watch the baseball game tonight. We need some father-son time."

Damn. Cue the emotion. Is this man for real? He's making his father his priority, and it only makes him more appealing to me. "There's nothing unfortunate about it. That's sweet."

He peers through the window shield, focused on the task of finding a place to stop. "If you say so. What's not sweet is the way I want to splay you across the hood of this truck and bury my face between your legs until you scream to the heavens." He finally turns to meet my gaze. "Would you like that?"

Oh, I see, we're going from zero to sixty tonight. The heat in his eyes lights a fire inside me. God, the thought of him going down on me as the night air cools my skin and I tug on his hair. It's too much. And probably not wise. I'm squirming in my seat trying to be a responsible person. "I'd really love that, but I also don't want to get arrested, so a kiss is our next-best option."

"Is it?" he asks. "What if you took off your panties, pressed your back against the door, and opened your legs for me?"

I wrinkle my nose. "I need a shower. And I have pants on. And someone could see us."

He pulls over on a service road by the reservoir and cuts the engine. "All valid reasons not to do it. But I fucking love your sweat. The pants?" He shrugs. "Yeah, I got nothing." He raises a finger as though he's just remembered something. "Oh, and I'll be on set in Irvine the early part of this week, so the next time we can see each other will be—"

I'm shoving my pants down before he finishes his sentence.

"Keep the panties on. I'll work around them. Plausible deniability."

With my pants discarded on the floorboard, I turn to the side and pull him in for a kiss. It's a hot and desperate joining of our mouths that leaves us both panting. Around us, the scent of our arousal—likely more of mine than his—mingles with the salty sweat on our skin. I breathe all of it in, wanting to remember every detail of this moment so I can relive it in my head for years to come. This is us. Daring. Spontaneous. Just a little reckless.

"Anthony, please," I say as I raise my left leg against the window that separates the cab from the truck bed. "We need to hurry."

He places his right knee on the seat cushion. His left leg is bent at an awkward angle so his foot can touch the floor, but he doesn't seem to care; if he can handle it, far be it from me to interfere. I push my panties aside, giving him the access he needs. "I'm shaking just thinking about your lips here."

He doesn't say anything. Tunnel vision prevents him from being deterred from his mission. With a low growl, he grabs my ass and lifts my bottom to bring my pussy closer to his mouth. And then he proceeds to tongue my clit with such precision and enthusiasm that I'm repeatedly banging my hand against the seat back as if I'm recreating the steamy window scene in *Titanic*. "Oh God."

The flicks across my nub slow, until he draws it into his mouth and sucks on it gently, sliding two fingers inside me. My wetness stops him. "Fuck. You're drenched and I love it." As proof, he inserts his index finger in his mouth and sucks it clean. "Delicious. I will never get tired of this taste."

"Oh, God, I want to come so badly. Please Anthony, make me come." I can't imagine what I look like, but I know how I feel. I'm tight and achy everywhere, and my clit is pulsing like it has its own heartbeat.

He returns his mouth to my pussy and laps at it relentlessly. Over and over, and over again. I massage his scalp as he sucks on my nub, and soon I'm circling my hips against his mouth, grinding myself against his face. The familiar tingle starts in my belly and descends to my clit, where it gathers in the center before it fans out in pleasure-soaked waves, my body shaking uncontrollably. "I'm coming, Anthony. Oh God, I'm coming. Yes . . . yes . . . yes . . . yes . . . *yes.*"

He doesn't stop licking, nor does he stop pumping his fingers inside me. And at this point, all I can do is squeeze my eyes shut and let the sensation run through me. Eventually, I manage to raise my lids and regain my breath as he strokes the inside of my thighs with his nose and mouth.

"See there?" he asks, rising from between my legs. "Better than just a kiss, wouldn't you say?"

"I will be unable to form coherent sentences for the remainder of the evening. Ask questions at your own risk."

He looks at his watch as he wipes a finger across his bottom lip. "I hate to eat and run, but I need to get home. I promised my father I'd bring the beer."

I'm struggling to get my pants back on and doing my best impression of a mess personified. I imagine this is what it would feel like to be a ball of cotton—fuzzy and soft and so delicate someone could pull you apart with little effort. My gaze falls to his crotch. He's sporting serious evidence of his own arousal. "What about you?"

"I got as much pleasure from that as you did." He leans over and kisses me, gently nipping at my bottom lip as our mouths separate. "Plus, I'm a big proponent of delayed gratification."

"Then expect to be very gratified the next time we meet."

He throws his head back and squeezes his eyes shut.

"Give me a minute. I'm picturing it." A few seconds later, he sits up, clears his throat, and starts the engine. "Seat belt."

I fasten my seat belt, and he shifts the car into Drive.

The memory of this evening will carry me through until we see each other again. I. Cannot. Wait.

TUESDAY AFTERNOON, ANTHONY sends me the fourth text he's sent since I saw him on Sunday. This one, unlike the others—all of which simply stated some variation of "I miss you"—asks a favor.

Him: They want me to do a few retakes of a combat scene Wednesday. Worried I might be late for class. Any chance you could cover for me? Already cleared it with Tori.

Me: What would I do?

Him: Anything self-defense related. Maybe lighten up the mood? Other than that one class with you, it's always serious.

Me: Sure, I'll come up with something.

Him: Thanks.

After Advanced Zumba, I remain in the studio, working on a routine for Anthony's self-defense class. As I noodle through an effective way to teach defensive techniques, I practice tae kwon do forms. Well, the ones I can still remember. In the stance for Form 2, it occurs to me that I enjoyed the class as a teen and in my early twenties because the forms were like dance moves. The repetitive sequence of steps made it easier to remember them, too. Two hours later, I've almost perfected a routine that blends self-defense techniques and cardio kickboxing into a powerhouse workout. I'm so excited that I text Anthony about it.

> **Me:** Came up with a great way to blend self-defense, kickboxing and dance. I'm on fire thinking about teaching your class tomorrow! We'll see if it works. Fingers crossed for me, okay?
>
> **Him:** It'll be great, no doubt. Let me know how it goes.
>
> **Me:** Will do.

The next day, I arrive at Every Body early and practice the steps until I'm comfortable with them. An hour later, Tori enters the studio while I'm in the middle of a sequence and waits by the door, watching and patiently waiting for me to finish.

When I'm done, she says, "Hey, you're here early. Getting prepped for Anthony's class?"

"Yeah, I'm trying something different . . . if that's okay."

She nods, drawing her brows together as though the question wasn't necessary. "I'm all for innovation and experimentation. What I just saw definitely qualifies."

I grab a towel and wipe my face. "Did you need to see me about something?"

She straightens. "Yes. I was just thinking that it would be nice if we could hang out this weekend. Maybe order takeout and binge-watch the first season of *One Day at a Time*. I could even stay over and bring my jammies with me."

How could I turn down a perfect date with my best friend? It's impossible. "If I could offer one friendly amendment?"

She rolls her eyes at me. "Yes. What?"

"We add *Nailed It* to the mix."

Tori grabs my hands and shimmies in excitement. "I *love* that show. Yes, amendment accepted. I'll be over by eight, okay? And I'll bring wine."

"Perfect."

"Good luck today. I hope they enjoy it." She waves as she walks out the door. A few seconds later, she sticks her head back in. "You know what's been a constant since you moved here?"

"What?" I ask.

"You're always ecstatic to be here. You know how

we're always talking about being each other's person? Well, I think Every Body is your place. Just a thought." She slips away before I can respond.

She may be right, but I'm still left wondering: Is that enough?

Chapter Thirty

Anthony

Me: How was class?

Eva: Fantastic! They loved it. One woman said it was like a millennial version of capoeira. Combat hidden in dancing. Told her not to get ahead of herself. 😊

Me: I'm not surprised they loved it. See you soon.

UNFORTUNATELY, "SOON" IS during stunt class, so there's not much more I can do than enjoy being in her presence again. I bet she'd freak out if she knew how much I missed her. How much I've thought about her while we were apart. Almost three days. A lifetime in Anthony-being-whipped-by-Eva years.

I hold up an article of clothing so everyone can see it. "This is a jerk vest."

Eva laughs. "Jerks have their own line of clothing now?"

Everyone joins in her laughter. As usual, I hold up a hand to quiet them down. I'll make her pay for that interruption later. Given the wink she gives me when no one's watching, I can safely say she's looking forward to my plans for retribution.

"We're introducing you to the ratchet today. The device uses piston and cable action to propel you through the air. It's the thing that makes a fight scene come to life. No human can punch someone so hard that they're thrown back fifteen feet, but with the ratchet system and the magic of movie editing, anything's possible. It enhances our ability to create truly memorable stunt work, but as with anything else, the more variables you introduce into stunt work, the more dangerous the stunt. So let's talk about safety. In general and in the context of any kind of stunt that uses a harness."

Before I begin, Kurt slaps me on the back. "I'll take the safety talk today."

I nod and lean against the nearest wall. He does a better job at it anyway. The last boot camp, the trainees complained my style was too graphic. I don't see what's so offensive about seeing precisely how a bone breaks if you're not too careful. It's useful information.

Kurt grabs a folding chair and swings it in front of him. "Gather around, folks. There's nothing flashy about this discussion, but it's an important part of your training."

The trainees find spots on the large mat in front of Kurt. True to form, Eva plops down dramatically as though she's finally succumbing to exhaustion. Tonight I'll make sure her exhaustion is real.

"Safety first is one of the most important principles in the stunt industry," Kurt says. "Your career hinges on your ability to perform dangerous stunts without getting injured or worse. We talked about this weeks ago. If you don't protect yourself, your career will be short-lived. But the good thing is, you're not alone. And that's what I want to talk about today. The people on set who will do their best to ensure that you're safe."

Kurt's given this speech dozens of times. At this point, he typically draws a flowchart on the chalkboard showing the relative positions of the people on a stunt coordination team. This is also when I usually zone out and read emails on my phone. But to my surprise, Kurt's decided to switch things up today and takes a seat instead.

"In fact, safety issues come up even before you get on set. Take last Sunday, for instance."

I jerk my head up when Kurt mentions last Sunday. Fuck. I'd put that episode out of my mind, but now that he's going on a safety tangent, I'm reminded that Eva knows nothing about it. Shit, shit, shit. What the hell is he planning to say?

"See, we got an emergency call for an underwater helicopter stunt," he continues. "It's a maneuver with a high degree of difficulty and a high risk of complications. But the qualifications were simple. A woman who could get out of a harness underwater while pretending to be in distress and terrified of drowning. The role called for a woman, race unimportant, in her twenties or thirties."

Eva laughs. "Why didn't you call me? My swim team experience alone should have been enough."

Kurt furrows his brows. "You were on a swim team?"

She nods. "Two years at Drexel. I can hold my breath for an impressively long time, too." Then she playfully brushes her shoulders as if to signal that we all should be dazzled by her talent. "Anthony says it might come in handy someday."

Kurt casts a veiled glance my way. "I wish I'd known that." His voice vibrates with annoyance plainly directed at me.

Heat creeps into my cheeks, and my stomach knots. I glance at Eva to see if she's picking up on any of this. Her gaze is assessing, curious, but she's not acting out of the ordinary otherwise. She's a smart woman, so she'll figure it out soon enough. I should have mentioned the job to her, explained why I didn't think she was the right person to perform the stunt, but I didn't, hoping it would just go away, and now she's learning about it from Kurt. Dammit.

Kurt shakes his head as he blows out a harsh breath. "Anyway, we had to find someone quickly, but the person we had in mind wasn't available. Still, the biggest factor was safety. We could have proposed one of you"—he points at Kim and Eva—"but we made the decision that neither of you had the skill set or experience to handle this as your first stunt." He gives me a bitter smile. "We ended up giving the assignment to someone else. Because the main objective is to keep everyone safe without hindering your ability to secure the assignments that will help you build a career. So you see, it starts with us, too."

In my head, I'm running through the sequence of events that day and trying to figure out a way to explain this so she doesn't think I tried to screw her. But that's not really the point, is it? The inescapable truth is that I purposefully withheld information because I didn't want her to be a viable candidate for the job.

Eva slides me a guarded look, slowly nodding her head as she undoubtedly considers the moral of Kurt's story. It's not hard to figure out the upshot. I interfered with her ability to get an assignment that could have been a springboard for her stunt career. As I see it, the moral is this: I'm just as manipulative as the other men in her past. Maybe I'm even worse, because I *knew* this type of interference would be a deal breaker for her, and I did it anyway.

Eva

AFTER CLASS, I pace the bathroom, trying to convince myself to relax and not jump to conclusions. Anthony thinks he'll be my ride, so I know he won't leave without me. And it's important that we talk now, because I'm not spending another second in his presence without finding out what the hell happened last Sunday. My gut tells me I'm not going to like what I discover. The scared-shitless expression he wore as he scrambled to the office is another helpful clue that something's amiss.

When I reemerge, only half of the overheads are on. Listening for the voices of anyone who might still be here, I plod across the warehouse floor to the small office in the corner. The glass window reveals that Kurt and Anthony are having an animated discussion, one neither is happy about, judging from the way they're both standing with their arms folded over their chests. I knock on the door. "Everything okay?"

Kurt gives me a smile that doesn't reach his eyes. "Come in. All's good." He grabs a set of keys off his desk and tells Anthony, "We'll talk tomorrow."

Anthony nods, a grim expression on his face, and then Kurt walks out.

This isn't how I expected we'd be spending our reunion. He's been gone only three days, but I've been anticipating his return like he's been gone for three months. Ridiculous, I know, but it's true.

"Do you have a minute?" I ask.

He nods and looks around. "Of course. Do you want to sit down?"

"This isn't that kind of chat."

He scrubs his face. "Right. I should—"

"Let me ask the questions, okay? I think this will go

a lot more smoothly if I can get the answers I need and not simply listen to what you want to tell me."

His face clears, as though he's relieved that he doesn't need to do the heavy lifting of explaining himself. "All right." He steps back and sits on his desk, legs crossed at the ankles. I hope his posture is a defense mechanism, because the alternative—that he believes we're having a casual, inconsequential conversation—would make me want to split his balls in half.

People who regularly encounter manipulators develop techniques for dealing with them. My mother is one source of handy tips; TV's another. A few years ago, I contracted the flu and spent two weeks stuck at home, unable to do anything but eat, bathe, and watch TV. Some days, frankly, only bingeing in front of the TV occurred. During a particularly rough point in my recovery, I watched a daily talk show segment on how to catch a liar. The guest, an experienced administrator of lie detector tests, said the best way to get people to tell you the truth is to give them no room to lie. This meant asking rapid-fire questions with only yes or no answers or very little wiggle room. I've used this strategy often, and I use it with Anthony now.

"Okay, so if I'm understanding what I heard Kurt say earlier, someone contacted EST looking for a stunt person."

He nods. "Yes."

"They wanted a woman specifically."

"Yes."

I scrutinize his demeanor for the next few seconds, knowing his answer here is critical. "And my swimming experience would have at least made me a decent candidate for the assignment."

He averts his gaze. "It would have been a point in your favor, yes."

"And did you and Kurt discuss me as a possibility?"

"Yes."

"But you didn't tell him about my swimming experience."

"I didn't."

"It wasn't that you forgot, right? You decided not to tell him."

He uncrosses his legs and stands. "I didn't tell him."

That's a squirrely answer. "At the time, though, you remembered I had that experience, yes?"

He sighs. "Yes."

At this point, I discard the strategy because it's working too well, and I just want an answer that will explain it all away. "Why?" The rasp in my voice makes the question barely audible even to my own ears. Or maybe the pounding between my temples is interfering with my ability to hear clearly. Who the hell knows?

He holds the back of his neck as he answers. "I didn't think you were ready. It's a dangerous stunt, not ideal for a first-timer."

"We all need to start somewhere, isn't that what you told the class?"

"Yes," he says, crossing his arms. "But I meant a roll

down a flight of stairs. A combat scene. A stunt that doesn't include the risk of drowning."

"But why do *you alone* get to decide that for me?" I ask, pointing a finger at him accusingly. "If you had discussed it with Kurt, and both of you, knowing *all the facts*, decided together that it wasn't a good idea, I could have lived with that decision. But you took it upon yourself to manipulate the situation to your desired effect without any concern for what I might want. You *promised* to treat me like everyone else."

"There's no excusing what I did," he says. "I wouldn't even ask you to. But I can try to explain. If it matters at all, I was terrified you'd get hurt. And yes, I'll admit I let my personal feelings get in the way here. Because you're not just any student to me. I care about you, Eva."

Jesus. He cares about me, and so it's okay? Every man in my life has tried to control my choices, tried to make me bend to their will. And it's always because they supposedly care. Because they want what's best for me. I thought Anthony was different, but now I know he's not. God, when I think about how I was *this close* to finding my person, to investing the time and effort to make this relationship work, while he was busy trying to rob me of a job opportunity, I want to smack myself for being so gullible. "That just might be the worst answer you could have ever given me. Congratulations, you've just joined the long line of men who know what's best for Eva."

His head snaps back as though I've slapped him.

The silence that follows is so uncomfortable my skin prickles. I force myself not to scratch away the itchiness, wanting to stand strong and appear unbroken.

Anthony grinds his jaw as he considers me, while I throw daggers at him with my eyes.

"So what does that mean?" he asks, his face absent of any expression whatsoever. "You're done?"

"I can't tell you one way or the other," I say, honestly.

He scowls at me. "I would have expected you to know exactly what to do in this situation. Don't you have a handbook for dealing with guys like me? Because let's be honest, Eva, you were expecting me to fuck up, weren't you? Because *everyone* fucks up eventually, according to you."

Heat courses through my body. And not the good kind. The gall of this man. "We are not going to play this game, Anthony. We're not going to flip this so that I'm the bad guy in this scenario. That's not how it works."

He scrubs the back of his head, ruffling his hair every which way. "Look, if I can admit that I was wrong, you can admit that you *wanted* me to be wrong. My mistake is just further proof that you shouldn't give your heart to anyone, isn't it? I will accept that I'm the one who did something wrong here. I'm *not* denying that. But Eva, in many ways, you're just as unavailable as I am."

I point an unsteady finger at him, inwardly cringing at the way my voice breaks when I speak. "No, I will not let you pin any of this on me. You made this problem, not me."

A muscle in his jaw twitches, and then his expression dulls. "You're right. It's my fault. I didn't want to hurt you, but I did it anyway. And unfortunately, it'll happen again and again, whether or not I mean to. Every bit of this proves what I've known all along. I can't be in a relationship. I'm sorry I made you think it would work when I should have known it wouldn't."

He's talking over me, not with me. As though he's working off a script and he's plotted out how this discussion will end. Whatever I say, he's going to redirect the conversation to fit his goal: ending this relationship. But what future do we have if he's always going to run when things are messy? Relationships *are* messy. Who the fuck told him to expect otherwise?

He gathers a few papers on his desk and stuffs them in his gym bag. "Let me take you home."

I snort at that suggestion. "Um. That's okay. I'll take the bus."

Sadness clouds his features. "Eva, I can give you a ride."

"No, really. I'm good. It'll give me plenty of time to think. I'll see you soon, I'm sure."

Unfortunately, unless I drop out of the training program, soon will be as early as Sunday of this week. The possibility of seeing him again with all this unresolved tension swirling between us is too much to consider in my present state. But I do know one thing: I need to buy a used car. It's *not* a dramatic exit if you end it by boarding a bus.

Anthony

FIVE MINUTES AFTER Eva leaves, I'm still standing in the same place, my hands resting on the top of my head. A dog barking outside the warehouse jolts me out of my daze. Somehow I generate enough brainpower to complete my lockup routine, lumber out back to the lot, and climb into the truck.

"No Me Ames," a Spanish-language ballad, is playing on the radio when I start the engine. In the song, Marc Antony tells Jennifer Lopez not to love him; it's a serenade tailor made for my drive home.

Hitting the steering wheel with the palms of my hands, I let out a deep growl of frustration. I *know* I messed up. I'd never pretend otherwise. And I hate that Eva's hurting because I made a poor and thoughtless choice. But this breakup is for the best. We both know the confrontation in my office was a formality, the obligatory showdown before Eva inevitably decided she didn't want to be with me. I simply sped up the process so that neither one of us would get too invested in a situation destined to fail.

I will say this: Hats off to the people who brave being in a committed relationship. I respect them. But if I've learned anything from my experience today, it's that

I should trust my instincts. I can live a comfortable, mostly stress-free life if I avoid romantic connections and stick with the random hookups that have served me well in the past. If I'm honest, no one gets hurt. Why would I ever want or need anything more complicated than that?

Chapter Thirty-One

Find yourself a best friend who'll help you eat
your weight in pizza to make you feel better.
Bonus points if they bring wine.

Eva

DESPERATE FOR REINFORCEMENTS, I pace my living
room as I wait for Tori and the delivery person Friday
evening. When they do arrive—at the same time, as luck
would have it—I jump up from the couch to buzz them
in. A minute later, I open the door, anxiously awaiting
the three pies I've ordered. Oh, right, I'm excited to see
Tori, too.

As they climb the stairs, their conversation carries
down the hall.

Tori: "You must be mistaken. We don't need three
pizza pies."

Delivery guy: "You may not need them, but that's
what she ordered. See here?"

Tori: "Well, we can straighten this out in a sec. I'm sure it's just a misunderstanding."

Tori's head of curls appear at the top of the landing, and I breathe a sigh of relief. Although I joked in my head about pizza being my priority, she's the person I need to see the most. She strides down the hall, already wearing her jammies—God, I love her so much—and the pizza delivery person trails behind her like a lovesick fool. When she spots me, she mouths, "Oh shit, your hair," and then she turns around and grabs the pizza.

"It's paid for," I yell as I tuck a few—okay, many— errant strands behind my ear.

"I'm giving him a tip," she yells back.

"I already did that, too," I point out while shaking my head.

Tori and the delivery person chat a bit, and then she arrives at my door, a duffel bag on her shoulder and three pizza boxes in her hands.

For a few seconds, my heart quickens. This night wouldn't be complete without liquor. "Where's the wine?"

She dips her head toward the bag. "In there. Will you let me in?"

I step out of the way and hold the door open for her.

She places the pizzas on the counter in my tiny kitchen and drops her bag by the couch. "What's going on? Why do we need three pizzas?"

"I broke up with your cousin." There's no point in

being evasive about it. If I'm going to get beyond this, I need to debrief, discuss, and disengage. Tori knows the steps as well as I do.

"Damn," she says. "That's fast even for you."

I stamp my foot and throw out my hand. "Shut the hell up and give me the wine."

Unmoved by my tantrum, she pulls me in for a hug. "Sorry, I shouldn't have joked about it. I know you're hurting. The pain's right there in your eyes."

I disagree. The pain's all over. It hangs around me like my own personal cloud, ensuring sadness wherever I turn. It's seeping into my body, weighing me down so that even typically simple tasks require more effort than I want to expend. "It's nothing a pepperoni pizza and a bottle of wine won't soothe," I say into her shoulder.

"*Bueno*, let's get started, then."

After she changes into fluffy socks, we work side by side preparing our meal. There isn't that much to do: pizza on plates; wine in glasses. Still, it's comforting to know we'll soon be sitting on the couch, legs up on the coffee table, as we devour my go-to crappy mood lifter.

"TV on or off?" I ask as we settle in.

"Keep it off while we debrief." She bites into the pizza and rolls her eyes in appreciation. "This crust is delicious. It's flaky and soft and that touch of sweetness takes it over the top."

"Okay, Gordon Ramsay. Tell me more."

"Ha. That's not Gordon Ramsay. This is Gordon Ramsay." She impersonates the famous, eternally crabby chef. "What the fuck is wrong with this pizza? The crust is hard and lacks salt, and the tomato sauce tastes like ass. I wouldn't feed this to my dog."

I laugh at her antics, momentarily setting aside my troubles. "You're too much."

She sobers quickly, though, and I brace myself for the conversation to come. "Okay, talk to me. What did he do?"

I recount the story, stressing the similarities between Anthony and the manipulative men in my past. There are differences, of course—many, in fact—but that's not the point of this discussion. We eat pizza and sip wine as the narrative unfolds. Tori listens, periodically asking a question for clarification. Because she knows my history, it's no surprise to her that his interference hurt me deeply.

When I'm done, I'm emotionally exhausted all over again. "I specifically asked him not to undermine me, but that's exactly what he did."

Tori, now facing me and sitting with her legs tucked under her, says, "You also asked him to treat you like everyone else. How could he? He kept his heart locked away for years, thinking it was safer not to love anyone. With you, he wanted to try. Sorry to break this to you, Eva, but you weren't like everyone else from the beginning."

That's one of the most frustrating aspects of the situation. He *knows* me. Is fully aware that I'd be crushed by what he did. And he did it anyway. It's like I handed him my heart and he threw it right back at me. "It may be true that I was different from the beginning, but he doesn't get a pass simply because he cares about me. That should have given him even more reason to let the process play out and raise his concerns with me directly. Like an adult. In a relationship. I might have heeded his warnings. But he took that choice away from me."

She reaches for my hand and squeezes it. "I don't disagree that he's the bad guy in this scenario. I just want you to think about what's really going on here. And before you throw Anthony in with the rest of the men who've fucked you over, ask yourself what he gained from doing what he did."

I draw back. "What do you mean?"

"Well, let's think about this. In college, the douche canoe tried to trap you into pregnancy because he wanted to bind you to him forever. And what about Nate? He didn't want to release you from your contract because he wanted to force you to stay. He's an asshat for sure. And your father withdrew his support because he wants you back in Philly. I'll refrain from calling him any names, but you get the idea. Now let's think about Anthony here. What did he want, and what did he get?"

Honestly, the question stumps me, which only makes me more agitated. And if Anthony hadn't shut down on me, maybe I would have realized this sooner. We could have talked about a way forward. I don't think he knows how to work through his feelings, though. He runs—and I'm not a chaser.

I fall over onto my back in frustration. "I don't want

to think about this anymore. I'd rather watch awful bakers try to recreate fabulous cakes and fail spectacularly."

Tori picks up the remote, pulls up my Netflix account, and locates the latest episode of "Nailed It." Before she hits Play, she turns to me and bites her lip.

"Say it, Tori."

"I just want to point out that sometimes people do remarkably stupid shit when they care about someone. Remember the stuff Carter pulled when we were first together?"

Do I. The man screwed up so badly he took to national television to admit his mistake. "Oh yes, neither one of us will ever forget that."

"Doesn't excuse it. But relationships are about working through these kinds of issues. No one's perfect, you know, yourself included."

The thing is, if relationships are about working through these kinds of issues, then maybe Anthony's had the right idea all along: They aren't worth this kind of turmoil.

Chapter Thirty-Two

Anthony

THIS SHOW IS wild. Too bad my father won't let me watch it in peace.

Once again, he shuffles past me, his bathrobe hanging loosely from his shoulders. "Antonio, *mijo*, the lawn's looking really bad. When are you planning to cut it?"

I'm lying on the couch watching *Westworld*, and I have no interest in doing anything, let alone mowing the front yard. But yeah, I know it's my responsibility. "I'll do it this week, okay? I've got some other things I need to do first."

He plants himself in front of the TV. "Oh yeah? Like what?"

"Just a few errands I've been meaning to take care of. Don't worry, Papi, I'll handle it." I grab the remote and turn up the volume. "Not today, though."

My father snatches the remote out of my hands and turns off the TV.

I sit up slowly, knowing that if he wants my attention, he'll make sure he gets it no matter what. "Okay, I'm listening."

"It's Saturday afternoon," he says, gesturing toward the light coming from the living room windows. "You should be out somewhere with your pretty girlfriend. Instead, you're moping around here in your boxers, scratching your ass and watching television."

I throw up my hands. "What? A man can't relax in his own home?"

He narrows his eyes. "What happened?"

I drop my head and run my fingers through the hair at the nape of my neck. How can a simple question like that hit me in the chest like a two-by-four? Eva happened. Or didn't happen. Who the fuck knows? When I look up, he's still standing there patiently waiting for a response. "I'm not in the mood to go out, okay? And FYI, Eva's not my girlfriend."

He slices his hand in the air. "Pfft. I don't know what you kids call it anymore, and I don't care. My point is, you like her, she likes you, and you shouldn't be in this house. And if you *are* going to be in this house, you should cut the grass."

I roll my eyes at him. "I'll take care of the grass, okay, but you won't be seeing Eva around. We decided it was best to stop hanging out."

That's the CliffsNotes version, at least. I don't have it in me to explain any more than that. The shit that's been popping into my head since we broke up on Wednesday has got me all kinds of fucked up. Everywhere I look, I see a memory of our time together, a joke we shared, something I want to point out to her. Even now, as I look at Papi, I'm thinking some people wear robes much better than others. And just like that, the night she greeted me on her couch in nothing but an open robe slams into my consciousness. I squeeze my temples trying to interrupt whatever frequency is sending me these cruel messages.

"Did she do something wrong?" he asks, the tenor of his voice tentative.

"Nope."

He widens his eyes. "Did *you* do something wrong?"

"Yep."

He pinches me on the arm. "Did you do something stupid or worse?"

I smack his hand away, pissed off that he's reminding me of Eva in yet another way. "Will you quit it? You know me better than that."

He means did I cheat on her or abuse her. When I was growing up, my father would always tell me if I cheated on a woman, I was cheating on myself. And if I ever abused a woman, verbally or physically, he'd defend her himself by kicking my ass. He knows there's a thousand more ways to screw up a relationship, but those are his three Thou-Shall-Not dating commandments.

Letting out a deep breath, he nods. "Then love will make a way for you to get back together."

Oh good God. This man needs to get a grip. "Right. Is that why you can't let go of Mami? Because you think *love* is going to get you two together? News flash, Pop. Love doesn't conquer all. You can love someone all you want, but that doesn't mean it'll work out. If anyone should know that, it's you."

My father avoids my gaze and shuffles his way back to the kitchen.

Fuck. That was so uncalled for I should slap myself. "Papi, sorry, I shouldn't have said that. Don't listen to me. I'm clueless in the love department. I'm just mouthing off because I don't know what else to say."

He shrugs behind the kitchen counter and picks up a plate, rinsing it before placing it in the dishwasher. "There's no need to apologize, *mijo*. You can't help but to see what's right in front of you."

I watch my father as he pretends to be unaffected by my rant, his shoulders nevertheless sagging as he undoubtedly considers what I said. Okay, now I'm bringing my negative energy into this house, and that's not fair to Papi. "Again, I'm sorry, Pop. If you need me, I'll be outside, mowing the lawn." I can't really hurt anybody doing that.

SUNDAY MORNING, I can't stop asking myself the same question: Will Eva show up this afternoon?

I want her to. I'd hate to be the reason she decided not to complete her training. Her raw talent deserves to be honed. And the film industry needs more women like her in it.

Then why'd you mess with her chances to get a job?

"Great question, dumbass," I mumble to myself.

"What's that?" Kurt says from his desk seat.

"Nothing. Just thinking out loud."

I've been doing a lot of that in here lately. Because Kurt and I haven't talked much since Wednesday. He's excellent at giving me a modified version of the silent treatment: He speaks when I speak to him and gives me curt instructions only when necessary. The morning after he found out I didn't disclose what I knew about Eva, he asked me one question: "Are you screwing around with her?" I told him it wasn't what he was thinking; he walked away in the middle of my explanation.

But I'm not letting him ignore me today. "Kurt."

"Hmm," he says, not looking up.

I drum up the courage to inject a tenor of authority into my voice. "Kurt, look at me."

He raises his gaze to the ceiling and slowly brings it down to meet my stare. "What's up?"

"Ready to clear the air? Because unless I'm mistaken, you've got a business to run, and not speaking to your right-hand man isn't conducive to doing that."

He places his elbows on the desk and clasps his hands together. "I'm listening."

I look him dead in the eyes and say what I should have said immediately after he discovered what I'd done. "I'm sorry I didn't tell you about Eva's swimming experience. I should have, and for a number of reasons, I regret not saying anything about it. I can admit my feelings for her clouded my judgment, but my analysis was sound. She hasn't finished training. Underwater stunts aren't ideal for first-timers. Production was running on borrowed time because they wanted to minimize the equipment rental costs. And Simms is an asshole who cuts corners. We had all the makings for a disaster cocktail. I didn't want her to be a part of it. And I didn't think the job was worth it—to her or to us—no matter how much you like Simms."

"Why didn't you share all this with me, then?" he asks, tilting his head to study me closer.

"I'm human, Kurt. I make mistakes. I made one here. A big one. And I'm sorry."

The air is thick with tension as I wait for him to respond.

A few beats later, he leans forward, resting his upper body weight on his elbows. "Can you see now that a policy barring relationships with trainees makes sense? Do you see how things went wrong?"

Here's when I should clarify mine and Eva's relationship, but I hesitate to do that because I'm not sure how to. "I don't want to say too much, but Eva and were together before training started. And this won't be a recurring issue. She's been different from the beginning. I just didn't want to admit it to myself. The point is, I did something you're understandably upset about, but that doesn't mean I don't care about the business, or you. I'm going to fuck up. It's part of life. What matters is how I respond to it. So tell me how to fix this."

Kurt smiles. "You just did it."

"What does that mean?" I ask, scrunching my face in confusion.

"You want to be a co-owner, *act* like a co-owner. Show me that you're thinking about the business. Exercise good judgment. And when shit doesn't turn out right, accept your responsibility in the situation and figure out how to move on. That's all I've ever expected of you, and that's just what you did. It's a start, at least."

It's not enough, though. Because Kurt isn't the only person I hurt in this situation. And more than anything, I don't want Eva to suffer because of me. "Kurt, there's one other thing I need to do, and I need your help to do it."

He raises a brow. "Yeah?"

"Yeah. I'm guessing my presence would cast a cloud on the remainder of Eva's experience during the training program. Would you be willing to take over?"

Kurt strokes his chin as he considers me. "I couldn't pay you for those classes."

I nod. "I know."

"It means that much to you?" he asks.

"It does."

We may not be together, but yes, Eva absolutely means that much to me.

Chapter Thirty-Three

So if I'm understanding this poem correctly, it
doesn't really matter which road I take? Well,
shit, Robert Frost was an asshole.

Eva

ON SUNDAY, TORI invites me to lunch before my training session at EST, and because she's working today, she asks me to meet her at the café around the corner from Every Body.

We choose to sit on the covered patio of the Mediterranean restaurant that's popular with the studio's staff and clients, both of us donning our sunglasses, not because it's sunny but because we want to people-watch. The gray weather matches my mood, and the neutral expression on Tori's typically vivacious face isn't helping to improve it.

After we order, she squeezes a dollop of sanitizer on her palm, and when I hold out my own hands, she squirts sanitizer on them, too. We rub in silence, until I realize this is how Tori acts when she's noodling through an issue.

"Out with it, Tori."

She flinches, as though I've pulled her out of her thoughts. But if the wistful smile on her face is any guide, they're good thoughts.

"Sorry," she says. "I'm not being a very good lunch date, am I?"

"What's going on?"

"Several members came to see me this morning. To discuss you."

Shit. People are already complaining about me? *Those backstabbing bastards.*

"They were raving about your self-defense class takeover," she continues. "Said they wanted to take that class on a regular basis and asked why it wasn't available. Apparently most of the class agreed."

Those amazingly intuitive geniuses. I can't help knocking my knees together in excitement. If I'm not too careful, I might float away. Is Tori for real? "Seriously?"

She nods. "Seriously. I haven't thought all of this through, but I was thinking we could try a full schedule of cardio self-defense classes. Call it Kickass Power Hour or something."

I wrinkle my nose at her. "Let me work on the name."

She shakes her head. "Fine. Point is, you've come up with something that you're uniquely qualified to teach, so I can justify giving you more hours if you want them. I'm thinking evenings, three times a week. And if the class works, we can add another one at a different time of day in winter. What do you say?"

I lean over and grab her hands, flailing for us both. "I think I couldn't be more excited than I am right now."

She gives me a wide smile. "I figured you'd say something like that."

My enthusiasm wanes when I think about Anthony, however. "Would I be replacing the current self-defense class?"

She shakes her head. "No, not at all. That class is a community service, for members and nonmembers alike. Your class would be a member benefit only. Plus, I was using Anthony's class to gauge interest in self-defense classes generally. It just turns out the interest veered in a different direction and now I have someone on staff who can meet the need. It's perfect."

My experience at Every Body has been nothing but positive, and I'm beyond excited to spearhead a new set of classes at the studio. I'm bringing value to the business and loving the challenge of this new venture. "Tori, this is the best news. When would you like me to start?"

She pulls out her phone and opens her calendar. "How much time do you think you'll need to come up with the routines?"

"I'd probably want three in the bag before we get started, so I'd say a few weeks at a minimum."

She swipes the calendar ahead one month. "Okay, and when does stunt training end?"

Our server arrives at our table, delivering a basket of pita triangles and a wide, shallow bowl of hummus with olive oil and spices drizzled on top. "This looks amazing," I exclaim as I dig in.

"Eva, look at me."

Reluctantly, I place the pita on my bread plate—it really does look amazing—and meet her gaze.

She frowns at me, her features scrunched in confusion. "Are you thinking about not finishing the training?"

"The thought had occurred to me."

She shakes her head, blinking owlishly and pretending to be shocked by my reluctance to resume training. "Whoa, whoa, whoa. You're doing your post-breakup ritual wrong. Debrief, discuss, disengage, remember? This is the disengage stage. You should be turning off your emotions and moving on."

I drop my head, exhausted at the mere thought of showing up for another class and seeing Anthony again. "I know. Believe me, this isn't easy for me. But how can I show up there? He's one of my instructors."

"*He* is now a part of your past. Or he would have been any other time. Is there something about this breakup that's different?"

This time, I shove a pita triangle in my mouth, chewing as I speak. "No."

She places her elbows on the table, rests her chin on her hands, and stares at me.

I'm not sure she can hear me when I finally, quietly, say yes, but her tender expression tells me she did.

"So what's different this go-round?" she asks.

Everything's different. I can't recall another time when a breakup affected me like this one has. Anthony and I had *so much promise*. It's as if I had a few weeks of being with the perfect person for me, and then he was snatched away for no good reason. "He's different. I'm different with him. This go-round, I can't shake the sense that I was *so* close to finding my forever person." Until he fucked it up. "Tori, I think I'm in love with him. But he won't let me in. So, of course, I want to smack him upside the head and tell him to grow up." I wipe my eyes. Fucking inconvenient tears. "And there's this teeny, tiny part of me telling me I can't handle being in the same training room with him. Not when I'm still raw."

Tori's wearing this *awww* face that makes me want to puke. "Sweetie, you're entitled to feel everything you're feeling. But I've said it before and I'll say it again, as to whether you should finish your training, that teeny tiny part of you needs to shut the fuck up."

She says this with an evil grin that scares even me. But not really. Because this is Tori. And she knows *exactly* what to say to clear my brain of my negative thoughts. "No, you're right. I'm going. Giving up is not an option." I raise my glass of water in the air. "Besides, how else would I prove to my father that he's wrong about my future while simultaneously pissing him off."

Tori lifts her glass and taps mine. "To pettiness."

Indeed.

MY FATHER CALLS when I'm on the bus traveling to EST. This time, I answer.

"So how's my Eva Knievel?" my father asks.

I'm glad we're not face-to-face; this way, he can't see my reaction to the silly nickname he's made up for me.

"I'm doing great, actually," I say in a singsong voice.

"Oh? Why's . . . that?"

"I received some wonderful news about my work. I substituted for a class at Every Body and it was so popular, Tori wants me to teach a new class. More classes means more money."

"More fitness classes. How exciting."

His sarcasm stings. With just a few words, he snatches away the joy I felt when Tori told me people were clamoring to take my class. It's one thing for him to ridicule my stunt training, but his disdain for the one thing I'm *truly* passionate about rankles.

It takes me a few moments for my thoughts to sink in. But when they do, I'm seeing the past several weeks in stunning clarity. The one thing I'm *truly* passionate about is fitness. It's always been enough for me. But it's never been enough for my father. And as much as I'd like to think I can dodge a manipulator with my well-trained eye, I *still* chose to undertake stunt training to prove that I could be *more*, and even then it wasn't enough for him—because it'll *never* be enough for him.

Anthony suggested as much when I told him why I wanted to train, but I didn't want to admit that I could be manipulated that easily. Joke's on me. But no more.

What I do is enough to pay the bills. What I do is enough to keep me engaged. What I do is enough to fulfill me in all the ways that matter. And if my father can't respect that, he's the problem, not me. "Dad, I love you, but—"

He chuckles. "Well, that sounds ominous."

"Let me finish. Dad, I love you, but I'm not coming back to Philly, no matter how much you want me to. I'm choosing to settle somewhere that's going to help me be the best version of myself, and for now, it's here. I'm doing what I enjoy, and I'll find a way to make it work financially. If that doesn't meet your approval, then so be it. I'm almost thirty years old, and it's time I worry more about meeting my own approval."

He sighs. "Sweetie, it's not that I don't approve of your choices, I just want more for you. And I think you could have it. In Philly." He clears his throat. "I never imagined you . . ."

"What? Never imagined what?"

"I never imagined you wouldn't be here," he says. "With me. Or near me."

"I'll call more, I promise."

"But what about our dinners?" he asks sullenly. "And who's going to drag me out to the movies?"

Oh God. Why didn't I see this before? My move to California affected him just as much as it affected me. And now he's lonely. He wants me back there because he doesn't know what to do with himself. "Dad, I'll come back for the holidays and to visit other times, too. And you can spend some time here with me. For a couple of weeks over the summer, maybe?"

"Sounds nice," he says.

"And let me ask you this. When's the last time you went on a date?"

He answers in a huff. "What kind of question is that? What does that have to do with anything?"

"I just think you need to focus your attention on someone other than your daughter."

"Well, now you're being ridiculous," he says in an affronted tone. "I'm your father. Of course I care about your welfare."

"Dad, I'm fine. It's time to let go and do your own thing. I mean, isn't there someone you could take out for coffee or dinner?"

My father's voice crackles on the other end of the line. "Hello? Eva? Are you there? I think I'm losing you. Hello?"

When I hear the dial tone, I almost slide to the

ground realizing he's taken a page from my playbook and is pretending that we lost our phone connection.

Well played, Dad. Well played.

THANKS TO THE Metro bus, I'm a few minutes late to class. Today, we're learning about harness and wire work. I'm excited to fly around and pretend I'm Storm from the X-Men.

I slip inside and join everyone in the circle. Kurt, with the help of a gentleman I've never seen before, is demonstrating how various harnesses and cables work together to create the pulley system for high-flying combat scenes.

My gaze bounces around the room. Anthony's nowhere to be found. All the stress of seeing him again slowly leaves my body, although it's replaced with a big question mark as to his whereabouts. I lean over to Megan, whispering as softly as I can while still being audible. "Hey, where's Anthony?"

She raises an eyebrow. "I don't know where he is, but I know he's not here. Kurt says he'll no longer be instructing this session. He did emphasize that Anthony would be back on board after this boot camp, so I don't know what happened."

I'm stunned speechless and can only respond with a nod. So, rather than see me again, he withdrew from the class?

No. Stop it, Eva. Think for a minute. He may be avoiding the class, but I refuse to believe he's avoiding me. If I had to guess, he's no longer teaching the course because he wants me to finish it and doesn't want to interfere with my progress. This time, I'm giving him the benefit of the doubt. Because in my heart, I know he's a good person.

See there, Satan? I'm finally on to you.

Chapter Thirty-Four

Anthony

I'M IN THE middle of watching an episode of *Caso Cer-rado*, a beer in my grip and a bag of chips by my side, when my father enters the living room.

I eye the overnight bag in his right hand with suspicion and frown at him. "Where are you going?"

"I'm spending a few days away. I'll come back for the rest of my things soon."

I glance around the living room, noticing for the first time that he's tidied up the place and some of his stuff—books, playing cards, even the case for his eyeglasses—are gone. "What are you talking about?"

My father sighs heavily, drops the bag by his recliner, and motions for me to give him space on the couch. After he lowers himself onto the cushion, he slowly rubs his hands. "Antonio, it's time for me to go."

I sit up and frown at him. "Go? Go where? You're not making any sense."

"I don't think we should live together anymore, Son."

That's not a statement I ever thought I'd hear my

father make. And it pisses me off to hear it. "Why the hell not? That's always been the plan. You, me, a dog maybe." I nudge his shoulder with mine. "Is it the dog? Because if it is, we can buy one this weekend."

He sucks his teeth. "It's not the dog. It's you. Me. Us."

My chest feels tight and there's a ringing in my ears I can't explain. "Well, damn, Pop, why don't you tell me how you really feel?"

He doesn't look at me as he speaks. "*Mira*, I don't doubt that you love me, but we're living together for a reason, and it isn't a good one."

"Which is?"

"I'm here to remind you what happens when you try and fail at love," he announces as though this nugget of wisdom should be obvious to me. Newsflash: It's not.

I draw back and stare at him. "What does that even mean?" Smiling, I say, "You need to stop watching *telenovelas* all day."

He throws his hands up in frustration. "*Mijo*, take a good look at yourself. You've created this life that makes it impossible for you to fall in love. You tell women you don't date, don't want to get married, don't want to have kids. You do those crazy dangerous stunts. You live with your *father*. *Dios mio*, what woman would ever see you as someone she could live the rest of her life with?"

My heart feels like it's skittering to a stop. Eva would. She'd put the same energy into making our relationship work that she puts into everything else she does.

Papi strokes his chin, looking more thoughtful than

I've seen him in a long time. "You tell yourself it's because love doesn't last and you don't want to hurt anyone
when it doesn't work out, but . . ."

"Don't stop now," I prod. "You're on a roll."

"But I really think it's the opposite . . ."

I know what he's going to say before he says it, the
truth slamming into me like a wrecking ball. I'm not
afraid of hurting someone. I'm afraid of being hurt.
And when I realized Eva might not forgive me, I ran,
figuring that I could avoid the pain of her leaving.

"You saw what getting hurt by your mother did to
me," my father says. "The man I became. And I don't
blame you for thinking I was a failure because I couldn't
let her go. And when that woman—"

"Melissa."

"Yeah, yeah," he says with a dismissive wave. "You
know what it felt like when Melissa broke up with you even
though you did nothing wrong. And *mijo*, you know what
it felt like when your mother left, because as much as you
pretend it didn't bother you, the truth is, your mother left
you, too. But never letting yourself fall in love isn't going to
change the past."

It kills me that he thinks I'm disappointed in him
in any way. Nothing could be further from the truth.
"Papi, I don't think of you as a failure."

"Maybe not in life, but in love, that's a different story.
And you know what? That's my fault. I've been living in
the past, too. I haven't been a good example for you. But
that's going to change starting right now. I don't want

you to use me as a shield to stop yourself from living. I'm not miserable. And I think it's time I do my own thing for a while."

The thoughts bouncing around in my head refuse to merge into a coherent whole, so I'm compelled to ask the most basic question while my brain tries to catch up. "Where will you go?"

He dips his chin and stares at the floor. "Berta has an extra room at her place. Says I can stay there."

There's that woman again. Popping out like a jack-in-the-box. "What has this woman done to you?"

He smiles. "Maybe the same thing Eva did to you."

Hearing her name is like having someone hit my chest with a battering ram. It hurts too much. Because I realize I messed up twice. Not only did I manipulate a situation to her detriment, but I also gave up on us when she confronted me about it. And I did all that because I was terrified that she wouldn't love me the way I love her.

He reaches over and taps my hand. "The time for your mother and me has passed. But you can still work things out with Eva. Apologize. I don't know what happened. Whatever you did, tell her you were wrong. Don't stop fighting for her because you're too scared to lose her. Try this time, *mijo*. If you love her like I think you do, *try*."

I doubt Eva would even want me to try. "I want to, Pop, but it's not that simple."

"Who the hell ever told you anything about love is simple, Antonio?" He pokes me in the forehead.

"*Piensa*. Love like the love I have for you is worth all the messiness in the world. And I bet the reason you've been moping around this week is because you got a little taste of what that could be like and now it's gone. Get it back."

Jesus. Have we been enabling each other this whole time? The thought turns my stomach. I can confidently say he's right about one point, though: Now that I've experienced what it's like to be with Eva, the alternative—never being with her again—makes me want to crawl up inside myself and shut down. "All right, Papi. I'll try."

Chapter Thirty-Five

Find someone who makes your heart soar.

Eva

MONDAY MORNING, I decide to immerse myself in preparing the cardio defense classes I'll be rolling out in a month. Not even a trip on the Metro dampens my enthusiasm for choreographing the new routines. Only reflecting on my relationship with Anthony would do that, and I'm making a valiant effort to curb such thoughts.

When I enter Every Body's lobby, I see Tori behind the desk speaking on her cell phone. Her mouth is moving at top speed, and her eyebrows are drawn together. Within seconds of my arrival, she ends the call and drops her head, and then she repeatedly taps her fist on the desk.

I jog to the counter. "Tori, what's going on?"

She looks up at me and worries her bottom lip with her teeth before she answers. "I don't know. I'm not sure if I should be concerned or not. It's Anthony."

CRASHING INTO HER 369

I'm rooted to the spot, but my heart is banging against my chest as though it's trying to force its way out of my body. "What do you mean? What's happened?"

She stares at me, an incredulous expression on her face. "Nothing yet. But he asked me to come to Griffith Park. To Griffith Observatory, specifically. Says he's doing the biggest fall of his life, and he wants me to be there. For moral support."

My knees buckle, and I grab onto the desk to keep me upright. "The eighty-foot jump Kurt's been trying to convince him to do?"

Tori gawks at me. "You knew about this?"

I shake my head, trying to remember what he said about it. "He mentioned it once in class. In passing. Said he didn't think he was ready for it."

Tori grimaces. "I'm worried he's being reckless. Maybe doing something he wouldn't otherwise do because he's chasing an adrenaline rush." She grabs her car keys off the counter and shoves them in her pocket. "I need to talk to him in person. See for myself where his head's at."

"I'm going with you," I say, striding beside her to the exit.

"Fine," she says, her face buried in her phone as she pulls up directions.

Once we're in the car, the thoughts about Anthony I'd been trying to suppress flood my brain. What if he's doing this because we argued? Because he's not thinking clearly about the risks? Because he needs the rush to get out of his head? I'd certainly understand. I mean, isn't that what I've been trying to do? Trying to numb myself so that I can function without him? We're both being ridiculous, and one of us needs to break the logjam.

I spend the rest of the drive rehearsing what I'll say to him when I get to the park. I want him to give us a chance. I want him to be my partner in every sense of the word. I want us to love each other, challenge and support each other, give each other our honest opinions knowing they may not always be agreed with or appreciated. And if he'll listen, I'll make sure he knows how special he is to me.

The car winds around a seemingly never-ending road up the slopes of Mount Hollywood. I'd planned to come here for sightseeing one day—my LA bucket list is long—so I only glance at the view of the Hollywood sign from the Observatory's parking lot, knowing I'll be back when I have fewer pressing matters to attend to.

Tori searches for cash in her wallet to pay the parking fee. "Go ahead. I'll catch up with you. I need a minute to text Carter anyway."

I stuff my bag under the seat and climb out, turning back at the last minute to ask where the hell I'm going. "Did he say where exactly they'd be filming?"

"The East Terrace. Up the front sidewalks. Said it would be closed to the public, but he'd make sure someone would let me in."

I run up the ramp, and with the help of several staffers along the way, find the sidewalk to the East Terrace.

In my head, I consider how to finagle my way onto the set, ultimately deciding the easiest approach would be to claim that Anthony's my boyfriend. But when I get to the East Terrace, I don't see what I expect to see—there are no people milling around, no cameras on scene, no safety checks in process. And now that I think about it, how the hell is someone going to perform a high fall off the deck of the Griffith Observatory? Did Tori misunderstand where in the park Anthony would be?

I spin around intending to march back to Tori's car, and that's when I spy a lone figure leaning against the deck rail. Anthony. My heart squeezes in my chest at the sight of him. He's wearing his shades, this time for good reason, and a hesitant smile. I give him a tentative wave, wondering with equal amounts confusion and hope whether his goal was to bring me here.

He saunters over, the easiness in his gait mirroring the casualness of his attire—a royal blue T-shirt and loose-fitting jeans that do little to hide his powerful thighs. "You're confused."

It's an odd way to greet me, but it's accurate, nonetheless. "I am. Are you doing the eighty-foot jump or not?"

His smile grows, as though it'll reveal its true meaning when it widens completely. "What did Tori tell you that made you think I'd be doing that jump?"

I try to think back to what Tori said. "She . . . um . . . she said you'd be doing the biggest fall of your life."

He nods. "Right. That's true." Licking his lips, he

inches closer, running a hand along my jaw. "The biggest fall of my life, though, is falling in love with you."

Oh. My. God. I couldn't feel any more cherished than I do in this moment. I'm also mindful that I spent the last thirty minutes imagining his untimely demise. I shoot out my hand and jab him in the stomach. "Wait. So you're not doing a high fall today?"

"Ouch," he says on a laugh. He removes his sunglasses, revealing eyes glowing with affection. "There are no death-defying jumps in my immediate plans. No, I'd only pull a stunt like this for you." Then he closes one eye, scrunches his nose, and twists his mouth in amusement. "Too cheesy?"

I can't help snorting. "Cheesy? Yes. Too cheesy? Nah. It means you'll make a fool of yourself for me, and that makes me want to swoon."

He wraps his arms around me. "Swooning is good."

I look up at him and smile, feeling more content than I have in a long time. He's my person. I know it. My heart knows it, too.

We stand there in silence, enjoying the rightness of being together. The quiet moment doesn't last long, though, because he pulls back and clears his throat, pinning me with a serious stare.

"You asked me once why I perform stunts," he says, "and I don't think I ever told you. When I'm free falling, there's a split-second of fear as I take the plunge, but then I let my body catch the air. For an instant I feel weightless, absolutely free. It's exhilarating. I chase that perfect feeling each time I free fall. But it doesn't hold a candle to how I feel when you're with me. I love you, Eva. And I'm so glad you crashed into my life."

I smile at that description. "I beg to differ. You're the stunt performer, so I think it would be more accurate to say you crashed into mine."

He looks up at the sky and says, "I'm getting used to never having the last word." Then he lowers his head and taps my nose. "I kind of like it."

I give him a saucy smile. "You should."

Before I can ask what led to this soul-baring epiphany, his expression clouds, the brightness in his eyes dimming. "I want you to know that I never doubted your abilities, and I never wanted to control you. I honestly thought I was keeping you safe. Making a reasoned decision based on what I knew about the totality of the situation. But I should have gone about addressing it differently. Should have talked to you. I won't make that mistake again."

I know this: Anthony's never made me feel incapable of doing stunt work. In fact, he's been my cheerleader even when he worried I was training for the wrong reasons. I trust that if he were presented with a similar scenario now, he'd speak to me about it first. "And what about the running? Because I'm going to need you to hang around if we're going to make this work."

He threads his fingers through mine. "I was scared. I kept telling myself that relationships were messy, that I didn't want to hurt someone else the way my mother hurt my father, or the way I hurt Melissa. But really, I was afraid that *you* would hurt *me*. The way my mother hurt me. The way Melissa did, too. And here's the thing. If I hadn't met you, I would have been okay continuing to run away from that possibility. But that perfect feeling I mentioned? I want it. With you. And if it means I keep my ass planted wherever you are to fix a problem or talk something through, then I'll do it." He cups my face. "So, are you willing to give me a second chance? I promise not to need a third."

He's in love with me. This gorgeous, funny, sensitive man is in love with me. Is that what I'm feeling? Does that explain the ache that won't go away, or my inability to shove him in the memory box of Relationships Past? It must be. I reach up and cover his hands with mine, suddenly forgetting the speech I practiced on the way here. But it's okay—the truth is simple. "Anthony, I can confidently say that you're my person, and yes, I'll give you a second chance. Because I'm in love with you, too, and I don't ever want us to be apart."

He lifts me up—thank goodness I'm wearing yoga pants—and I wrap my legs around his waist, my body anchored by his big hands palming my butt.

"You're dying to kiss me, right?" he asks.

In answer, I brace the sides of his face and lean in for a long, slow kiss. It's a tender one, and this time, I'm overwhelmed by the promise in it.

When our lips separate, he gives me a devilish smile, his eyes suddenly blazing with undisguised lust. "So,

Ms. Montgomery, are you finally ready to admit that I rub you the right way?"

I snicker at the reminder of our shenanigans outside Bradley International several months ago. "You do, Mr. Castillo. You absolutely do."

Epilogue

Eva

One year later

TORI STUDIES HER swollen belly in the dressing room's full-length mirror. Her thick, dark hair and dark brown eyes make the blue of her dress appear even paler.

"No pregnant woman should be forced to participate in a wedding beyond the seventh-month mark," she says.

Standing beside her and making last-minute adjustments to my hair, I singsong my response. "You could have said no."

"Oh, right. Like that was even an option." She sticks out her tongue at my reflection. "You make it sound so simple. As though my presence wasn't a foregone conclusion."

"Everyone would have understood."

"Ha. I thought you knew the Castillo men. They're not good at letting things go."

"They're both getting better at it, though."

As soon as I say the words, I smile, knowing how true they are. Anthony no longer assumes he'll be hurt by love. He accepts that there are no guarantees and appreciates that our relationship must be nurtured to grow. When we fight—and it's happened a time or two (or three)—his first instinct isn't to run but to communicate. And I've become less defensive, less apt to assume his suggestions are anything more than his opinions, which I can accept or reject depending on the circumstances.

We're living together now, in the house he once shared with Luis. Paying only half the rent has been a boon to my savings account. The occasional stunt job when I'm not teaching classes helps, too. We're also working out a rent-to-own agreement with Kurt's sister. It'll be interesting to see how my father reacts to my and Anthony's living arrangement when he visits next month.

Anthony isn't a partial owner of EST yet, but Kurt's been dropping hints that it'll happen soon. Now that Julian represents him, though, he's less dependent on EST income anyway. And Luis? Well, Luis has changed, too, his divorce from Anthony's mother having been finalized several months after he became Berta's roommate.

Tori turns around and fans herself. "This little girl is going to be a handful. I can already tell."

"Serves you right, *chica*." I bend over and talk to her belly. "And your godmother is going to teach you all the ways to annoy your mother."

Tori playfully covers her belly to protect it and turns away. "Give me a few years before you start in on her training."

I put a hand on my chin and pretend to think about it. "Maybe."

She smiles at me and pulls me in for a hug. "Ready?"

I nod. "Absolutely."

We walk past several dressing rooms, and then she precedes me into the reception hall's vestibule, where a photographer snaps a few candid shots while we wait for our cue.

Ashley appears in the doorway leading to the garden. "We're ready for you."

Carter appears behind her and holds out his hand. Tori takes it with a smile.

"Still breathtaking," Carter says. "Then. Today. Always."

She grins at him. "Oooh, you're going to get you some tonight, baby."

Then Luis appears behind me, looking dapper in a black three-piece suit. "Ready to walk with this *viejito* down the aisle?"

"I'm honored to, and yes, I'm ready." I take his arm in mine, enjoying the way my vintage tea-length dress flutters against my legs as I shift in place.

To the left of the gazebo, Ashley subtly nods to the organist and the enthralling sounds of "Ave Maria" fill the garden. Having served as an event planner in one of her many jobs before she settled in LA, Ashley's brought that experience to bear here and has taken on the planning of this wedding as if it were her own. Julian sits in the third row, proudly paying attention to no one other than his partner. He's nothing if not consistent.

Ashley nods, using a hand by her side to motion us forward. Luis and I follow her cue and walk down the garden path, smiling at the friends and family who have gathered to witness the marriage. When we reach the officiant, we separate and take our designated places.

My gaze immediately lands on Anthony, who's now standing in the doorway, in the same place Luis and I just stood, with Berta by his side. I glance at Luis to witness the moment when he first sees his bride. A misty-eyed Berta smiles at her husband-to-be.

I can't help meeting Anthony's gaze and holding it. This is a special moment for his father, and I'm so glad we're taking part in it. But more than that, this is a special moment for us, too.

It's an affirmation of the joy of loving someone and letting them love you.

It's proof that one can let go of the past and find love again.

It's confirmation of the rightness of us.

After the wedding, we proceed to the reception hall, where a banquet-style feast awaits us. And yes, Tori's mom, Lourdes, and her sister, Bianca, are overseeing the menu. Their only restriction? No baked empanadas.

A DJ spins a remixed version of Sister Sledge's "We Are Family" at my request. I'm still annoyed it's one of the top fifty songs couples ban at their weddings according to one survey. What is wrong with people?

Anthony leads me to a dark corner beyond the dance floor, not bothering to find our table. There, he raises my hand to his mouth and plants a soft kiss across my knuckles. "I love you, Eva Montgomery."

I've gotten used to the little flutter that skips across my belly each time he says it—and he says it a lot. "And I love you, Anthony Castillo."

He wraps one of my curls around his finger, toying with it as he stares at me with smoldering eyes. "You're the most beautiful woman in the room. I wish I could take you away from here and make love to you all night."

I pull him close, sliding my arms inside his jacket and resting my hands on his waist. "We can't leave yet. I have a surprise for everyone, especially you."

He draws back, his wicked smile coordinating perfectly with the devilish glint in his eyes. "A surprise. I'm intrigued."

I stand on my toes, placing my mouth near his ear. "I hired a reggaeton band."

Instead of laughing at the news, he staggers backward, his eyes widening to comical proportions. "Shit, I did, too."

For a few seconds, we stare at each other in silence, and then we fall over in laughter.

See? A perfect match, indeed.

Acknowledgments

CONFESSION: I'M TEARY-EYED as I write this. The Love on Cue series holds a special place in my heart because it reflects my true voice as a writer. I'm beyond grateful to the people who helped me navigate my journey to this page.

To my sweet, supportive husband: Your love and encouragement (and thirty-minute dinners) mean the world to me. Thank you for always holding it down and making me smile. You're my person. Always.

To my daughters: I'm blessed to have you and so proud to be your mommy. Thank you for all the ways—big and small—you helped me finish this book. I'm able to make readers laugh because *you* make me laugh. I love you more, okay?

To my fierce, independent, and stylish mother: Look Mami, I'm doing the thing. *Eu te amo muito.*

To my agent, Sarah Younger: I can't imagine doing any of this without the benefit of your sage counsel and excellent GIF game. Thank you for making my dreams come true.

To my editor, Nicole Fischer: I can already predict how this will go. I'll say you're a magician; you'll say it's your job. And although to a large extent that's true, you perform your role with such love, attention, and skill, that I do believe there's some sorcery going on. Can't wait to see what happens next.

To my beta readers (Ana Coqui, Susan Scott Shelley, and Soni Wolf): You've read every book in the series. Wow. I can't thank you enough for your invaluable feedback and thoughtful advice. I owe you *empanadillas*, don't I?

To my trusted reader, C. Lee: Thanks for sharing your expertise and good sense.

To my critique partner, Olivia Dade: Not even a move to Sweden could keep us apart. Thank you for always being "there" in the most important sense of the word.

To my partner in publishing crime, Tracey Livesay: Thank you for cheering me on, keeping me accountable, and making me cackle. We did it, woman.

To my 4 Chicas posse (Alexis Daria, Priscilla Oliveras, and Sabrina Sol): There are not enough pages to catalog the ways in which you've helped me grow as a person and a writer. You're all amazing, and I'm thrilled to be traveling on this journey with you.

To the rest of the Avon Books team: Although you often work behind the scenes, your love for the romance genre shines through for everyone to see. Thank you for helping me share my stories.

Bianca, you're *still* a gem.

Would it be weird if I thanked my four-legged writing buddy, Zoe? Never mind. She can't read anyway.

Do you love Mia's sexy and hilarious novels?
Well, you're in luck. A brand-new,
stand-alone romantic comedy
is coming soon . . .

The Worst Best Man

Coming Spring 2020
Mark your calendars!

About the Author

MIA SOSA was born and raised in New York City. She attended the University of Pennsylvania, where she earned her bachelor's degree in communications and met her very own romance hero (spoiler alert: she married him). Mia once dreamed of being a professional singer, but practical considerations (read: the need to generate income) led her to take the law school admissions test instead.

A graduate of Yale Law School, Mia practiced First Amendment and media law in the nation's capital for ten years before returning to her creative roots. Now she spends most of her days writing contemporary romances about imperfect characters finding their perfect match. Mia lives in Maryland with her husband, their two pop-culture-obsessed daughters, and an adorable dog who rules them all. For more information about Mia and her books, visit www.miasosa.com.